THE

BUDAPEST

ESCAPE

THE BUDAPEST ESCAPE

A COLD WAR THRILLER

Bill Rapp

coffeetown**press**

Seattle, WA

coffeetownpress

Epicenter Press
6524 NE 181st St.
Suite 2
Kenmore, WA 98028

www.epicenterpress.com
www.camelpress.com
www.coffeetownpress.com

For more information go to: www.billrappsbooks.com

Cover design by Dawn Anderson

The Budapest Escape
Copyright © 2019 by Bill Rapp

ISBN: 9781941890721 (Trade Paper)
ISBN: 9781603815116 (eBook)

Library of Congress Control Number: 0002019945289

Produced in the United States of America

For my parents, William and Nelda Rapp,
may they rest in peace.

———⚮———

Also by the author

Cold War Thriller Series

Tears of Innocence

The Hapsburg Variation

Suburban Detective Series

Angel in Black

A Pale Rain

Burning Altars

Berlin Breakdown

Acknowledgments

M Y DEBT OF gratitude for the appearance of this book—as with all my books—is a large one. First of all, I want to thank the editors at Coffeetown Press, Jennifer McCord and Murray McCord, for helping this manuscript become so much better than the one I originally submitted. Jennifer in particular pressed me to address questions of substance and character that if unanswered would have left this book a less satisfying read for all concerned. My wife Didi and my daughters Eleanor and Julia endured the challenges of having a husband and father who periodically locked himself away and stormed through numerous drafts and revisions before he found a story worth sharing. I hope they enjoyed some of the satisfaction as well. And thanks to her editing suggestions and research my wife was instrumental in creating a book that was correct, complete, and interesting. Quite simply, I could not have done this without all their help.

Chapter One

⁂

As soon as the man stopped in front of him on that cool, sunny morning of October 20, 1956 Karl Baier knew that he would have to go into Hungary himself to rescue his agent. Maybe not today or tomorrow, but still soon enough. He knew deep inside that this was something he had to do, despite the risks of running headlong into the KGB and its Hungarian ally, the even more brutal AVO security service. He had snuck into Budapest once before, and Baier had been lucky to escape with his life. He realized, though, that this was part of the job, one of the responsibilities and obligations he had accepted when he signed his name to that contract and secrecy agreement the day he joined the Central Intelligence Agency.

His superiors in Washington would take some convincing. Fortunately, Baier would have the opportunity to do just that when he flew back this week for "consultations," as many in Washington liked to refer to these kinds of discussions. He was supposed to leave later in the week, but he would move that up, maybe even leave this evening. If he could book a flight soon enough. He had been the Deputy Chief of Station in Vienna, Austria for almost three years, and acting Chief for about the last fifteen months. He knew that it was time for him to rotate to a new assignment, hopefully a step up to a larger, more important post. Maybe even get his own position as chief, not just an 'acting' one.

Now the consultations would have to cover this as well. Regardless of what came next, Baier was certain there was one more thing he would have to do before he packed his beer mugs and wine glasses that final time. The look of fear and anguish on the face of the Hungarian refugee standing not more than two feet from his own, told Baier all he really needed to know.

Baier had been pacing in small circles for nearly two hours. Either that or beating a steady rhythm of impatience with his feet while he tried to stand in one spot as he squinted, studying face after face set against the pale blue sky broken by intermittent patches of gray. The air shone almost like a pastel watercolor that could be found in any of the artists' stalls lining the banks of the Danube back in Vienna, the ones that attracted the tourists. Baier simply passed them by, giving them no more than a glance and a shake of his head. He wondered momentarily just why he thought of them today of all days. Then this stranger had stumbled toward him, his arms outstretched, the skin on his hands dried and cracked, as though he had been wandering the countryside for days. His face was marked by a days-old stubble crawling up his chin and along his cheeks, reddened eyes, and a carpet of tousled grey hair. The man had approached Baier slowly, breathing hard, as though he was out of breath. Or very, very nervous.

"Josef could not come. He needs you now. Things are becoming desperate there."

The stranger said no more. He just as quickly turned away and started to disappear into the crowd. Baier was too stunned at first to say anything. He had never seen, much less met the man before, and alarm bells rang in the back of his mind. Why this man? Why now? Why not Josef? How did he know to confront Baier, to select him alone among all the people there?

"No wait. Who are you?" Baier reached for the man's arm. "How do you know Josef?"

The wanderer's eyes turned white with fear and pleading. "No, there is no time. There may be others here among us." As though to confirm this, he glanced in every direction, searching through the sea of faces. "Please."

Then he was gone, disappearing within the wave of humanity that had carried him here to the Austro-Hungarian border.

Baier realized that he had no choice. Eventually, but certainly soon, he would have to follow.

Chapter Two

———

As Baier made his way back to the estate that he and his wife Sabine maintained a little over a mile from the border separating Austria and Hungary, he reflected on the events and the history that had led him to this day and this place. The plan had been to meet Josef Kovacs, the asset he had recruited over a year ago. The trip was similar to many Kovacs had made in the past. They would meet at the border, then travel together to Vienna, where Kovacs would deliver his report and the two would discuss how safe it was for the Hungarian to remain in place as Baier's—and the CIA's—agent within the Hungarian government in Budapest. Moreover, the risks to Kovacs from travelling here would not be that great. He and made the trip before, and today he would have blended in easily with the surge of refugees streaming west. But apparently today he hadn't even begun his journey.

The wave of humanity and the stories they carried told of more than the personal tales each person brought. It was a time, he thought, when the phrase about the sum being greater than the whole truly applied. Taken together these personal stories formed part of the history and politics that were so inescapable in this corner of the world: changing governments, states reformed and borders redrawn, communities ruptured and rebuilt, lives threatened or shattered, some rescued and dreams revived. It had been that way for centuries, and it had only intensified with crash of ideologies and sweeping armies that had passed through Europe over the last forty years. The same could probably be said for many parts of the world. But this was one that Baier had come to know and understand best. Baier's own family had experienced much the same upheaval, but they had been fortunate to land in America after fleeing Nazi Germany. Situated on the front lines of the Cold War, this part of the Europe remained immensely important for his country and its role in the world. It remained important for Baier, too.

The group surging toward the Austrian border today was larger than usual, although it was hard to imagine what one would consider normal in times like these. He guessed their numbers to be in the hundreds, perhaps as many as a thousand stretched out before him. There would certainly be more as the day wore on. Tomorrow and the day after as well, he guessed. Unless things changed.

They were coming from Hungary, the country that lay just to the east. The vast majority were, at any rate. Initially, when Baier and Sabine had arranged for the escape network that had opened a hole in the border with the connivance of several friendly Soviet security officers and well-paid border guards roughly a year ago, the flow from the east had been little more than a trickle. It was actually tougher to get people across the border back then, and Baier had needed the cooperation of the KGB border guards to smuggle Kovacs and other assets from further east safely across without the cover of large refugee flows. In those days, there had been a spring of hope in the political atmosphere inside Hungary, easily more than anything Hungarians had felt since the end of the war. It was

different now. Baier could not claim to know everything that
had been going on further east, but he had been able to gather
enough pieces of the puzzle from scattered press reports and
stories from various refugees, as well as Kovacs, to put together
a rough picture of what had happened over the last year and
a half.

The rulers in the Kremlin, who followed Stalin after his death
in 1953, had tried to instill a sense of reform and renewal.
In June of that year, the new Soviet leaders had even deposed
Matyas Rakosi, the Hungarian premier and Communist Party
leader and perhaps Stalin's most loyal henchman and imitator.
Rakosi had been forced by Khrushchev and others in the
Soviet Politburo to share power with the popular reformer
Imre Nagy.

Rakosi, it was well known, despised Nagy and had worked
to limit and undermine the latter's reform program at every
possible step. Nagy was a committed Communist, but
he was no Stalinist. If there was one thing he saw that the
party henchmen had missed, it was the need to loosen the
stranglehold the Soviet system had placed on Hungarian
life. The people of Hungary remembered Nagy as the man
who had broken apart the huge estates of the Magyar nobility
after the war and redistributed it among the peasants, many
of them landholders themselves for the first time. When he
came to power, however, Rakosi had quickly taken it all back
and established the dreaded—and ineffective—collective
farms on the Stalinist model, the same ones that caused so
much hunger and death in the Soviet Union, the Ukraine in
particular, during the 1930s. Then, Nagy was dropped to some
insignificant post before he was recalled in 1953. Rumors—
true, actually—had begun to spread within a few years that
the Soviet masters had become bitterly disappointed in the
failure of Nagy to instill some life in his country's moribund
economy this time around. Of course, Rakosi had virtually
ruined his country by insisting on imposing on Hungary the

model Stalin had deployed to force the Soviet Union's own rush to industrialization after the Bolshevik seizure of power. Like the USSR, Hungary had been largely agrarian. If it was good enough for Papa Joe, then it must be good enough for Hungary, Rakosi had reasoned. Besides, it testified yet again to the Hungarian leader's slavish dependence on Stalin, which Rakosi had hoped would secure his own power. It worked, as long as Stalin lived, that is.

Now it was October 20, 1956, and the worried, exhausted faces in the small mob that tumbled toward the opening in the border testified to the failures of Rakosi and the emasculated reform efforts that had followed. Back in April, Nagy had been forced out and Rakosi restored. Then Rakosi's second demotion followed in July, just three months later. No wonder people were confused about where their country was heading and what they could expect of their own future. The appointment of Erno Gero, every bit as hardline a Stalinist as Rakosi, had done nothing to revive the country's economic life or suppress the intellectual and political ferment in Hungary, most evident in the Petofi Circle, a group of writers, artists, and students who had rallied around Nagy. He, however, had been exiled to the provinces once again and this time expelled from the party.

These refugees streaming westwards before Baier's watchful eyes were obviously not members of that rebellious group. You could not tell by their clothes, though, since nearly everyone in Hungary made do with a limited supply of hand-me-down parcels and re-patched articles that gave the citizenry the look of a country still struggling to emerge from the brutality of Nazi occupation, the horrendous fighting in 1944 and 1945, and now Soviet domination. Most of the dresses, pants, and jackets looked as though they had not seen a washing machine or dry cleaners since the end of the battle for Budapest. It was the haggard and hopeless look on so many of the faces, the drawn cheeks and sunken eyes that told the true story. These people had lost hope in their country's future. The shifting political winds in Moscow and Budapest appeared to make little difference in their lives. Baier wondered if Kovacs had also lost hope. For his country's future and his own. Perhaps, that would explain today's confrontation. The man had said the situation was desperate. Maybe the hope had been taken from him by those bastards in the KGB and AVO. If so, it really was a desperate situation.

Ironically, Kovacs had long been a committed Communist and loyal party member in Hungary. He even worked at the headquarters of the AVO, Hungary's brutal and widely feared security service. He was close to Gero himself, having served with the man in Spain during its civil war in the late 1930s. It was the same war in which Gero had earned his well-deserved reputation as "the butcher of Barcelona" for his work liquidating Trotskyites and other left-wing opponents of Stalin's rule over the international communist movement during Gero's tenure as the local chief of the NKVD--the KGB's predecessor—in Catalonia. But Josef Kovacs, even as close to Gero as he had become early in his career, had proved to be a valuable asset for Baier and the CIA. How that could be was a mystery that the few who knew the man's identity and personal history struggled to comprehend.

Normally, Kovacs's features made him easy to distinguish, even in a crowd this size. He was tall, Baier guessed at least 6' 3", maybe even 6' 4" if he had on a pair of new shoes. He was also thin, like most Hungarians at this point—except for many of the party bosses, of course, who made sure they never had to do without in a land of shortages and rationing of even basic foodstuffs. Kovacs had worn his tight, thin features almost like a badge, a sign of his sacrifice for the future of his country. There was a limit, of course. When Kovacs first started working for Baier and the CIA he had occasionally requested sticks of butter as part of his compensation, explaining that even such a basic article of food had become a luxury inside Hungary. In any case, the man's long, aquiline nose, wide green eyes, and his greying mane of thick wavy hair were usually enough to mark him out as singular and separate.

Baier thought back again to the day the two men had met. It been a little over a year ago in Vienna, shortly after the signing of the State Treaty in May, 1955 that ended the Allied occupation of Austria and restored the country's independence. Kovacs was on an official visit to the Hungarian Embassy, a convenient cover for his meeting with Hungarian intelligence agents working in the Austrian capital. This visit was just the latest in several such trips abroad that Baier had noticed since he had begun to survey the visitors to the newly-opened embassies from the behind the Iron Curtain in hopes of identifying their intelligence agents.

It had not been that difficult in Kovacs's case. There was something in his manner and street smarts that set off Baier's instincts and suspicions. Not only that, but the regime clearly trusted the man, allowing him to travel so frequently and alone. Baier had noticed him on several occasions, five in the first six months alone following the signing of the State Treaty, which gave Austria its sovereignty back and brought in a host of foreign embassies. He had initially followed the Hungarian to see with whom he met, part of Baier's attempt to get a more complete picture of Soviet and East European assets operating in the Austrian capital.

Then on a bright sunny day in July the Hungarian had stunned Baier by approaching him on the street to inquire about the possibility of applying for political asylum in the West. The man was definitely a real professional, having made Baier in spite of the American's best efforts to remain discrete and hidden among the many pedestrians of the Austrian capital. Kovacs claimed he did not want to leave Europe and that he had appealed to an American because he believed that was the surest and quickest way to have his case heard. It was obvious, he also said, that the richest and most powerful nation in the West was running things on this side of the Iron Curtain. In order to demonstrate his bona fides, Kovacs had given Baier an organizational chart and personnel list not only of the Hungarian intelligence network inside Austria, but also a list of Soviet intelligence officers as well. He promised that there were more things he could divulge once safely ensconced in a protected CIA hide-away.

Baier's tradecraft may have been less than perfect during his surveillance, but he recognized a gold mine when it stood open in front of him. He convinced the man to return to Budapest to continue his assignment at AVO headquarters in Stalin Avenue. It marked the beginning of a very productive relationship that had led to a series of reports on developments inside the government and Communist Party in Hungary, and on the relations between Budapest and other East European capitals. There were even periodic reports on policy guidance from Moscow, which served as a window that opened once in a while into the broader developments within the newly-established Warsaw Pact.

There were doubts, of course. Baier had been impressed by the man's tenacity and courage, demonstrated in his own surveillance of the American Embassy, recognizing Baier and then approaching the American in an unexpected appeal for help. It was what was known in the business as a 'cold call.' But there was still the need to validate the man and his claims. One had to be certain he was not what was also known as a 'dangle.'

"How do I know this is all credible stuff and that you're not a provocation, some kind of operation to confuse our own efforts to track the work of the Soviets and their puppets in the West?" Baier had asked.

"Surely you have some other information against which to test at least parts of this," Kovacs had replied, pointing to the envelope in Baier's hand. "You will learn quickly that this is truly damaging to the Soviet Union and its operations in

Austria and Germany."

"But why are you doing this?" Baier had asked. "A sense of your motives would help us understand you."

The Hungarian simply smiled. "You will have to leave me my personal secrets for now. Trust the information in there." Again, he nodded toward the envelope.

The Station in Vienna did test it, and they learned to trust it. The Americans did not have much on the other Warsaw Pact services operating in Austria, but what the Americans did hold corresponded to bits and pieces of Kovacs's gift. This packet from the Hungarian volunteer was the sort of thing that helped pull more of it together.

Baier stopped to catch his breath. He hadn't realized that his hike had turned into a fast trot. Another two hundred meters on the horizon, he caught sight of the estate he and his wife had purchased in the province of Burgenland near the Hungarian border. Not only was it a pleasant retreat in the heart of Austria's wine country; it also served as a cover for welcoming and debriefing assets like Kovacs, after they had snuck their way through the narrow passage in the fence or blended in with the refugees from the east, just before they made their way back to Vienna and possibly the CIA station with whatever tidbits they had acquired on their trips in eastern Europe or the Soviet Union. The estate provided an ideal location, sitting a little over a mile from the border. He would discuss his plans with Sabine as soon as he walked through the door. Then a call to the Station in Vienna and the drive to office, where he would reach out to Headquarters to prepare them for his change in plans.

Baier was determined not to let Kovacs down. Looking back over their joint venture in providing the America and its allies with the sort of information needed to understand Soviet policies in the region, Baier decided that he would do all in his power to save the man from the AVO torture chambers. He felt a cold shiver run through his chest and spine as a light breeze from the east swept across the border as the afternoon wore on. Baier pulled his jacket tighter around the sweater that suddenly felt thin and threadbare.

Chapter Three

～～～

"**K**ARL, MUST YOU go to Washington?" Sabina asked.
Baier shifted his weight uncomfortably on the chair at his kitchen table. He and Sabine had just finished a late lunch, and scraps of bread, cheese, and salami littered their plates. Baier's fingers circled a glass of mineral water, which was now half empty. They had taken the roughly two-hour drive from their estate to the Austrian capital in about an hour and a half, conscious of the need to get to the office to send a cable back to Washington. Baier wanted to explain his concerns over Kovacs's security and what he planned to do about them. His head swam with unpleasant scenarios of Kovacs's unmasking, his seizure, and the torture and execution that would inevitably follow. Or perhaps, he had been compromised, turned by the KGB and AVO, then exploited as a double agent and source of disinformation for the CIA and the American government. In Baier's mind, this made it all the more imperative for him to get into Budapest as quickly as possible.

"Yes, and I'm afraid I have to leave tonight. This trip was laid on last week to discuss my follow-on assignment, Sabine, and it can't be avoided. It's how we work, for better or worse."

"But why must you, and why must we leave Vienna? I thought you enjoyed living and working here." She let a small laugh drift across the table to her husband. "I know I certainly do." Her hands reached across the table. "What about our place in the countryside? Who will look after that?"

"Sabine, you know it's not about liking or disliking Vienna, or Austria even. The Agency chooses your assignment based on its own needs and logic. It's like any large organization. And the powers that be have determined that it's time for me to move on to something else, to develop new skills and new perspectives. Hopefully, at a higher level. They probably believe that if I stay in one spot for too long, I'll atrophy. You know, grow stale." He sighed. "I just won't get promoted if I stay here."

"Why not? You've worked hard here."

"Yes, but I need to prove I can handle more responsibility and new challenges. That's why I need to go back, to discuss other options. It may mean leaving Europe for an assignment elsewhere, maybe even back in Washington. You only get promoted, Sabine, after you prove yourself at a higher level."

"But look at your background. Our backgrounds. Both our families come from Germany. We know this part of the world, and we know how important it is. We feel it, Karl, in our bones, in our souls. We're on the fault line here. Our families are."

Baier took a sip of his water, then leaned back away from the table. "Well, not mine, not any longer. But you're right, Sabine, and I think I've had some real success working along this fault line, as you put it. So have you. God knows we've had our challenges and setbacks, too. There is still a chance that I'll be asked to take on another job in Europe. Like I said, that's one thing I'll discuss back home."

"Oh, I hope so, Karl. It would make so much sense."

Baier shifted himself again, this time leaning forward. He reached for his wife's hands with both of his own. "Sabine, there's something else." He brought his wife's hands together in the palms of his own. "I may have to go back into Budapest again."

Sabine's head shot back, and her spine stiffened. "But why, Karl? That must be so dangerous. What can be so serious that you have to do this again? "

"It is dangerous, and certainly serious. It's why I need to discuss it back at Headquarters. I can't simply walk through the Iron Curtain on my own authority…"

"Why not? You've done it before."

Baier shook his head. "No, Sabine, that was with the approval and cooperation of the people back home. I'll need that again. You can't just run off on your own. Given the turmoil in Hungary these days, I can't be sure how they'll react to my proposal. Plus, I'll have to get the concurrence of our man in Budapest as well. The Agency tends to frown on adventurers acting on their own. I'll send a cable back as soon as I get into the office this afternoon, but I'm pretty certain I'll have to raise it with my superiors in person. They'll probably figure that as long as I'm coming back, I can discuss it with them there.

"But can you spare the time, Karl?"

"We'll see what they say. I doubt they share the same sense of urgency. Remember, it's still a large organization."

"And a large bureaucracy."

"Yes, I suppose that's true. And it's thousands of miles away. But I will not stay longer than a day. Two at the most, if I can help it."

"Why is this so important? Is this the man you've been meeting at our estate near the border?"

"Yes, we've have met there on occasion, but also here in Vienna."

"Why is this so important, Karl, that you must risk your own safety for his?"

"Sabine, I owe this man. He has done so much for us, and I guess for me as well. He's a very important source in the Hungarian government, very well placed. I can't say any more than that, but he is probably our best source—maybe even our only one—who can help inform us not only of the plans and intentions of the Hungarian leadership, but he can also shed some light on Soviet thinking as well."

"How can a Hungarian do that, Karl?"

"Sabine, ever since Stalin's death three years ago, and especially since Khrushchev's efforts at reform, the Warsaw Pact has been in turmoil. People are rejecting the old Stalinist system and demanding more freedom. Look at what happened in East Berlin, your old home."

"You mean the workers' revolt back in '53? When the Soviets had to send in their tanks?"

"Yes, yes. And in Poland there's been a change in the party leadership and the chance for some real autonomy."

"Yes," Sabine smiled. "I've read about their 'goulash communism.'"

"Well, it looks like Hungary could be the new flash point. It could have tremendous repercussions for Soviet rule in Europe. Hell, for the Soviet Union itself."

"But why this particular man, Karl? Why do you feel so committed to him? Surely there are others who can help."

"I seriously doubt that, Sabine. It's what we do. We have to protect our people. Who would ever work for us if we don't?" Baier paused as he studied the window above the kitchen sink. "Besides, he's an interesting man. We've grown close over the last year."

"Oh, Karl, how did that happen? He's just another Communist. Good riddance, I say."

"That's how the people back in Headquarters may well be thinking, Sabine. It's a big reason why I need to discuss this with them. Believe me, there were plenty of alarm bells going off as soon as I recruited this guy."

Baier thought back to those initial meetings when he shared some of those concerns. He pressed repeatedly to get to the heart of Josef Kovacs, his outlooks and beliefs, his motives behind the sudden turn in his own life and loyalties.

"You appear to be a longtime Communist, my friend. One who has worked closely with the 'the butcher of Barcelona.' You've even benefitted from being his protégé. What happened to bring you around to our side?" Kovacs had looked puzzled, hurt even. "I mean, surely you realize we have to question your motives, given your history," Baier had stated a month after their first meeting. "I told you this earlier."

"Mister Baier, you do not see and participate in the kinds of things I have and not have it leave an impact. Yes, I have always been a committed Communist, but what Gero and Rakosi and others have done in Hungary is not socialism. They have simply built a dictatorship for their own benefit. It is not good for my nation and its people."

Kovacs paused, studying the ground at his feet while his right hand massaged his forehead. When he looked up again, Kovacs's eyes were moist from the memories of his past. "It has been a long journey, Mr. Baier. You know the split between the followers of Leon Trotsky and those who pled allegiance to Stalin?"

Baier nodded. "Somewhat. Sure."

"Well, I was initially a follower of Trotsky. I believed in the prospects for world revolution after the First World War. I betrayed that belief when I decided that Stalin was necessary to protect the home of the Revolution, especially when it became clear the workers of the world were not ready to forego bread and prosperity for glory and the dictatorship of the proletariat."

"You got that right."

"Yes, and everything since then has shown me that Stalin and his henchmen have only their own interests and those of some defunct Russian empire at heart. Your country, Mr. Baier, represents a great hope for mankind, despite all your faults,and there are many of those. Still, you are clearly the lesser evil."

Kovacs, it turned out, was also inspired by a love of Hungary and a disdain for the "Muscovite" crowd. It was the label that those who had remained behind to work against Admiral Horthy's fascist regime and the alliance with Nazi Germany stuck to the likes of Rakosi and Gero, who spent the war years in the relative comfort of Moscow sucking up to Stalin and his crowd in the Kremlin.

Baier had found Kovacs's reporting invaluable, especially when one considered how little actual intelligence came out of the Soviet Union and the Warsaw Pact countries. An organization in its infancy, the CIA was still finding its balance and strength in the world of international diplomacy and espionage. The Soviet Empire was one area where it operated nearly blind. It relied instead on travelers' reports and photographs—little more than tourist information, really--or locals kept in place on meager contracts. There had also been agents parachuted behind the Curtain, but these were invariably scooped up by the host services. Kovacs, however, was the real deal: a recruited agent buried deep within the Communist power structure.

Baier couldn't help but worry about what sort of suspicions the periodic visits to Vienna might cause, although Kovacs appeared to travel with the blessings of his party bosses. Baier had never picked up any surveillance on the man. Moreover, given the tight operational environment in Budapest itself, Vienna had proved to be the safest and most productive place to meet whenever Kovacs's schedule allowed. Besides, Budapest Station, with only one man in place at the Embassy, was not equipped to run an asset like Kovacs. It was enough just to ask his colleague in place to maintain the communications Baier had established through a series of dead drops in a city like Budapest, controlled by a thorough and well-resourced service like the AVO. The man had to do it on his own.

The leadership within the European Division back home had never been comfortable with the whole operation and had resisted Baier's plan from the outset. They had also failed to come up with anything better, or more secure. Baier had scored a point when he argued that the surveillance in Budapest was simply too strict and too close, especially since Rakosi's ousting of Nagy. This made the meetings in Austria a necessity. There were always worries associated with an operation this sensitive, especially with the elevation of Gero to leadership of the party and the state. Even Kovacs expressed concerns at times.

" I thought you two were close," Baier had pressed.

"You can never be truly close to a man like Gero. If he even is a man." Kovacs had smiled at his own small joke. "Sometimes it feels like you are working with a steel trap. You know, the kind you set for a bear. You do not survive in that sort of environment without a naturally suspicious mind, Mister Baier. He has become even more wary and cunning with all the unrest and uncertainty."

Baier had demurred. With his mentor in charge, Kovacs's own access would only increase. "My God, you'll be sitting next to the throne," Baier had exclaimed. Perhaps Kovacs feared the kinds of things he knew the AVO were capable of in those dungeons at 60 Stalin Avenue. It was enough to frighten even the bravest person. And Kovacs certainly was brave. Baier had to give him that much, considering how many chances he had taken already and how much he had delivered.

"Karl, are you still with me?" Sabine asked.

"Yes, yes. I'm sorry. I was just thinking back to how much I have learned from this man, and how much he has meant to me, and to the West actually. I just realized how fond I've grown of him. It's strange, I know so little of his family and personal history. But I still feel as though I've known him for years as a friend."

"Is that wise, Karl?"

Baier sighed. "Wise or not, It's where I am. And it's who I am, Sabine. You should know that by now."

His wife smiled. "Yes, I do. And I love you for it. But I want to ask again. Must we go? Look at what you'll be leaving behind." She hesitated before continuing. "Karl, have you ever thought that it might be time to leave the Agency, to find something else?"

Baier shook his head. "What do you mean? Why would I do that? Where else would we go?"

"We could stay here, Karl. I know you'd find something else to do. Something without the danger, the separations."

He stared out the window over the sink, then shook his head again. "No, Sabine. I can't. This is what I do. It's what I believe in."

"Well then, I just hope this mission doesn't let you down, Karl. That it proves to be worth it for you. For us."

Baier nodded. "I'll find out soon enough. But whatever does come for us, Sabine, wherever we go, there is one more thing I need to do here."

Chapter Four

~~~

EVERY TIME HE flew into National Airport just across the Potomac from Washington, D.C. Karl Baier thought his plane was about to land in the river right before it touched down on the runway, and the very next morning was no different. The airport had been built on the minimum space available—Baier had long suspected it stood on reclaimed swamp land, like so much of the Washington area's riverside property—and the runways ran right up to the water's edge. He blew out a long, silent breath of relief as the plane taxied towards the terminal. Since this was a short connecting flight from New York,he hoped his bag would be waiting and a taxi easy to hail.

Instead, a flashy white Ford Fairlane convertible sat at the curb near his exit with Ralph Delgreccio standing by the driver's side door. At least it looked white in the bright Washington sun, or pretty much so, until Baier got close enough to pick out the teal-colored underside bordered by a silver shaft that ran the length of the car. He was surprised and pleased to find his former boss from Vienna there to greet him, a man Baier had come to like and respect during their two years together in the Austrian capital. Delgreccio had been his chief of station during a trying period when Baier had become engulfed in a murder investigation that had tossed him into the middle of a bid to undermine Soviet rule in southeastern Europe, through an old Austrian aristocrat and *Wehrmacht* officer. While all this was going on, Baier's wife Sabine had been kidnapped by a Soviet and East German team, then turned over to the Hungarians in Budapest as part of an attempt to pressure American intelligence to end its budding relationship with the Austrian intelligence services. That, in any case, was how the KGB colonel, the brains behind the operation, had explained it to his leadership.

A bright sun baked the lingering heat and humidity from the remnants of a Washington summer, which hung in the air despite the late October timeframe. Indian summers always seemed to appear later and last longer in Washington's semi-tropical environment. Baier tossed his luggage in the trunk, then hopped into the front seat on the passenger side. He rolled down his window to let some fresh air mingle with the breeze from Delgreccio's window as the car sped along the George Washington Parkway on its way downtown, coasting along a riverbank lush with multi-colored foliage and bright marble monuments. Rays of sunshine flashed off the car's sterling fenders, encouraging a sense of optimism that always seemed to pervade Washington in the fall. At least, when the Redskins were winning.

"How come the top's still up?" Baier asked.

"Too much rain lately. You'll just have to suffer a little while," Delgreccio replied.

Baier leaned out the window. "Is the trim on these things really stainless steel?" He pulled his head back inside as soon as he felt the heat of the Virginia sun along the back of his neck.

"You betcha, and there's a V-8 rocket under the hood of this baby."

"Wow, Ralph, you must be moving up in the world."

"Well, it sure feels like it, what with all this power under my seat." Delgreccio smiled. "And try not get any sweat on my upholstery."

Baier glanced around the car's interior. "It looks like it could use the polish. Do I get to check into my hotel at least before I report into Headquarters?"

Delgreccio smiled and shook his head. "Afraid not, Karl." He glanced over at Baier. "Since you're only staying one night, I thought you might as well stay at my place in Arlington. When do you fly out?"

"Tomorrow evening. I want to stop off in London for some discussions at MI6 to get their feel for what's going on in Hungary. As you no doubt recall, they remain very interested in developments in Eastern Europe, especially given their abiding distrust in those pricks in the Kremlin. Since we're practically naked in that part of the world, I want to check on their presence to see if they can help me out with something. They are, after all, our closest partners, despite all that crap surrounding Burgess, Maclean, and the rest of those Cambridge snobs."

"Something?"

"That's right. But you'll understand if I say no more. Sorry, buddy."

Delgreccio smiled. "Sure. Good luck with that. I gotta wonder just how interested they are in European affairs right now. As best I can tell, our British cousins are completely wrapped up in this Egyptian mess they've created for themselves. I doubt they've got the energy or the resources to look anywhere else at the moment."

"Well, I plan to find out how true that is." Baier turned to lean towards his chauffer. "So, how is life with your fellow Middle Eastern adventurers these days? You getting along with the fancy-pants East Coast types?" Baier broke into a wide smile.

"I mean, you don't exactly have the Groton-Harvard pedigree."

Delgreccio smiled in reply. "I get along just fine with my Catholic school upbringing. I can throw some Latin right back at 'em when they try to get too classical and snobby."

"Well, other than that, are you happy to be back in all that sand and oil and shit?"

"Hardly." Delgreccio sighed. "It's a real fucking circus right now. Copeland and Roosevelt are practically pulling their hair out in frustration with the Brits over their insistence that Nasser be removed. The limeys keep saying the guy's another Hitler. Can you believe that?"

"I doubt the other Europeans would agree. At least not those who had to suffer under a Nazi occupation."

"Working so close with the Israelis isn't helping matters either. It pretty much guarantees opposition from the rest of the Arabs, putting us between a rock and a hard place." Delgreccio shook his head. "A very hard place, I might add."

"And the French?" Baier asked.

The car swung along the wide curves that led from the Parkway to the Memorial Bridge, which crossed the Potomac and aimed for the Lincoln Memorial. No matter how many times he encountered this sight, Baier felt it inspiring. He remembered, too, how eager Delgreccio had been to return to Middle Eastern affairs, where he had spent the bulk of his career thus far with the Agency. Ralph had joined at the outset, like Baier, but Vienna had been an interlude of sorts. He had left Baier in nominal charge of the station in Vienna when Washington had called Delgreccio back to join a Middle Eastern Task Force led by Miles Copeland and Kermit Roosevelt, two of the leading lights in the Agency's operations directorate, in large part because of their proclivity for covert operations, like the Iranian coup Roosevelt had organized three years ago. Delgreccio served as one of two deputies in the group, where his talents for intelligence collection were admired and valued. It was a skill set that could be hard to find as the Agency worked to establish its presence around the world.

"Oh hell, those fuckers are even worse than the Brits. Sometimes I think Paris is the one pushing the Brits forward, not the other way around. They're scared shitless that some kind of anti-colonial virus will spread to their possessions in North Africa."

"Well," Baier added, "they're already infected in Algeria. It looks to me like they're all still stuck in the previous century."

Delgreccio smiled. "You got that right, my man. They're acting like it could spread to the rest of Africa, which would be a real blow after they had to scamper back home from Vietnam."

"Man, I hope we don't just step in after them." Baier shook his head. "What a mess that would be."

"It's one of the places where the new battle lines are being drawn with the Soviets and Chinese, Karl. Southeast Asia, a new up-and-coming place to see and be seen…"

"Oh, spare me. I mean, does it really need to be?" Baier studied the cars lining the Mall along Constitution Avenue. "But enough on that part of world…"

"You are such a Europhile, Karl."

"True, true. I also understand that you guys are pretty tight with Nasser, which can't help matters," Baier pressed.

"Oh, tell me about it," Delgreccio laughed. "I think we're actually missing out on a real chance to gain an important ally among the Arabs here. He's been pretty much pushed into the Soviets' hands by John Foster Dulles's stupidity over the funding screw-up for the Aswan Dam, and now Nasser's turning eastward with his military shopping list because we're giving him no alternative. If this Suez Canal invasion actually goes ahead, we can forget having any friends in the region for a long time."

"And the Israelis?"

Delgreccio glanced over at Baier and shook his head as the

car pulled into the parking lot at the front of the Navy Yard, which housed the head offices of the CIA. "Don't bet on that crowd. The Israelis are their own best friends, and nobody else's. They're not going to help us unless it serves their immediate interests." Delgreccio glanced over again. "And only for about that long, too."

"So, what do all our friends hope to accomplish?"

Delgreccio shook his head. "There's the rub, Karl. Nobody knows, least of all Paris or London. They seem to think that simply pushing Nasser out will open up a bright new future. There's no plan for the day after or who might serve as allies inside Cairo from what I've seen."

"Do London and Paris actually think it will be that easy to move Nasser out?"

Delgreccio nodded. "Apparently. But don't ask me how."

Delgreccio swung his car in a tight arc and into a parking spot that hugged the wall of a red brick building facing the Mall and the Lincoln Memorial. As they strolled from the car, Delgreccio reached out to hold the sleeve of Baier's jacket, as though he needed to hold his friend back for a moment. "Are you sure this was a good idea? To come back here for consultations, I mean?"

"Baier squinted against the sunlight. "It was already scheduled, Ralph. But, it turns out to have been a good thing, because I need to get Headquarters' agreement in case I have to go in pull my asset out of Hungary."

"Is that your 'something'?"

Baier smiled. "Yeah, I never could keep a secret from you. I need to argue my case in person."

Delgreccio dropped Baier's sleeve. "Good enough. You know, I may not need to point this out to you, Karl, but you should also be aware that we are coming to the end of a hard-fought presidential election campaign."

"And?"

"And nobody here or elsewhere in town wants to rock any

proverbial boats until after the voting is over. The attention of most higher-ups, especially with President Eisenhower and his crew over at the White House, is on the election, and they have little time or inclination for jumping into foreign adventures. Moreover, nobody, but nobody wants any unpleasant surprises." Delgreccio glanced at the building in front of them, as though trying to isolate some of the people inside. "Just keep it in mind during your meeting today."

BAIER WALKED AWAY from Delgreccio's car and waved at his friend. The two agreed to meet in the parking lot at 5:30. Baier ambled up the front steps and then climbed one more floor and headed for the back of the building to meet with his immediate boss. Gary Peters sat behind a grey metal desk that look as sterile as his pressed white shirt, green and gold regimental striped tie, and crewcut blonde hair. The walls were covered in an off-white paint that differed little from the original plaster board coloring. The office held little artwork on the walls beyond the reproduction of a Grant Wood landscape that hung directly behind the desk. At least he had a corner office that looked out over the Potomac and on to Roosevelt Island, midway between the District and the Commonwealth of Virginia. The space and location of the office made sense, given that Peters was the head of the Agency's European Division in the Office of Policy Coordination, the official title for the directorate that ran the Agency's overseas operations. He had been in this position for almost six months now, but at times still seemed to be getting himself familiar with the people and operations in his part of the world. The one thing he had no doubt learned, though, was that nice office space comes with the responsibilities of authority, especially over such a crucial region that formed the front line in the Cold War, as Sabine had called it last night. She was right. It often seemed as though the future of Western Civilization hinged on the outcome of the competition between the United States and the Soviet Union in the middle of Europe.

Baier had started to sweat again after the breezy car ride downtown when he walked to the square red brick structure at the rear of the complex of office buildings in Foggy Bottom, situated on a small hill that backed up against the Potomac. It was known as the E Street Complex, named for the street that ran in front and separated the buildings from the State Department across the road. The fan in Peter's window had cooled his office enough for Baier to relax and the sweat to evaporate. Eventually.

"Welcome to Washington, Karl. I read your cable last night, and I understand there may be a problem with your source in Budapest, and that you may have a solution, of sorts. So, tell me again how this guy Kovacs came to be working for us."

Peters leaned back in his chair while his hands played with a rubber band, he had scooped up from his desk top. A brown cardboard folder lay open on his desk, and Baier assumed it was the 201 file, or personal history of his asset. "I've read through the file, of course, and I have to say that his background hardly suggests he'd be a trustworthy asset of ours. Certainly not one that would find favor or much understanding, especially with Senator McCarthy and his crowd on the Hill. Have you been following that circus? Are we paying this guy?"

Baier leaned in towards the desk from his chair opposite Peters. "Yes, I have, although from a distance, thankfully. As for payment, well, yes and no."

"Come again."

"We are giving Kovacs a salary, but he's asked that it be deferred to an account in Vienna for his use when—or if—he exfiltrates to the West. We do pass along some commodities as well, like basic foodstuffs from time to time. The living there can be pretty deprived."

Peters nodded. "Well, that makes sense. Good tradecraft. I guess it would be pretty damn conspicuous if he had a lot of extra cash to spend in that hell hole."

Baier nodded in turn. "Absolutely. The guy's tradecraft has been truly exemplary. He's a real professional." Baier sat back. "Then again, you'd have to expect that of a man with his experience."

"You mean, the Spanish Civil War and all that?"

"That and more." Baier nodded. "He also survived several years living and working underground in Nazi-occupied Hungary. Then there's all the turmoil of Stalinist rule under Rakosi with the many purges. In fact, he owes his current standing and job to one of those purges. The previous occupant had been jailed and then executed for supporting some kind of Western conspiracy and sabotage."

"Did he?"

Baier shook his head. "I gather the man's principal crime was having been a Jew."

"That crap's still going on?"

"Apparently."

Peters leaned in over his desktop, dropping his rubber band. "Frankly, Karl, getting back to Kovacs himself, that's one of the issues. Not this Jewish thing, of course, but the guy has a real history as a committed Communist, active on their international front. You yourself mentioned how closely he worked with Gero in Spain when that bastard was butchering any non-Stalinist leftie he could find. You understand that that sort of thing obviously raises questions about Kovacs's ultimate loyalties here."

Baier sat back to give himself some additional space. "Gary, I'm not smart enough to talk about 'ultimates' here, and Kovacs's history in the communist movement is unquestioned. But it's what's happened to it under Stalin and his loyal satraps in places like Hungary that motivates this guy. I don't know for certain what exactly he did in Spain to win Gero's apparently undying affection, but the 'Butcher of Barcelona' has made a point of protecting Kovacs throughout the purges that followed the end of the war. In this case, it's played to our advantage. It has given us invaluable access."

"Why did Gero take such a liking to your guy?"

Baier shrugged. "I can't say for sure, Gary. But maybe Gero saw the young Communist in Spain as the idealist he had wanted to be in his own youth. That is, until he got the taste for power and blood. Or Gero may have found it useful to have a former Trotskyite in his camp, someone over whom he had leverage and could use to sniff out left-wing deviationists, as the Stalinists like to call the other side. Then I think he actually came to like our guy. What he seems to have missed was the personal turmoil Kovacs experienced working for the likes of him."

"How can we be certain that Gero hasn't figured this out and been using your man nowadays, especially if he has some leverage?" Peters had picked up his rubber band again. "Even if this Kovacs fellow is unwitting."

"Gary, I respect your concerns and counter-intelligence sensitivities, but look at the reporting. The guy's stuff has been spot-on. What about the report on Rakoski's pending departure and Gero's own elevation? He gave us some pretty good warnings of the building unrest in Posnan over in Poland." Baier glanced out the window at Roosevelt Island. He noticed a smattering of red among the leaves on the trees still full of their foliage. He realized suddenly that he would miss living and enjoying the autumn in Washington, perhaps his favorite time of the year. "Just to keep with our own security here, let's use Kovacs's cryptonym, Bluebird. I'd feel more comfortable."

Peters leaned back. "Yes, you're right, of course. Sorry." The rubber band was making wide and rapid circles around his fingers. "That information all came out in their press. Or he had to know it would eventually. It wasn't a great secret."

It was Baier's turn to lean in now. "That's just the point. 'Eventually.' We got advance notice. That should have been useful over at State and the White House, if they knew what to do with that sort of information. Let's not forget his initial reporting that gave us our best insight into Soviet and East Bloc operations in Austria. You know how tough it was to get a full picture of all that's been going on there since the end of the war. It's been a real haven for spies and intelligence services from all over Europe, not to mention our own work there. I mean these Four-Power occupied countries like Austria and Germany just invite that sort of thing, and it's nearly impossible to sort the trees from the forest. Or it was, until we had Bluebird's help."

Peters nodded and shifted his weight in the chair. "Yes, yes, I'll concede that much."

"What about his reporting on the inner workings of the Hungarian government and Soviet concerns following the popular demands for reform after Khrushchev's destalinization speech earlier this year was certainly valuable." Peters held up his hand, as though to keep Baier from adding more. He was not dissuaded, however. "How about the most recent report, the one about the Soviets putting their forces on high alert? Has there been any corroborating data out there?"

"Points taken, Karl. I believe the latest U-2 flight did pick up some additional activity at one or two Soviet garrisons. Unfortunately, most of those flights have been redirected to the Sinai. You are aware, though, that our man in Budapest is also skeptical of Kovacs's—excuse me, Bluebird's--motivation and his freedom to report as we'd like?" Peters paused to consider some point before looking up at Baier again. "Perhaps 'skeptical' is too strong a word. Let's just say that Stan Muller does share some of these concerns."

"Yes, I've had numerous conversations with Stan and others in Vienna who think like him. Frankly, I think they're too cautious in this case. I understand the need to be careful in such a tightly controlled environment. But, I know the man, and I'm convinced he's a valuable asset who is willing and prepared to provide useful information and insights, regardless of his background and personal history. You can't read all these guys the same way, Gary. Bluebird has proven himself. His loyalties have changed." Baier stared at Peters for a moment before continuing. "It's not like we've got lots of assets over there to choose from."

"But what is his ultimate—I'm sorry to use that word again, Karl—motivation? Why us? Or more specifically, why you?"

"Well, as for me, I think I was simply the guy available when he was looking for someone from our side to approach in Vienna. Sort of a target of opportunity." Baier took a breath before continuing. " I think he turned to us out of a sense of betrayal at what Stalin and his fellow butchers have done to a cause he believed in. He said as much when he explained his own journey from committed communist to dissident spy. He apparently believes America—and the CIA--can help right that ship by putting up obstacles to the Stalinist rule in his homeland."

"And us? The Agency?"

"Bluebird turned to an organization on our side that he was sure he could understand. Remember, Gary, he comes from the world of intelligence himself."

"Well, Budapest and the Hungarian desk are prepared to give you the benefit of the doubt, given your work with them in the past year. The refugee network you've established has proven to be a real bonus in terms of moving people in and out of there. Remind me again how you set that up."

Baier's gaze wandered to the window again, where he saw a sailboat that was making its way at a leisurely pace up river. It would presumably meet the Chesapeake Bay in a few hours and begin a proper sailing adventure. He wondered where his own Hungarian adventure would end. "It started up last year in Budapest. We met up again with a KGB officer in charge of border security in Hungary, someone we had gotten to know several years ago in Berlin. As you might have guessed, this particular officer is not a committed Communist. In fact, he's more of a capitalist than either your or me."

"So, he's in it purely for mercenary reasons?"

"For sure. Well, maybe not 'purely.' This officer has had his own problems with the Kremlin and the system over there. The fact that he's survived this long shows how capable he is of operating in the world of deception and subterfuge. I'm under no illusions regarding the guy's loyalties. Those rest with himself, and himself alone."

Peters let the rubber band sail across the room where it bounced off a picture of George Washington, America's first spymaster. "Karl, you need to be aware of the alarm bells that working with so many Commies and security types has set off back here."

"So many? You mean two?"

"Karl, there has got to be more people involved, or some who are at least aware of the operations. Do you really think just these two people can survive on their own for this long? Surely, you've thought about whether those few have been able to keep their circle tight enough and truly closed. How secure do you think these two operations really are?"

Baier smiled, then immediately regretted it. "Good point, Gary. My Russian does have some help, obviously, but as far as those people know this is all about the money to be made from the bribes they get to let people through. I continue to monitor any indicator I can find on how safe we all are out there. I do have some experience here, Gary..."

"Karl, I did not mean to imply..."

Baier raised his hand. "No, Gary, I get your point about the potential dangers to the security and integrity of the operation. I believe the benefits still outweigh the risks. Who else are we going to work with in that part of the world? Fictional opposition groups?" He also regretted the last comment as soon as it was past his lips. Under Allan Dulles and Frank Wisner, the OSS veteran and now the Agency's chief of operations, the CIA had squandered enormous funds and too many people in ill-conceived paramilitary type attempts to glean information from those closed countries or even to overthrow Communist rule in Eastern Europe. Those failures—and there were many--had cost the Agency dearly in resources and credibility.

Peters stared for what seemed like a full minute before he spoke. When he did, he leaned in close, his head extending beyond the halfway point of his desktop. "Karl, I'm going to forget that last remark. Wisner may or may not be fantasizing about opposition rebellions behind the Iron Curtain…"

"We're not the OSS, and the Second World War is over. We need to build a network of assets, not try to foment imaginary rebellions."

Peters held up a finger before continuing. "The Old Man is also taken with dreams of rebellions, coups, and rollback. In view of the successes in Iran and Guatemala, I think that's understandable."

"Despite what some around here may believe, those are also different parts of the world, Gary, societies that operate a lot differently than the Soviet Union and its satraps."

"There's an additional issue here."

Baier sat forward to close the space between them. "And that is?"

"Karl, you remember the Polish fiasco, don't you?"

"Vaguely."

"Well, I won't go over all the gruesome details, but in '52 we discovered that what we thought was a top-notch espionage operation in Poland, was actually a very clever ruse run by the Polish service into which we poured a lot of gold and allowed a number of Polish exiles to be lured to their deaths in Warsaw. So, you can imagine why people in this building are overly cautious towards an operation that has so many worrying aspects. I mean, this thing looks like it's cut from the same cloth."

"Fair enough. Let's not forget our Albanian fiasco, when we dropped all those exiles and supplies only to have them snapped up by the local service. That was another cocky-mammie scheme…"

It was Peters's turn to raise his hand. "I'm well aware of that unsuccessful operation."

"But those similarities to what we've got going in Budapest exist only on the surface. Bluebird is not trying to get us to bring resources and people into the country. Nor, is he trying expose our operational M.O., as far as I can see." Baier sat back against the chair as far as possible. "In any case, I stand warned. I still trust Bluebird and think we should stand by him if he's in trouble. Besides, we could be facing a real shit storm in Hungary, and Kovacs is placed to provide invaluable information and warning." Baier paused. "If we need to get him out, I can do it.

"Or die trying?"

"I prefer not to think of alternatives like that."

"You think it could be time to pull him out?"

Baier nodded. "I think it's a very strong possibility. We never got the chance to discuss it, since he failed to show for our meeting at the border yesterday."

"Well, dammit, Karl, that brings up another issue. Just who was the mystery man you met at the border yesterday?"

Baier shook his head. "I wish I knew, Gary, but I have no idea. He sure was convincing, though."

"Enough to lay a trap?"

"Believe me, I've thought about it. But, it's a chance I'm prepared to take. Hell, Gary, I don't see that we have any choice. If anything, I want to try to re-establish contact to make sure Bluebird's alright and see what he be able to tell us about the coming storm. At least, that's the positive side of it."

Peters pressed on. "You are aware, I'm sure, Karl, that our Embassy does not think things will come to a violent head in Budapest. They just don't see the Hungarians rising up in revolt against the Red Army."

"You know, there are analysts who think we could be in for some big surprises there."

"Like who?"

"Like Brian Quinn. I've come to trust that guy's instincts and insights. Besides, it's doesn't have to be a revolution to force change. Look at what happened in Yugoslavia in '48 when Tito broke away and established his independence from the Soviets."

"Look, Karl, Brian is a bit of an iconoclast. You can't put too much trust into what he says."

"Perhaps he is, but at least he's not like some people who have trouble conceiving of change. The trend lines aren't always straight, you know."

Peters shook his head. " Tito's still a Communist, and Yugoslavia is not on the Soviet border, or in a pathway of past invasions of Russia."

Baier sat upright. "But Yugoslavia is no longer a Moscow satrap, Gary. Tito causes more headaches for the Kremlin than anyone else in Europe these days."

"What about your KGB border guard in Hungary? How much do you trust him?"

Baier sighed. "Not all that much. Certainly not as much as I do Bluebird…"

"Now that is interesting. You say you trust a committed Communist more than someone you described as a real capitalist."

"He's a mercenary. Your own words, Gary. I've had a lot more experience with this KGB officer, not all of them good, admittedly. So, yes, I remain on my guard with him, and I believe he is still useful."

Peters stood and circled the desk, signaling that the meeting was now over. "Karl, you would be well advised to remain on your guard with everyone in this operation. I'll let you work things out with Budapest on what to do about Bluebird." He held up his hand. " I almost forgot. Your replacement has been named. The Old Man just approved it this morning. Gerry O'Leary."

"Not another Irishman?"

Peters smiled. "Yes, but he's also another Notre Dame grad, so you guys should have a smooth transition. Unfortunately, he's on home leave now back in Chicago, but we hope to get him out to Vienna as soon as possible."

"And my own assignment?"

Peters nodded and looked into Baier's eyes. "Nothing's been settled there yet. You have been discussed as a possible chief of your own station after the good work you've done in Vienna. It would probably be a small post, hopefully somewhere in Europe, given your background. Some place where you can get your own shop as a 'real' COS, Karl."

"That would certainly be fine with me."

Peters stopped on his way to the door. "Oh, yes. I wanted to ask you about one other thing from your cable last night."

"And that is?"

"You said you wanted to stop off in London on the way back. Is that necessary?"

Baier pulled his hands from his pants pockets and brought them together at his front, hoping to reinforce his argument, to help build his case. "Well, Gary, as we learned from the von Rudenstein affair, the Brits have had a presence in that part of the world for some time now, certainly longer than us."

"And you think they can help?"

"I can ask. Seeing as how scarce our resources are behind the Curtain, especially in places like Budapest with only one man there…"

"And given the difficult operating environment there…"

"Exactly. I got to know several of our cousins last year, one of them quite well, and I thought I'd sound them out to see if they could help." He paused. "If I need any, that is."

"Alright then. We'll let London know you're coming. You won't be entirely alone in Hungary, Karl. We're sending out two more officers to Budapest to help our man there, given all the uncertainty right now. You may remember one of them."

"Who is it?"

"Bill Schneider. You worked with him last year."

"Thank you, Gary. I couldn't ask for a better man."

Peters nodded. "Good then." He offered his hand to Baier. "In any case, we'll bring you back in the Spring after we've decided on your next job to get you ready. But be aware, Karl, that your next assignment could be riding on how this case turns out. Maybe more, depending on how deeply you get involved."

Baier stood and took the hand Peters offered. "I'm already deeply involved."

"I know." Peters returned to his seat and did not look up from his desk as Baier headed for the door.

Chapter Five

His buddy Delgreccio had been right. The British were far too absorbed in the mess they were busy creating in Cairo to be of any assistance in Hungary. Or elsewhere in Europe, for that matter. They weren't even sure all the attention in that part of Europe was actually necessary.

Baier's plane touched down at London Airport, southeast of the hamlet of Heathrow, on the morning of October 22. As his plane had circled overhead, Baier could see the crowd of workers busy with the construction of a permanent terminal for an airport that seemed always to be expanding. Or at least, it was under pressure to do so as travelers still flocked to a city that remained a cultural and political mecca for many, even with the Empire in decline. Hell, it had already lost its 'jewel' back in 1947 when India and Pakistan had broken away. The ride in, however, showed the same sea of green he remembered from his past visits to the British capital with the ubiquitous splashes of white wool from all the sheep that populated the countryside. At times, Baier wondered if the British Isles contained more sheep than people. Whichever way it went, he was pretty sure just from his various trips in from the airport—not to mention those around the countryside when he had served in London a few years back--that it would be a close call. Fortunately, a blue sky spread out along the horizon with only a few patches of white in the air above. On days like these it was a blessing to be in the United Kingdom. The pub gardens would certainly be full. He only hoped that the weather would hold for the next day or so before he returned to Vienna. There was a saying in Britain: if you don't like the weather, just wait an hour.

After dropping his bags at the Caledonian Club in Belgravia, just a few blocks from the Wellington Arch, Baier grabbed one of the iconic black bubble cabs for the drive to St. James's Square, the location for the office within Britain's famous— or at times infamous—foreign intelligence organization, the Secret Intelligence Service or SIS, that Baier dealt with most frequently. More popularly, the SIS was known as MI6, the abbreviation for Military Intelligence 6, the moniker it picked up at its founding during the First World War. Although the main MI6 headquarters were over on Broadway Avenue, the European office had been temporarily relocated to the more scenic Square just off Piccadilly Street. Baier had resisted the temptation to grab a quick nap after the 12-hour transatlantic flight, fearing that he might sleep through the day and miss his appointment with the new head of the European Division, Sidney Hargrove. As the taxi swung around Buckingham Palace and sped towards the light at St. James Road next to that palace, the traditional Court of St. James, Baier congratulated himself on dropping Sir Robert Sinclair's name to secure a reservation at the Caledonian. Baier had stayed there during his excursion to London a year ago, trying to dig to the bottom of the mystery surrounding the death of the Austrian aristocrat Herr Heinrich Rudolph von Rudenstein. Sir Robert, then-head of MI6's European bureau, had been polite, of course, but less than helpful to Baier. Still, he had arranged for the American to stay at one of the more comfortable London clubs during his visit. This one, as the name suggested, catered to London's strong Scottish community, and the selection of single malts at the bar was truly memorable. If he could, Baier might even try to swing the tab onto Sinclair's account. Not only would that save some money, but it would be a nice bit of mild retribution for Sinclair holding so much back on von Rudenstein's background. He smiled at the thought as the driver pulled up in front of the long, five-story stone building that occupied nearly the entire western side of St. James Square.

"Important business to attend to, Guv?" The cabbie inquired.

"I'm not really sure at this point," Baier replied, as he climbed out of the back seat.

"In any case, that'll be five quid."

Baier handed over the money through the driver's window, then trotted up the front steps, where he encountered the same receptionist behind the rich brown mahogany counter who had greeted Baier on his arrival over a year ago. Not much in the way of upward mobility in this service, Baier guessed. Baier gave his name and showed his passport. "Mr. Hargrove's office please."

The man smiled through the stiff white collar that topped his black butler's tuxedo. "I remember you from your previous visit. Wasn't that long ago was it, Sir?" He consulted a ledger at his front. "Yes, Sir, Mr. Baier. Sir Sydney is waiting for you. It'll be the same office that Sir Robert occupied on your last visit."

"Thank you." Baier was glad to see that some things continued to work well in this service. The people he knew remained friendly, informed, and occasionally helpful. Baier had reached out to another British colleague from the von Rudenstein affair, Thomas Harrison, to set this meeting up at short notice. That officer had turned out to be more than a colleague; the two had become friends as well. Harrison had come through again this time around. Baier had originally hoped Harrison would be joining him for this session, if only to broker introductions. Harrison, however, had regretted. "I'd love to, Karl, but I'm afraid I'm completely swept up in this Middle East thing. Have you heard much about it?"

"There have been rumors swirling."

"Probably almost as many as there are facts. None of them encouraging, I might add. But also between us, you understand."

"Of course. My lips are as sealed as Sir Robert's. How is the old man?"

"Hmmm. We'll have to see about that. As for the 'old man,' as you call him, I gather he's living well in a very comfortable retirement west of here in Warwickshire."

"Warwickshire? Isn't that Shakespeare country?"

"As a matter of fact, it is. Also, staunch Catholic country. At least historically. Like Sir Robert's family apparently. I hear his estate even has a 'priest hole' used to hide Jesuits during Elizabeth's reign."

"The previous one, right?"

Harrison chuckled. "Yes, yes, of course. Let's meet for drinks afterwards at the Club. Only this time we'll make it my place, The Travellers Club down on Pall Mall."

Baier had promised to make time later that evening. If that failed, then he offered to spring for drinks the next time Harrison found himself in Vienna. Harrison and Baier had both cultivated a taste for *Gruener Veltliner*, the fine dry white wine that was popular in Austria.

"Come in!" Hargrove announced.

Sir Sidney appeared to have deep, even booming vocal cords. Baier had not met the man yet, and he prayed that this was not another British aristocrat who had inherited a senior position in his country's civil service. To Baier's surprise, the body failed to match the voice. Hargrove was short, about five or six inches shorter than Baier, who measured in each morning at 6 foot 2. He did have a rich head of red curly hair, which

Baier had heard often signaled some roots from the Viking raiders who had plagued these islands back in the 9th and 10th centuries. Baier also doubted that Hargrove's pale skin was in any danger from the mostly overcast skies that covered the United Kingdom. The skin appeared all the more fair, set against the navy-blue suit that Hargrove was wearing. He had on the requisite white dress shirt for the day and a bright gold tie with some kind of crest at the center. Hopefully, not a family coat of arms. Sir Robert's had been enough for one career.

"Sit down, Karl. May I call you that?" Hargrove motioned towards the brown leather sofa that was a familiar sight from previous visits.

"Please," Baier responded, dropping into the corner of the couch farthest from the desk and closest to the door. He noticed that none of the framed portraits of past aristocrats and British luminaries, including the one of Winston Churchill behind the desk, had been exchanged from Sir Robert Sinclair's time, and Baier surmised that they must belong to the office, not the man. The burgundy wall papering and black curtains that hung from the tops of the long windows to the floor were also the same as when Sir Robert had occupied the post. Baier wondered just how far back in time they went.

"I'll get right to the point, as I'm sure you're eager to return to your home and office in Vienna. I'm afraid that we can be of little help for you in filling in any gaps in your knowledge of developments in Budapest. That is why you're here, isn't it?"

Baier nodded and resettled his rear end on the cushions. "Yes, in a way. You see, I'm most interested in your service's assessment of the prospects for stability or change in Hungary, and what you think Soviet intentions are." Baier shifted his weight. "Whether you have any information you might like to share on operations you're running there. I'd hate for us to step on one another's toes," he explained.

"I see." Hargrove settled back against the sofa and glanced

towards the ceiling before continuing. "Well, I'd say that we agree with our Ambassador's assessment that a revolt or any sort of violent rebellion is highly unlikely. The Hungarian populace is simply too passive and too cowed by their Soviet masters and their local Stalinist allies to do much in the way of rebellion. Look at how poorly Nagy was received and the failure of his reform program."

"Just what do you see happening to Nagy? Any chance of a comeback?"

Hargrove's eyes went wide, and the words seemed to bubble from his lips. "Nagy? My God, the man's lucky to be alive. I should think he'd be happy to end his days filling agricultural quotas for whatever Five-Year Plan they have in place. That is, after all, the man's specialty."

"Okay, he did specialize in agronomy, but in doing so he oversaw the agricultural reform and land redistribution that was so popular. I believe it's one of the reasons the Kremlin turned to him when they tried to popularize Communist rule after Rakosi's botched leadership."

Hargrove nodded as his gaze wandered to the window and back. "Yes, I read that report from your service's analytic branch. Interesting stuff. But he also created a new class of *kulaks*, which probably marked him in the Communist ledger as someone not to be trusted. No, I don't see that man playing any kind of significant role in Hungary's future. I'm sorry." He paused to consider Baier for a moment before continuing. " I gather that your State Department feels the same as we do. So why are you really here?"

Baier repositioned his butt yet again to buy himself a few more seconds before responding. "Well, it's an operational matter that I really can't go into at the moment. But I may need your service's assistance at some point, or someone's assistance."

"Can you tell me what sort of assistance you were looking for?"

"No, I'm afraid I can't go into much in the way of details. Particularly as it involves a part of the world where our two services have had their differences. Operationally, I mean."

"Ah, yes. You're referring to that unfortunate affair in Vienna last year, I take it."

"Yes. But that does not mean that you might not be able to help this time around. Given how few resources we have of our own in that part of the world, I may be looking for some assistance on the ground in the east at some point in the near future. I was hoping we might be able to work together, if it becomes necessary. If that does come to pass, I'd certainly be prepared to divulge more. We'd have to move cautiously, of course. It depends, in part, on how active your people still are behind the Iron Curtain." Baier smiled. "Wonderful phrase that, by the way."

Hargrove smiled, then frowned. "Ah, I see. And thank you. We rather enjoyed Mr. Churchill's speech back here. If it's any help, you know we have restricted Kim Philby's access until he is fully cleared."

"Which you expect to happen?" Baier leaned forward, trying to suppress the note of incredulity in his voice and the look of wonder on his face.

Hargrove nodded. "Yes, frankly I do. But I'm afraid that even then we can be of little help in that theater."

"Because of Suez?"

"Yes, I'll be honest with you. Our resources are fully committed there, especially as we are getting so little help from our special friends across the Atlantic. Any chance of that changing?"

Baier shook his head. "I'm not involved in that issue, and I do not speak for my Agency. But I seriously doubt it. I sense a lot of skepticism. I really can't say any more than that."

Hargrove nodded again. "Fair enough. But I'll also be honest and tell you that we really don't see any need or reason to divert resources to Hungary, regardless of how promising some may see developments there." Hargrove rolled his eyes. "As for operational work there…well," his hand rose and fell. "I'm afraid we cannot offer much help there either. Once burned, twice shy, as they say. Both our organizations have been burned more than once in that part of the world. I am sorry. I do wish I could be more forthcoming."

Baier stood. "Well, I do want to thank you for taking the time to meet with me today."

Hargrove rose from his seat and seemed to be studying the red and blue Persian carpet at their feet. He looked up at Baier, as tiny glint of light in his eyes. "Hold on. Perhaps there are some retired officers who might be able to help. At least, in the way of advice."

"That might be interesting. Can you recommend anyone in particular?"

Hargrove shook his head. "Not right off, but you might ask around. You still have some other contacts in the building, I take it."

Baier stood. "As you say then, fair enough." He started towards the door. "I'd like to wish you luck with your endeavor in the Canal Zone, but I doubt it would do much good."

Hargrove stood and accompanied Baier to the door. "Likewise, Karl. I doubt either of us are likely to find much success in our endeavors."

"I'M AFRAID YOU got the straight scoop from Sir Sydney, old man."

Thomas Harrison had just treated Baier to an excellent dinner of Scottish prime rib at his local society, the well-known Travellers Club, famous as the starting point for the bet involving the round-the-world trip in eighty days. The port and cigar stage had already begun, as Baier lost himself in the plush leather armchair that looked through the bar and out along the traffic crossing Pall Mall. The dark wooden paneling and tuxedoed waiters reeked of wealth and tradition. Baier had asked himself during the dinner just how Harrison could afford this sort of place. There must be money in the family, he guessed.

"Are you guys really so sure that nothing is going to happen in Hungary?"

Harrison chuckled. "It's probably more a case of hoping nothing will happen. We're already oversubscribed to this Suez Canal adventure, which does not bode well, in my limited consideration. I keep hoping someone upstairs knows better. But given our Prime Minister's fragile mental and emotional state, I doubt it."

"So, it's true. Eden is in well over his head. I hear that even Churchill is disdainful."

Harrison nodded as the smoke from his Cohiba drifted past his chin and rose slowly along his cheek. "Afraid so, my man. Anthony has been in over his head, as you say, for years. The surprising thing to me is that Churchill seems so well aware of it. Probably thinks it will make his own legacy look that much more impressive."

Baier expelled his own mouthful of smoke before sipping from his glass of port. "Is it true that the French and Israelis have been pushing their own agenda here?"

Harrison sipped some his own port and shrugged. "Well our agendas are pretty similar, or at least running in parallel. I can't say that either one has been all that helpful. The Froggies are hell bent on pushing a military solution, apparently in an effort to erase the stigma of their kidnapping the leaders of the Algerian revolt after promising them safe passage."

"And the Israelis?"

It looked as though Harrison might choke on his port for a moment. Then he rolled his eyes and moaned. "Bloody hell, Karl. Can you imagine?"

"What is it?"

"I guess it shows how things change. You know of the bombing of the King David Hotel in Jerusalem not that long ago?" Baier nodded. "I mean it wasn't all that far back that we lost ninety-one people to those sods in the Irgun. We literally had to scrape the remains of some of our people off the walls across the street. One typewriter was found with someone's fingers still glued to the keys. Now we're working with the bastards against the Egyptians."

"I'm sorry." Baier said. "I guess I had forgotten about. That must really be tough for many of you."

Harrison shrugged. "Well, that sort of decision is made well above my head, as I'm sure you're aware. I guess one can understand the Israelis' sense of fragility, surrounded as they are. But they don't seem to realize that their future would be much more secure with a peace settlement than military expansion."

"Then why keep pushing this thing?"

"You said it yourself, Karl. The PM is in over his head. And there does not appear to be anyone along Whitehall willing to step up and tell him that we're headed for disaster." Harrison paused to draw more cigar smoke, which he blew over his glass as he took another sip of port. "My real concern, though, is what this might do to our most important global relationship. That is, our one with you Yanks. I only hope it survives."

Baier was silent. He didn't know what to say to that.

Harrison leaned forward. "You see, I agree that our real nemesis is not some Arab potentate with delusions of grandeur. It's those clowns in the Kremlin. They're the ones that pose the real threat to our security and our way of life. It's playing out in Hungary as we speak. We need to be better informed, and we need leaders willing to be informed."

"You don't see much of that at present?" Baier pressed.

"Well, old man, do you?"

"So, is there nothing you can do to help?"

"Do you mean with our respective leaderships, or something closer to home?"

Baier smiled. "Well, the latter for now." He studied his

British colleague for a few seconds before continuing. "Sir Sidney mentioned how strapped you are for resources in the region right now. Much like we are, I might add. He did suggest, though, that there might be a retired old gent or two that could help. More in the way of advice, I believe."

Harrison drew a long breath on his cigar and let the smoke slip slowly from his lips. Then he reached over, raised his glass of port and swirled the deep brown liquid in the half-full glass. Before drinking, he spoke. "Well, that's certainly an interesting approach. Not that anyone springs to mind at the moment." He sipped his port. "Wait a minute. There is one old fellow who might be able to help. Probably nothing more than sage advice, though. He is a bit long in the tooth."

"Who might that be?"

"A chap named Oliver Rankin. He's retired now and lives up north in the Lake District. Pretty country that."

"I'm sure it is. I wish Sabine and I had had the chance to visit when we lived here during our assignment to London back in the early 50s. How am I supposed to meet this man? I leave tomorrow night for Vienna."

Harrison took another swallow of his port. "Well, it shouldn't be that hard, actually. The Lake District isn't that far. If you leave early enough, you can make it back for an evening flight."

"What makes this retired officer so useful?"

"Oh, he's lived quite an adventurous life, some of it working with our original spy ring in Moscow right after the Bolsheviks seized power."

"How is that supposed to help me? I mean, that was what, forty years ago?"

"Oh, I realize, Karl, that times have changed, and that we're dealing with a much different set of circumstances now. He may still have a few good lessons to impart. Maybe even a name or two to pass along if things get desperate. Can you tell me more about what you'll be up to?"

"Just that there's a source who may be in trouble. In fact, I'm pretty sure he is."

"Well then, this may be your man. He's had some exciting escapes of his own, should it come to that." Harrison drained his glass and stared at Baier. "Karl, you know I wouldn't recommend this if I didn't think it would prove beneficial."

Chapter Six

THE LAKE DISTRICT was indeed a beautiful piece of country. Famous, too, for several of its residents, like William Wordsworth and Beatrix Potter. Baier had wanted to visit the former's two residences in the area ever since his course in English Literature during his freshman year at Notre Dame, but that would probably have to wait for another visit. Time was at a premium for Baier on this trip, if he was going to make that evening flight back to Vienna. That meant he had to catch the afternoon train back to London, which included a tight connection in Kendal. And this was a country where the trains did not always run on time.

Oliver Rankin's house—more of a lodge or cabin, actually—was easy enough to find, especially with the aid of a taxi. Bowness-on-Windermere sat on perhaps the largest Lake in the District, Windermere, appropriately enough, and Rankin's place was just outside the village on a small plot of land, about half an acre, overlooking the Lake with a view across the water to a set of green hills that rolled above the opposite shore. He was also at home, it being 11:30, just before the lunch hour.

Not that a man who must be in his 80s, or even older, had a whole lot else to do. Still, he seemed friendly enough, eagerly inviting Baier inside for a 'spot of tea.' The man was tall—he had an inch or two on Baier—but he walked hunched over and with the help of a hardwood cane. Still, he looked to be quite limber and mobile as he rambled toward the kitchen at the back of the house. His worn brown sweater and heavy cotton pants seemed to flow through the hallway. Baier was also struck by the man's clear-headedness and mental agility after only a few sentences between them.

"So, you're in the middle of the game? I gather things are about to break loose once more."

"Yes, it would seem so," Baier answered.

"You think I can be of help? Who did you say sent you?"

"Thomas Harrison. We worked together on a case in Vienna last year."

Rankin laughed lightly. "Well, bless his heart. It's nice to be remembered. Even if it has been a while." Rankin puttered around the sink and stove, filling a pot of water and setting it over the fire he lit. "He must have attended one of those lectures the higher-ups brought me in to deliver on operating in Russia after the Revolution. I'm not sure how my experiences in the Soviet Union would help, though. Not right off, anyways."

"Could you tell me what you did while you were there? What sort of operation were you involved?"

That drew a heartier laugh. "Oh, that. Well, I got involved because I was working with George Hill. Do you know of him?" Baier shook his head. "He was an RAF officer initially sent to Russia to train pilots for their own air force when they were in still in the fight with us against the Kaiser. Then Sir Andrew Cummings…you've heard of him, of course"

Baier nodded. "Sure. The famous 'C,' the man who established MI6 during the First World War."

"That's right. He drafted Hill, or convinced him, is more like it, to work for this new service, and George convinced me to come along. So, I worked with George and that scoundrel Sidney Reilly to set up a courier network to get all the information we were collecting out to our people in London."

"Was there a lot?"

Rankin whistled. "Oh, absolutely. It was no trouble in those days to find people with access who wanted to help us. It's amazing, when I think back on it, how open things were in those days. I guess it comes from being in the middle of a revolution." Rankin chuckled. "Most of the people I met hated the damn Bolshies. It's a wonder they ever survived." The pot of steaming water whistled. Rankin poured a stream over a small tray of tea leaves in a ceramic pot on the table. Heraldic portraits of British royalty under wreaths of green decorated the sides of the teapot. "The ones working for the Bolshies, I mean. A lot of the others didn't."

"I guess it's a wonder the Bolsheviks survived as well, if there were so many willing to work against them."

"Yes, well, those bastards proved to be the more ruthless side, willing to do whatever was necessary to survive and ensure they stayed on top. Keep that in mind son."

"No need to worry there. Why do say Sidney Reilly was a scoundrel? I thought he was nicknamed 'The Ace of Spies.'"

"Because we had a damn fine operation going that smuggled all kinds of valuable stuff out that kept His Majesty's Government pretty well informed about things in the middle of that Revolution. And right from the top. But Reilly let his ego get in the way."

"What did he do?"

"Tried to overthrow the Bolshevik government, is what he did. Not only was it foolhardy…it was really poorly planned, you see. He wanted to put himself in charge." Rankin shook his head in disgust. "No, just being a good and useful intelligence agent wasn't enough for the likes of him."

"I take it that put an end to your own collection and courier program."

"Damn right it did. We were lucky to get out alive. We

even had to make a swim for it through one part of the Gulf of Finland. Cursed Reilly's name the whole way, we did." He poured Baier a cup of tea. "The whole plot was exposed from the start. Played right into the Cheka's hands. Pitiful!" He eyed Baier with a squint. "You know what the Cheka was, young man?"

"Yes, of course. The forerunner to the NKVD and today's KGB. I am truly sorry to hear about the end of your operation back then. I wonder if there's any lessons for me in that today. Is there anything else?"

"Well, I did go back briefly and helped set up another courier route, but that all went to shit when the Trotsky's Red Army threw the Whites out of the country. Those that he didn't kill."

"I get the sense that you did not have a lot of luck with running complicated courier operations."

"Well, not over the long term, of course. It was all too chaotic back then. That was the downside of a situation like that. Sure, you got access and information for a while, but it could change overnight. They would work for a little while, but eventually you have to worry about breakdowns in the hierarchy or along the routes. Things were very uncertain and changing all the time.' Rankin shrugged. "Still, we didn't have a whole lot of choice. It would have been nice if we could have carried the material out ourselves, and we did try sometimes. But that wasn't much of an option either. Plus, we wanted to be there to protect our people if we could."

"I see."

Rankin returned the pot to stove and held up an index finger as he turned back to Baier. "But there were things we learned about moving people back then. Is that what you're interested in?"

"Perhaps. What about afterwards? Any other missions to the East?"

"They sent me in to help pull some of our people out of Tajikistan."

"Why were you active in that godforsaken place?"

Rankin looked at Baier with some incredulity. "Good God, man, have you not heard of the Great Game?"

"Is that what you meant earlier when you spoke of being 'in the game'?"

"Absolutely, son. We were worried that the Bolshies would instigate a revolution in our Indian possessions. The jewel in the crown and all that. Couldn't have it, of course. So, we were busy doing what we could to block their efforts on that front. They had quite a lot going on in that arena, I can assure you."

"Not like now, though, is it?"

Rankin waved his hand, as though he wanted to dismiss the passage of time. "No, but we did learn not to trust the same methods for too long. Those bastards can catch on quick."

"What sort of methods?"

"Oh, concealment or false documents." Rankin frowned. "If I remember correctly, it was the latter that seemed to work best. But that was probably because the Bolshies hadn't really set up a functioning government yet. Wasn't hard to produce fakes, you see." He shook his head and stared at the tea in his cup. "No, those days are gone. At least for us. That's why we'll probably leave whatever's happening in Europe with the Bolshies to your folk. Can't be bothered with it all these days. Especially not with all this silly shit down in the Sinai and the Suez Canal. Just a sign of how little we matter anymore, in my opinion."

"Miss it, do you?"

"Absolutely. I was proud to be part of our mission back then."

"What did you mean earlier when you asked if I was in the 'game'? This has nothing to do with India or that part of the world."

Rankin shot a look of surprise at his guest. "Hell, man, it's all part of the game. The geography doesn't matter that much. We're in competition with the Russians still. It's that simple.

The arena just moves on." He poured himself a cup of tea, then cradled it both hands before taking a sip. "But we've got an ace up our sleeves this time."

"What's that?"

Rankin pour some tea for Baier. "You Yanks, of course."

Baier dumped several spoonfuls of sugar into the tea in an effort to make it palatable. He would have killed for a cup of coffee just then. He took several sips to be polite before continuing. "I see. That is helpful. Actually. Any more words of advice on moving people? You seem to have done a lot of that."

Rankin limped over to a chair across from Baier and settled in. "Sure. Good documents can be critical. But even more important is having a solid network of people to help along the way. It's nearly impossible to do it alone. Much depends, of course, on where you're operating and how far you need to go." He took a surprisingly long drink from his cup of tea. "I doubt you'll want to say much about what you're up to, though. Can't say as I blame you. Not with all the nonsense that's been going on in our service these days."

"No, it would be best for me to say as little as possible on that score. But may I ask if you still have any contacts in the area?"

"What, you mean in Moscow?"

"No, I was thinking more of Austria or Eastern Europe."

"Oh, most of the people I worked with are long retired or dead even. Let me think. There may be one or two still kicking around." Rankin sipped from his cup and studied the table top. After a minute, he looked up at Baier. "If I think of anyone should I pass the name and contact information along through this Harrison fellow?"

Baier smiled. "That would be great. I really appreciate this."

To show how much he did appreciate Rankin's help, Baier finished all his tea.

BAIER SPENT THE better part of the evening of October 23

scrambling to get a flight out of Heathrow, or any London airport for that matter, back to Vienna. He had been too late to make his original reservation, and he did not find a seat on a Pan Am flight until later that night, which got him back to the Austrian capital around 11:00. It was after midnight when he made it home. A wide-eyed Sabine greeted him at the door, holding it open but not moving back or aside to let him in. Baier could see that her lips were trembling.

"What is it, Sabine? What's wrong?"

"It's begun, Karl."

"What has? What's begun?"

"The students and workers have taken to the streets of Budapest, Karl. The country is in revolt."

Chapter Seven

~~~

"**S**ABINE, WHAT HAPPENED?"

"Karl, what's wrong? You look upset, or worried. Angry, even. Aren't you happy for the people of Hungary?"

"I'm not angry. I'm worried because nobody saw this coming. At least not anyone I spoke with in London or Washington. It means we're not prepared, that we're flying blind here."

Baier stepped inside and dropped his suitcase in the hallway. Then he headed for the kitchen. Baier turned to his wife as she hung back by the front door, draped in a loose, green cotton nightgown and red and black flannel robe. Her feet were bare, and Baier realized she had not bothered or even thought to put on slippers. Her face shone with that light of expectation and excitement that one would expect with news like this, her eyes like small illuminated globes. Her hands were folded tightly together at her front. It was as though there was a disorientation mixed in with all the excitement. When he reached the refrigerator, Baier pulled out the open bottle of Riesling and poured two glasses. "Tell me what you know, Sabine. Please. How did you find out?"

"Karl, it's all over the news here. Haven't you heard?"

He shook his head. "No. Not yet. I've been traveling all day, trying to escape from various English airports so I could get back home."

Sabine slumped into a chair at the kitchen table and reached for her glass of wine. Baier noticed the weariness under the excited glow for the first time since he had arrived home, and he cursed himself for keeping her up so late. First waiting for his return, and now this. Then again, revolutions don't happen every day. Things were only beginning. God knows what awaits us all, he thought. He thought of Kovacs. Was it now safer for him? Or did he face an even greater threat?

"I was down at the border this afternoon, searching for the man you've been expecting," Sabine began. "There were so few coming across that I thought I would easily be able to pick him out by your description. I didn't know if you had arranged anything, but I thought it was worth a try."

"I take it he didn't show."

Sabine shook her head, then sipped her wine. "That's right. I'm hardly surprised at this point. So, I started to ask some of the people what was going on over there. They all looked more shaken and fearful than before, Karl. Many were crying, and others had eyes red from weeping and rubbing."

"Shouldn't they be happy?"

"Karl, they're frightened. They don't know what will happen to their homes, their families."

Baier took a seat opposite his wife and drank some of his wine. He noticed immediately afterwards that he had drained nearly half the glass. It had gone down almost like water. But, the sour aftertaste helped sharpen his attention. "Yes, I can imagine. Has there been fighting? How did it all start? Is the Hungarian Army involved?"

Sabine stared at her own glass for a moment before continuing. "I don't know about the Army. I think there have been some shooting and deaths, but mostly between the demonstrators and the AVO."

Baier sighed. "That figures."

"From what I could gather, it all started with a demonstration by some students and intellectuals. There were separate protest marches in Budapest, three, I think. Eventually they all converged on the Parliament. I guess it started up sometime in the afternoon."

"Was it just students and writers? The intellectuals?"

Sabine shook her head. "At the beginning, yes. But the refugees said they were soon joined by workers and office types as the crowd made its way through the capital. Karl, these people at the border said there must have been hundreds of thousands protesting in Budapest."

" I still don't understand why these people at the border would be fleeing? Isn't this what so many had hoped for?"

"Karl, of course they had hoped for this. Not everyone is so brave, especially when they have so much to lose. Can you blame them? Look at what they're up against."

"So where was the fighting, and how heavy have the casualties been?"

Sabine shrugged. "Karl, these refugees would not know all that. They did say that there was some fighting at the main radio station, which I believe eventually fell to the demonstrators."

"Where did they get the weapons? What's the Hungarian Army doing? Are they neutral or even supportive?"

"I guess they've stayed out of it, for the most part. Although some have gone over to the rebels' side, and many others have given up their weapons. The rebels have also raided some police depots."

"Is there any word of Nagy and where he stands?"

"Oh, Karl, the crowd was calling for him, but when he spoke at the Parliament he was booed."

Baier pushed his glass to the side and leaned in over the table. "But why?"

"He told the people to go home and trust the party. He has

no credibility now. He's fallen behind where the demonstrators are going. He refused to endorse the Sixteen Points."

"The what?"

"The rebels have put together a string of demands. The biggest are for free elections and departure of the Soviets."

"So, the revolt is essentially leaderless."

Sabine nodded. "It appears that way. But, so is the Party. Some at the border said the leadership initially banned all protests early in the day, but then allowed the demonstration to go forward." Sabine shook her head. "Karl, those people in the Party do not know how to respond to something like this."

Baier leaned back and reached for his glass. He finished his wine in a single swallow. "And just how confused are they in Moscow? First East Germany, then Poland, and now this. Khrushchev must really be regretting his destalinization speech and openings to reforms, no matter how small." He remembered the work of his own agency in smuggling that famous, supposedly secret speech denouncing the crimes of Stalin out from the Soviet Party's Twentieth Congress and publicizing it around the world. He smiled.

"Karl, what is so funny?"

Baier looked at his wife. "I'm sorry. I'm just smiling at my own foolishness. I know you could not have learned all the details from the people at the border. But you have picked up a lot. I'm just thinking out loud."

Sabine stood and carried her half-full glass of wine to the sink. She set it aside. "And Karl, they have a new flag, at least in Budapest. Someone at the border showed it to me and claimed that everyone in the capital was carrying these now."

Baier stood and moved towards the sink with his own empty glass. "What does this flag have on it?"

"It's what it doesn't have. It's like the old one. They've cut the hammer and sickle out of the middle."

"Oh, Jesus, that's not going to help. That will have the Kremlin pissing nickels. Were there any Soviets at the border?

I don't suppose our "fucking Russian" friend was anywhere around."

Sabine stepped in close to her husband and circled his waist with her arms. Her head fell to his chest. "That has me worried even more, Karl. Early in the day there were perhaps a dozen or so there, and they let the refugees move freely. I assumed they had their orders from our friend Chernov, or maybe they were some of his handpicked accomplices. By evening, they had all gone."

"The Soviets?" Sabine nodded. "Did you get a sense of where they might be heading? Did you overhear anything?"

Sabine threw her head back, shook it, then rested it on his chest again. "No. I'm sorry."

"Shit," Baier exclaimed. He stroked his wife's hair. "No, Sabine, I don't mean to criticize what you may have missed. I doubt I would have gotten anything either. I seriously doubt they were on their way home to Moscow."

Just what did Chernov know? Baier would have to find the Russian now, as well as Kovacs. He was almost certain that he would have the chance to learn just where the loyalty of Chernov-- the 'fucking Russian, as Sabine had named him during their time in Berlin--lay and how deeply they ran in the shifting scene in Budapest, another piece to an increasingly dangerous puzzle.

HE GOT LITTLE sleep that night. Two, maybe three, hours, although he spent the early hours of the morning in a daze and couldn't be sure how long he'd lain awake and how many minutes of fitful sleep he had been able to snatch from the gray dawn outside his window. When he arrived at his office, it looked as though his compatriots were in much the same condition. In fact, when Baier stumbled over to the coffee pot next to the internal office mailboxes, he found only a thin sliver of black crud on the bottom of the pot.

"Hey, who forgot to brew fresh coffee? You guys know the

rules. Last man makes new stuff. This crap would work better as paving for the parking lot out front." He held up the pot for all to see. "If you take the last cup at least turn the damn machine off."

Bill Nelson, who had been in Vienna for a little over a year, having arrived the previous summer, hustled over. "Sorry, Chief. I was in a hurry to get a cable back to Washington. It's on your desk ready for you to sign off. There's also a rush message for you from Peters. You'll want to look at it right away."

"Okay, thanks." Baier marched over to his office as Nelson scrambled to get fresh coffee grinds in the percolator. "Let's assemble in my office in ten minutes to collect what we know about events in Hungary and what we might be able to do about the information gaps out there."

The message from the Agency's European Division chief sat on the top of a pile of paperwork on Baier's desk, resting inside a manila folder marked with a deep red sash at the top that said, 'Top Secret.' As he might have expected, Baier could almost feel the tension and excitement emanating from the sheaf of paper that Nelson had run off the teletype for him. Words like "urgent," "immediate," "drastic," and "woeful," leaped out at him from the page with its brief text in bold type. There were two sentences that stuck out more than any others for Baier, ones that left him eager and gratified, but also frustrated and angry. "In the absence of a permanent chief of station in Vienna at this critical juncture, it is Headquarters' belief that efforts to contact Bluebird should be left to our representative at the Embassy in Budapest. Additional personnel have been dispatched to assist Budapest to respond to mission requirements. Recognizing the value of Bluebird's access and reporting over the past year and the woeful lack of insight into Hungarian and Soviet government planning and intentions, Headquarters directs those personnel in Budapest to begin efforts to re-establish contact immediately."

Bluebird, the code name for Kovacs. 'Son of a bitch,' Baier mumbled. At least Washington recognizes the guy's value. Peters and those other clowns need to get their heads out of their collective ass. Just who do they think is going to be able to dig this guy out besides him? What makes them think this asset will report to just anyone? Kovacs was likely to be more cautious than ever with all this turmoil surrounding him. He would almost certainly be looking for a friendly face, one he knew and trusted. And that would be me, Baier thought, not some new guys from Washington.

"So, what's up, Chief? How much longer do we get to call you that?" Nelson asked. He grabbed a seat by the window. Sunlight framed him in a bright yellowish glow that stung Baier's eyes. At least it helped pump some additional adrenalin through his body. Three more colleagues entered Baier's office and took places along the wall.

"Not that long. A new station chief has been selected. Gerry O'Leary. He's had plenty of experience in European affairs, especially in Germany. He's also a good guy..."

"Not to mention a fellow Domer, right Chief, one of your own from Notre Dame?" Steve Clay added. Baier glanced over at the Fordham graduate.

"True, and I know you'll all give him the deep respect and reverence you've shown me." Baier smiled and waved away the low chuckles that greeted this last statement. "He's been at home in Chicago closing out some personal business, but my guess is that his departure will be accelerated now. Being a bachelor should help untangle any knots in the States." Nods and raised eyebrows all around. Baier took in a deep breath before continuing. "So, what do we know about developments in Budapest?"

Nelson, as usual, was the first to speak. "Well, the Soviets have gone in. Not in a big way, mind you, only about five thousand, could be a few more, and maybe a couple hundred tanks. At least that's what the journalists are reporting.

Our State colleagues down the hall have been talking to the Embassy there."

"The journalists?" Nelson nodded. "That makes sense, of course. And it squares with what I heard on the radio this morning," Baier continued. "Have our new people arrived there yet? If so, what have they had to say?"

"Not much," Nelson continued. I don't think they've had much of a chance to get out and about yet. The Embassy has put a tight rein on all personnel there for now."

"What's the word on Nagy? I take it he didn't make much of an impression at the parliament yesterday. Is it true we're all relying on newspaper people and other travelers for our information?"

Clay jumped in. "Well, Nagy's back, in any case. There are some reports from the Embassy in Budapest that he's about to be renamed as Prime Minister. According to what I've heard from our State colleagues down the hall, though, I gather he has yet to fully embrace the demands of the rebels."

Baier nodded. "That makes sense. The guy's still a committed Communist. He's probably hoping he can avoid alienating the Soviets to the point where he won't be able to engage in the modest reform program he tried to install when he was last in office."

"Good luck with that," Steve Miller added. Baier looked over at the most junior member of the office, a first-tour officer who had arrived in Vienna that July. He still dressed to impress in a charcoal grey suit, white shirt, and solid navy-blue tie. He looked the part of the Boston Brahmin that his family represented. The other members of the staff were in slacks, open-necked shirts, and jackets that were arrayed on the backs of desk chairs throughout the station like soldiers in a morning formation. Given the emergency that had erupted in the heart of Central Europe the day before, function--not style--had been the order of the day for most, as it was for Baier, who was wearing the same sort of business-like casual attire of grey slacks and an open-collar blue shirt. Just to be safe, though, he had stuck a red necktie in the pocket of his blue blazer. You never knew when you might be called upon to attend some high-level meeting or give a briefing.

Miller continued. "I mean, it's not like he had much in the way of support from the Kremlin or others in his own party the last time he tried. It also looks like the revolt is beginning to spread to the countryside and even some of the industrial towns, where the proletariat is supposed to remain loyal to their government's Communist ideals."

"Yeah, that's gotta sting," Clay added.

"Any idea what Washington plans to do?" Nelson asked.

Baier shook his head. "Not that I know of. Or heard, back in Washington when I was there. People in London and Washington seemed pretty certain that just this sort of thing would not happen, that the Hungarians' unhappiness would not go this far. As a result, I doubt any of our policy people have had the chance to look very far ahead."

"It looks like they underestimated the popular determination there," Nelson added.

Baier nodded. "As well as the degree of government, or Communist Party control. That's easy to do on the other side of an ocean." He sighed. "That is, if you're not listening. Our job is to find out as much as we can to keep Washington informed, preferably ahead of the curve, in hopes it will help them come up with a decent policy. Let's see what the Austrians can tell us, if anything. They should be better plugged in than we are, sadly."

"Are we going to offer the rebels any support? Eisenhower and Dulles have been making a lot of noise about 'roll back' ever since they got in office," Clay said.

"I guess we'll find out soon enough," Baier answered. Although the prospect of a conflict with the Soviet Union would surely have them thinking twice about that, he added to himself. This when our closest allies appeared ready to invade

Egypt, for chrissakes. 'Great timing,' he mumbled half out loud.

At that moment, Hank Freeman burst into the office and tossed a sheet of paper atop the small hill on Baier's desk. "Rush note from Budapest for you, Karl." Freeman, on his third tour, was one of the few who felt comfortable addressing Baier by his first name. He was rumored to be in line for a chief of station posting in the not-to-distant future, perhaps some place in the Far East. Baier could see it happening, and he could see it being a good thing.

Baier pushed these thoughts aside and glanced at the cable. Contact had been made with Budapest Station regarding the whereabouts of Bluebird. It wasn't Kovacs himself who had reached out, even though the contact had come through the emergency mechanism Baier had established with Kovacs if there was ever a need to get in touch immediately, or if the man's life was in danger. At least, it didn't appear to be from Kovacs. The author, whoever he was, may have made the pre-arranged dead drop, but he had failed to use any of the code words Baier had given him to signal distress, a change in plans, or a recognition of his last set of instructions regarding the failed meeting at the border. More significant, the handwriting appeared to be different. Actually, it wasn't even handwriting. Just a series of oversized block letters cut from a newspaper.

Bill Schneider, the officer who had met Baier at the train Station in Budapest over a year ago had checked the dead drop. Schneider was first officer Headquarters had sent into Budapest to support the Agency's one-man operation there. Baier had been happy to learn of this from his discussion with Peters back in Washington. Baier had been impressed by Schneider's street smarts and ability to pick up patches of Magyar, a very difficult language. It had allegedly been the language of the Huns. They hadn't had a chance to speak with each other yet, but Schneider had been instructed to check on the dead-drop site at least once a day, preferably twice, if it

was safe as a way to re-establish contact in the flash cable from
Washington.

The message from Kovacs--or whomever--included a
request for a personal meeting to re-establish contact and
impart valuable information. Only Baier would do. Up until
a few days ago Baier hadn't been aware that anyone else in the
Hungarian government was aware of the man's relationship
with Baier. In fact, Baier had expressly forbidden Kovacs from
sharing any information about his work for the Americans,
with anyone. Kovacs should have known better in any case,
given his own history of living underground. So, who the hell
had written the note? How did he know about the dead drop
arrangements?

First the meeting with the mystery man at the border, and
now this. Baier grew even more doubtful that Kovacs was even
alive, much less safe. There was an even stronger possibility
now of this all being a trap. There was only one way to find
out. Baier unconsciously crumpled the note from Budapest
in his hand.

Chapter Eight

SABINE REACHED OVER to grab Baier's hand as they stood gazing out across the border and into Hungary. A steady stream of refugees flowed through the gap in the barbed-wire fence that separated Austria from its eastern neighbor. The wooden posts framing the open space had been pushed back at right angles to the wire to allow the refugees through. According to Sabine, their numbers had grown over the last twenty-four hours, probably because of the fighting that had broken out in Budapest and elsewhere. The crowd still seemed thinner than the one Baier had witnessed just a few days ago when he had waited in vain for Kovacs, only to meet the frightened and elusive mystery messenger. The day had begun with a rich blue and nearly cloudless sky spread over the horizon, but in the last hour or so, patches of grey had begun rolling in from the east. Riven with anxiety, Baier hoped this was not an omen of some kind. He no longer looked for his Hungarian asset. The man was obviously back in Budapest, but Baier could come up with no positive explanation for all that had happened over the past few days.

Still, he was not prepared to give up on a man he had come to like and respect. Lord knew there was enough going on back there to keep a man occupied, both in his real job, as well as collecting information to pass to the Americans. It certainly helped Baier and the CIA to have an asset in place, providing first-hand information on the plans and policies of America's principal adversary and its loyal satrap at a time of growing turmoil in Europe and the Middle East. That is, if he was still an American asset, and in place.

Chernov, their Russian contact and co-conspirator in running the escape channel through the Austro-Hungarian border, had also not put in an appearance, but this was, in itself, not unusual. He rarely showed at the border, having an apparently reliable set of underlings in the border force to ensure that the operation ran smoothly. Infrequent appearances also served to keep his own role hidden. Nor could Baier expect regular meetings since the Russian was not what you'd call a controlled source. He must have made a small fortune through the bribes he accepted from refugees and dissidents fleeing west, along with the small and periodic payments Baier provided to ensure ready access for the occasional CIA agents passing through. Baier could count on one hand the number of times they had met in person over the past year. It made little difference to do so, since their arrangement had run smoothly. At this point, it was anybody's guess if that would continue.

Baier and Sabine had driven down from their home in Vienna the evening before. They had spent the night at the von Rudenstein estate, a vineyard property they had purchased the previous year to use as a headquarters for the smuggling operation that served as a cover for the infiltration and exfiltration they needed to run the Agency's intelligence collection program in Hungary and further east and south into Soviet occupied Europe. Sabine did not seem to mind the frequent travel. She had told her husband that she actually enjoyed helping run the center they had set up to debrief and care for returning assets before they moved on to other destinations in Europe. She also liked the beautiful countryside in this part of Austria, a welcome relief from the urban tangle of a major city like Vienna. Baier had used the drive down to explain to his wife why he needed to go back into Budapest after having snuck in a little over a year ago in search of her.

" Karl, they must know you now. They would love to get their hands on you, I am sure. You know what the AVO does to its prisoners. Can your people engineer another escape, and so soon?"

"Sabine, I really have no choice. I owe it to my man over there, and to our government in Washington. They are absolutely blind back home."

"Karl, do not forget that your country has an Embassy there."

"Yes, but what can they accomplish right now if no one will talk to them or can even reach them? It's not like they were able to get around much before."

"Perhaps that is changing."

"Sure, perhaps. Until I know more about what is happening, I have to do what I can."

Standing at the border with all the memories she carried of that place and the land further east, her own worries and anxieties refused to fade away. She reached out and squeezed his hand hard enough to make it hurt. "Karl, how can you be sure that he will be telling you the truth? Even if you can find him, which will not be easy in all this chaos."

Baier was silent for a moment. It was a question he had been asking himself. "If he is still alive, I will find him, Sabine. That alone will be no small victory. I'll only know the truth of it all when I meet him. There are some code words he can use when we communicate to let me know if he's being coerced. I'll have to see how reliable his information appears. I won't be able to do that sitting back here in Vienna. I need to meet the man face-to-face."

"How will you get to the capital from here?"

"One of the fellows from our office is there in place who helped me last year when I had to sneak in. He's picking me up a few miles from the border. I'll walk to the meeting point from the crossing below."

"It's not one of those guys who accompanied us to the border, I hope. The ones with the guns. If so, I'm sure I'll never see you again."

Baier smiled. "No, they're all back in Washington. They did help, Sabine. You could show a little more gratitude." Sabine groaned. "No, I'm meeting my colleague, Bill. He's more level-headed. He's a real professional. Like I said, he's had some experience in that capital, and he was sent back in recently. You'd have to have some pretty good skills to avoid getting compromised in the sort of environment you have to work in over there, which he has been able to do." Baier gestured in the direction of Hungary with a nod of his head.

Sabine stood on her tiptoes and kissed Baier long and hard on the lips. "Please be careful, Karl. I want to see you home in Vienna again. You know I'll be anxious and frightened until you return. Don't make it too long."

Baier circled her shoulders with his arms and pressed his face into her hair to get one last scent of his wife before leaving. "I know, Sabine. Believe me, I do not want this to go on any longer than it has to. I promise to return as soon as possible."

THE AUSTRIAN AND Hungarian border guards barely gave Baier a second glance. The Soviet advisers ignored him. The first look from the Austrians and Hungarians came only because they must have wondered why anyone would be going into Hungary, instead of the other way around, like all the others there. Baier had also made sure that he did not look like a prosperous Westerner, but rather like an ex-patriot who was returning home for whatever reason. He had the fake identification documents he would need in case he was challenged, although they had been hastily drawn up at the

Station and might not pass very careful scrutiny. According to these papers, he was a member of the German minority that had been expelled after the war, returning to check on some family left behind, but preparing to leave, themselves. Baier could not be sure the guards he encountered would be part of Chernov's operation, so he was banking primarily on a lackadaisical attitude on their part. To build a more convincing appearance, he had made sure that his clothes looked worn and dirty, as though he had been on the run and struggling for weeks. The old cotton trousers he had found in a flea market had grime around the cuffs and smudges at the knees, while his white shirt collar was turning to brown. The jacket was worn at the edges of the sleeves and ripped on the elbow.

"Well, I can say you look authentic," Schneider said, when they met by his car in a wooded grove just under three miles from the crossing. "I hope you don't smell as bad as you look. Did you bring a change, at least for underneath?"

Baier shook his head. "I don't plan to stay that long. I just hope to find Bluebird alive, and then assess the guy's access with all the turmoil in your town and his continued reliability. Then I'll head back."

"Do you think he's still among the living?"

"God, but I hope so."

"Well, there is good news, of sorts."

Baier turned his head sideways. " Are you going to keep me waiting?"

Schneider shook his head and smiled. "Nope. Bluebird has reached out. He responded to my note at the dead drop."

Baier whipped his entire body around to face Schneider. "How did it sound? Do you think it was him?"

Schneider shrugged. "I'll leave that to you, but it is a positive sign at least."

Baier settled back in his seat. His grin felt like it could cover the entire windshield. "That's really great."

"As long as it's not a trap."

"Well, I guess we'll find out shortly." In his excitement, Baier's words came tumbling out. "Any information he can pass along will be greatly appreciated in Washington, I'm sure. Not to get too far ahead of ourselves, but if he is safe we might also think about setting you up as his control in the meantime. I imagine things are going to stay pretty hectic, and we'll need to get reporting as frequently as we can." He shifted his weight and turned to face Schneider again, moving so quickly that he nearly bounced in his seat. "Will you be here long? When do you have to return to Washington?"

Schneider shrugged. "Hard to say. I guess it depends on the situation. My orders don't have an end date."

"Good. Because I'm not going to be able to come here all that often."

"No shit. You won't believe what you're about to find in Budapest."

"Like what?"

"I'll let you see for yourself. We're just under two hours out. Tell me how you got Headquarters to punch your ticket for this thing. They sounded pretty adamant about you staying back in Vienna, given all the confusion and fighting going on. We were copied on the cable you got, of course."

Baier looked out the windshield and shrugged. "Yeah, I figured as much. The bad news is that I didn't get anything approved by Headquarters."

"Come again?" The car slowed and drifted to the side. Schneider had inadvertently braked, and his hands fell from the steering wheel in his surprise. He blew out his breath, looked around, and then quickly resumed driving.

Baier looked over at his companion. "That's right, I didn't. Fuck those guys. Bluebird is my recruitment, my asset. I'm the one responsible for his safety. I'm not letting anyone else make this call or get him out if needed." He reached over to pat Schneider's shoulder. "No disrespect intended, Bill. You've been a great help to me in the past and maintaining contact in

Budapest with Bluebird will probably fall to you, if that's how we decide to go. But as far as I'm concerned, it's still my call."

Schneider grinned and studied the countryside ahead. "None taken, Karl. But when the shit rolls in from Washington, just make sure I've got an umbrella of some sort."

"Don't worry." Baier paused to glance over at his companion. "I'll take the heat on this one. I doubt it would go any other way. If necessary, I'll tell them I lied to get you to go along."

"Gee, thanks. As though that will do any good with those bureaucrats."

IT WAS OCTOBER 25th, and the Hungarian revolt was less than two days old. So Baier was not really surprised by the absence of large-scale destruction in the capital. There were still plenty of burnt out ruins from the fierce fighting in 1944 and 1945 when the Soviet army rolled in to take the city from the Germans. That battle had gone on for months. Baier spotted what looked like new rubble near the city center on the Pest side of the Danube, where fighting had erupted around the radio station, a couple telephone exchanges, and the Eastern Railway Station. A tense standoff appeared to be holding additional violence off at the Corvin Cinema and the Killian barracks, two focal points of the revolt, for a little while at least.

"The rebels will want to seize those spots," Schneider said, pointing towards the cinema and barracks. "They're pretty strategic locations, especially with a fuel depot nearby."

"They don't have any tanks of their own."

"Ah, but they do have plenty of bottles for Molotov cocktails. That's their artillery at the moment."

Baier wondered about the utility of that weapon. From the journey through town he guessed that there were considerably more than the few hundred tanks he had heard about in Vienna. Even if they were the older World War II-era T-34's. Those things had reportedly given the *Wehrmacht* fits fighting in the dust and mud and snow in the Russian countryside, but they didn't look all that useful in a modern city. Even during the war when the T-34 was considered perhaps the best tank in the field when it first came out, the Germans had destroyed almost 45,000 of them. Maybe the cocktails would prove effective.

"So where to now?" Baier asked.

"I had thought we might drive to Buda and then back to check on surveillance, but it's getting risky to cross the bridges now. We'll stay on this side of the river, so we can go straight to our rendezvous. I had replied in the dead drop that we wanted to set up an early meet at a safehouse with Bluebird."

"The reply? Where are we supposed to meet Bluebird to take him there?"

Schneider grimaced and stared straight ahead. "Nowhere." He glanced over at Baier. "I mean, I gave him the address."

Baier nearly jumped out of his seat. "You what? Bill, what the fuck were you thinking?"

Schneider's fist slammed against the front of the steering wheel. "He insisted, Karl. He said he wanted to go there directly by himself. He claimed that was the safest way, given all the turmoil going on. He insisted on cutting down on our time and travel in the city together."

"That is not a good sign, Bill. It's like he or somebody else is trying to run this thing."

Schneider shrugged. "Okay, okay. I'll guess we'll see when we get there. Besides, it's an older spot, one that we were thinking of getting rid of anyway."

"Shit, Bill. This smells more and more like some kind of trap. What else did the note say? Any indication of coercion?"

Schneider shook his head. "Not that I could tell. It was very short and sweet."

"Yeah, sweet all right. We'll have to find a new safehouse after this. That's sweet for you."

"Do you want to abort?" Schneider asked.

Baier stared out his window. "No. It's too late for that. We need to go through with this now. Bluebird is too important for me, for us."

THEY DROVE THROUGH the city for over an hour. It wasn't so much the rubble or the roadblocks, or even the presence of Soviet armor and troops, most of whom were staying out of sight. At least on the side streets. Instead, it was the counter-surveillance that Baier insisted on. He kept requesting that they make several detours and additional runs through the neighborhood to check on any unwanted visitors or followers, given the chaotic conditions in Budapest and the uncertainty surrounding this meeting, even the very nature of the contact. The drive in to the city had all seemed too easy, especially in view of the troubling note and the circumstances surrounding this meeting. Schneider eventually argued that too much driving around would make them look even more suspicious. He drove into a side street lined with older, turn-of-the-century apartment buildings that seemed to draw their inspiration from the Opera House that Schneider had left just three blocks behind. He pulled up in front of a gray stone building of four stories that was turning to brown from the city's polluted air, its front pockmarked by what had to have been shrapnel and rifle fire. Those marks also looked to be fresh. One of the top-floor windows had been blown away and resembled a yawning gap of anger—or sorrow—as it looked down upon the street below.

"I hope that's not our safehouse," Baier said.

"Nope." Schneider looked over at Baier with a sly grin. "It's the flat right above it. Let's go see what we find."

Schneider parked a block away and around the corner. They climbed out of the car and halted momentarily to take in the streets to the front and on either side of their location. Then both men entered the building through the front door together, cautiously climbing the wide stairs that allowed them to walk side-by-side until they reached the third floor, where the stairway narrowed. The entire building appeared to be deserted, which Baier found odd, given its size and location. There had to be some inhabitants.

"Maybe they're all out protesting, or tossing welcoming gifts at the tanks," Schneider explained.

"So, who's running the revolt? Is there any kind of unified command?"

Schneider shrugged. "Got me. It's all just getting started, so there isn't a lot any of us know. We have to be very careful about reaching out to those people, because we don't want to give the government or the Kremlin an excuse to crush these poor suckers. You know, claiming it's a western-inspired coup."

"Maybe you're right about the people being out on the streets," Baier said. "Not only are all the doors closed, which you might expect, but there's not a hint of noise coming from any of the apartments." He tried one of the doorknobs and found it locked. "Almost like they're out shopping or at work."

Schneider stopped and held out his arm, nodding toward a dusty wooden door with the number 326 set above the frame. "Here we are." He tried the knob. This one turned in his hand. He pushed it gently inwards. The Americans slid into the apartment and stood stunned just inside the door. "Good Lord," Baier whispered. "What the hell happened here? I hope this isn't your idea of housekeeping."

The furniture in the first room, which appeared to be the living or drawing room, lay scattered and overturned. The sofa had been flipped on its back, and two arm chairs were resting on their sides, one them with its arms splintered. All the cushions had been ripped open. A bookcase was sprawled on its front with a handful of books scattered on either side. A desk against the far wall had been emptied of its drawers, the contents spread along the floor.

Off to their right was a brick fireplace that looked like it had not been used in years. It was remarkably clean. Baier couldn't be sure if it was even connected to a chimney. Or maybe there was no firewood to be had in this workers' paradise. The immediate area in front of the fireplace was surprisingly clear and clean, however. Except for the corpse, that is. A middle-aged male in dusty and wrinkled brown trousers, a black leather jacket, and white shirt hung limply from a noose that stretched from a chandelier in front of the fireplace. His black tie had been twisted to the side on his neck, and the body rotated slowly from side to side. If the slow, circular movement was still going on, Baier figured that he could not have been there long. The movement could mean that the killer or killers were still in the flat.

"Please tell me that is not Bluebird," Schneider whispered.

Baier shook his head, staring hard at the swollen face of the dead man.

"Thank God for that small favor, at least," Schneider added.

The Americans checked the corpse to make sure the man was dead, then moved as silently and cautiously as possible through the rest of the apartment. It was empty, and the remainder of the rooms were undisturbed. It took only minutes, since it was a one-bedroom apartment with a single bath and kitchen.

"How long has the Station had this place?" Baier asked.

"I think it's been about a year or two."

"Well, they won't have it any longer, that's for sure."

"Any idea who this guy might be? His clothes scream AVO, especially the black leather jacket."

"Yes, I've seen him before," Baier answered. The words came out barely above a whisper as his spirits sank. "We met at the border crossing."

Chapter Nine

IT WAS THE sound of approaching gunfire that forced them to hurry. Not just rifle fire and the occasional sound of breaking glass that came from a Molotov cocktail tossed from a rooftop. There was that, for sure, but there was cannon fire as well, the kind you hear from a piece mounted on a tank.

"This is the guy who gave you the warning about Bluebird?"

"The very same one," Baier replied.

"Shit, Karl." Schneider's head swerved in the direction of the window. "That sounds like it's coming from the direction of Parliament," Schneider said. "It's getting pretty damn close to here. Too close, in fact."

"Then we'd better hurry," Baier said. "Give me a hand going through this guy's pockets. It might help identify him and explain how he ended up here."

"Shouldn't we cut him down first?" Schneider asked.

"That depends on whether we plan to report the death. How about if we leave him as is and call it in anonymously? I mean, this place is obviously blown as a safe house now. So, who cares if the cops come?" He studied the corpse. "It's going to be hard enough reaching up and holding the body still to get him down. Let's just leave him hanging here. It will look more authentic."

"Which it is, in any case."

"True. But I think we can manage all the same."

Schneider stepped forward and got ready to grasp the dead man's legs. "Hopefully, the locals will chalk it up to the revolution. You know, these things tend to happen in times like these."

"Wait a sec. I think our priority should be to give the safe house a thorough search first. Let's make sure we remove any trace of an American presence here or our previous use of his place."

"That should be easy enough. I got the distinct impression that whatever use it provided to the Station in the past must have been fairly light."

"Yeah, and he apartment itself is pretty bare. Hardly any furniture. It looks as though next to nothing has been stored here."

Only when they had completed that chore did they decide to search the corpse, fingering their way through his pockets with a light hand, mostly out of a sense of decency and respect for the dead. They also moved quickly, given the morbid feeling of their task. Schneider had drawn the short straw and grasped the dead man's legs as Baier searched the pockets of the pants and jacket. The big surprise—and a good deal of confusion--came when Baier discovered a slip of paper in the man's pocket. It was no more than a single page, folded over twice, and slipped into the outside jacket pocket that covered the man's heart. "How ironic," Schneider noted.

The note contained a brief message in German that Baier read out loud. "Gero gone on Moscow's orders. Nagy still uncertain. Janos Kadar new party boss. Be very careful of a man for whom power is more important than principle. Soviets also reinforcing. Over 10,000 more troops and 250 more tanks. Khrushchev adviser Mikoyan and KGB chief Serov in town to direct Soviet response."

"What the hell are we supposed to do with this?" Schneider asked. "We don't know who put the damn thing there or how reliable the information is."

"It's something we can verify easily enough. Some of this stuff will become public soon. At least ,the part about Gero and Kadar. The rest, I admit, is pretty cryptic, but it could be pretty valuable."

Schneider nodded. "This sounds consistent with what we're hearing about Nagy." He paused and considered the floor, as though the answers might be lying there. He looked back up at Baier. "What's the purpose of this note and the timing?"

"What do you mean?"

"Why didn't whoever killed this guy take the note with him when he, or they, left? Presumably, that's why this guy was killed, isn't it,to cut off the communication? Why didn't they wait for us if it was a trap? Wouldn't that have been more useful for them?"

"Maybe they were surprised or rushed," Baier replied. He paused. "Plus, we don't even know who this guy was or why he came. He told me nothing at the border. This makes it even more imperative that we get in touch with Bluebird. God knows what's happening with him."

"Or, if he's even still alive. This is hardly proof, one way or the other," Schneider said. He pointed to the note. "This does throw some positive light on things, though."

"Yeah, I suppose so. This is exactly the kind of stuff I had expected to get from our man. It would have been very helpful to have met with him for more details and follow-on tasking on just this kind of thing."

"Well, we won't be getting in touch with anyone if we don't get the hell out of here." Schneider trotted to the door. "Let's get a move on. We should run this stuff by Barnes."

"Who's he?"

"The charge. We don't have an ambassador at the moment. He's the number two and acting ambo right now. He'll find this useful, for sure. He might be able to throw some light on this if he's heard anything else. It could help verify the information."

"If it's from Bluebird, I'm pretty sure it's valid. I just wish we could get the chance to press him for some additional info, especially on the Soviet advisors."

"Yeah, you said so already. This guy may also have taken the note off Bluebird, assuming that's who wrote it."

"I'm sure it is. It just feels like the kind of thing he'd tell us." Baier motioned with his head toward the body hanging still now, his feet pointing down toward the floor. "If so, then who killed this guy? I seriously doubt it was our friend."

"Too damn many questions," Schneider replied. "We'll just have to work that much harder to find the son of a bitch."

ON THE DRIVE to the embassy, Baier and Schneider found plenty of evidence of new fighting. Bodies littered the streets and sidewalks along with a handful of burning tanks. The Molotov cocktails were obviously a potent drink. Small bands of Hungarian rebels darted in and out of building entrances or down alleys, occasionally pursued by Soviet soldiers. For the most part, though, the Russians hung close to their tanks, probably hoping the armor would somehow protect them, as well as the crews inside. If they actually were Russians, that is. During his time in Berlin, Baier had learned not to automatically equate Soviets with Russians. He guessed that many of the troops here were probably from the Central Asian or Caucasus republics, more expendable as cannon—or cocktail—fodder in this kind of chaotic urban fighting.

One thing that impressed Baier was the age of the rebels, who seemed to be on some sort of school vacation. Some appeared to be as young as grammar school age, even wearing shorts and school caps as they ran from building to building. The majority looked a bit older, though not by much. Tattered and dusty sport coats or sweaters provided their only armor, with long hair either slicked back as a sort of makeshift helmet over the tops of their heads. An occasional curl fell across many of the foreheads, but for the most part, the hair hung like a mop from the tops of their skulls. Almost all were carrying rifles and machine guns that appeared to have been looted from government military depots. Baier wondered if they'd had any training on how to use and maintain their weapons. Maybe those who had served in the army. Most would need proper military assistance for that sort of thing, especially if they hoped to carry on with the fighting and the rebellion. He wondered just where that was supposed to come from.

"Sit tight, Karl. It looks like we've got a blockade up ahead." They had just turned down Tusolto Street on their way to the American Embassy. Baier leaned forward to get as close as possible to the windshield. "It looks like it's a rebel roadblock, though. We should be all right."

Schneider shrugged. "Who knows? Anything can happen in this kind of fight."

Baier had been right about the occupants, in any case. He was relieved to discover that it was a roadblock set up by the rebels, although Baier asked himself what they would do if a Soviet tank decided to challenge their authority. Schneider rolled down his window and flashed his American passport at the tall, thin young Hungarian who approached the car.

"Hallelujah!" The student shouted when he reached the window. "Americans!" Those were the only words Baier understood. Schneider tried to carry the rest of the conversation all by himself, but his Magyar was too rudimentary. He seemed to succeed only in creating more confusion. The student rescued him by continuing in halting English. "When will we see your troops? NATO is coming, of course, right?"

Schneider nodded eagerly. Too much so, for Baier's taste. He wondered what his colleague was agreeing to, if he knew something that the folks in Vienna or even Washington with whom he had spoken previously had not known or learned yet. "For sure, for sure. Any day now," Schneider agreed. Maybe he just wanted to get through the roadblock.

Arms and hands reached inside and pulled the two Americans from the car. Amidst the concern and confusion, Baier was surprised to feel hands and fists pounding his shoulders while he was greeted by smiles all around. Someone ruffled his hair from behind. A young woman pushed through the crowd and planted a long, wet kiss on Baier's lips, then embraced him in a crushing hug as her legs rubbed up against his own. He pushed his right hand inside his pants pocket to make sure the note he had found on the corpse was still there. He craned his neck to the side, so he could find Schneider and plead for an escape only to discover his colleague in a similar embrace by a young woman much more attractive than his own. Just my luck, he sighed.

"But wait, comrades," Schneider shouted as he broke free. Apparently, he had had the same thought. "We need to get to our embassy. We must go."

The group of Hungarians turned unexpectedly sullen. The rebel who had shown such warmth toward Baier strolled over the Schneider. "We no longer use that term here." She surveyed her companions. "We are not Communists. That is over in Hungary."

"Then let's say 'friends'" Schneider shouted. "We are not Communists either."

Smiles slowly returned, and Baier received more encouragement as more hands rubbed his hair and fists continued to pummel his shoulders. He and Schneider pushed their way back into the car, and Schneider edged it forward until they were free of the crowd and the makeshift blockade of furniture and two burnt-out car hulks.

"I guess you'll have to learn a new vocabulary here, Bill," Baier said.

"Yeah, but for how long?" Schneider smiled. "In any case,

we need to report this kind of thing to the charge. I don't know how much the State weenies are getting out right now."

"I'm not sure it's fair to call those people 'weenies' right now, Bill. We're all in this together, and under the gun. Literally."

"THAT'S SOME INTERESTING news." Stephan Barnes, acting as Chief of Mission at the embassy in the absence of an Ambassador, sat at his desk in his office. He had remained in the Deputy Chief of Mission's confines, probably thinking that Tom Wails, who had already been confirmed as the new ambassador, would be arriving soon. At least, that had probably been the plan until a few days ago. He sat slightly slumped forward, with a look more haggard than Baier's even. The office ran the length of a large living room and had the comfortable furniture that would go with it, as well as a large wooden roll top desk. The three men sat in a circle with a sofa, two arm chairs, and a long rectangular coffee table in the middle, over which Barnes had spread picture books of the Carpathian Mountains that advertised the region like a travel brochure. Barnes looked as though he had not slept for days, which was probably true enough. His white shirt had lost most of the starch it might have once held, and the striped tie was pulled down several inches from his neck. The pants were also wrinkled, and the black wing tips looked scuffed and badly in need of a thorough polish. He almost made Baier feel clean. Baier realized for the first time that he probably smelled like he had just come from a locker room.

"We can hear the spread of the fighting just sitting here, but it does help to know how serious or vicious it is and the extent of it all. The use of roadblocks by the rebels is an interesting point."

"Is there any organization among the rebels yet?" Baier asked.

Barnes shook his head. "Not that we know of. It's mostly just small gangs that melt away and regroup—and not always with the same people—somewhere else. In one sense, this probably presents more of a challenge for the Red Army here. They are certainly not used to this sort of resistance."

"No, that's certainly not how the Germans fought them," Baier agreed. "Not until they got to Berlin, anyway."

"Which makes the information in this note all the more interesting," Barnes continued. "It says something about Soviet intentions, which I might add, do not look promising from our point of view. How reliable is it, and where did you say you got it?"

Schneider shook his head. "We'd like to hold off on the latter question, Sir, at least for now. Until we know more we really can't give you an answer on the first part either. It's something Karl and I plan to run down as quickly as possible."

"How do you plan to do that?"

"You'll have to trust us on that one, Sir," Baier answered. "But we do promise to keep you informed of anything else we find out about what's going on out there. I take it your own communications with the government have probably dried up."

Barnes nodded. "That's one way of putting it. The Hungarians were not the friendliest hosts to begin with. That's why this information could prove so useful. In fact, I'd like to use this in a report back to Washington. Appropriately caveated, of course. Are you going to report this through your channels as well?"

Schneider nodded. "Yes, Sir. As soon as we get back to our office, even if it is a pretty short note."

"What can I tell the Department of its origins?" Barnes pressed.

"Just tell them it's information we picked up on the street," Baier said. Which in a way it was, he thought. "I do have another question, though, if you can answer it."

"Sure. What is it?"

"The shooting over by Parliament. Do you know yet what

happened there?"

Barnes swung his chair to look out the window behind his desk. Clouds drifted by, mingling with the patches of smoke that climbed from isolated blocks of the city below. When he spoke, it was as though he was addressing the people of Budapest.

"There are all sorts of rumors right now, and no one seems to know for sure. It broke out in front of Parliament, in the square there. A large crowd had assembled, and it was all peaceful enough at the beginning. Then some shooting started, which killed scores of innocent bystanders in the square. Some say the bastards in the AVO started it, with snipers firing from the rooftops of buildings nearby and even the Parliament itself. Others blame it on the Soviet tanks, claiming that the fatalities and wounds could not have come from rifle fire alone." He sighed and ran a hand over a head of uncombed light brown hair. "The short of it, though, is that we really don't know for sure. Our movements are pretty restricted, as you can imagine."

He turned back to the sofa to face Baier and Schneider. "I also doubt we'll ever know for sure, at least for some time yet. You can rely on the Soviets and their puppets to try to shut this up as tightly as possible." Barnes paused, as though to heighten the effect of his words. " I'll say one thing. If their intent was to suppress the revolt, they've badly miscalculated."

"How so?" Baier asked.

"From what I hear," Barnes continued, "the locals are rushing to join the fighting in droves now. This incident at the Parliament has only inspired them."

"Do you think it will push Nagy further along?" Baier asked.

"Hard to say. He's still lagging behind the street. His most recent radio address didn't do anything to inspire the public here. He apparently continues to think he can keep a lid on things and move forward slowly with his old reform program."

"Your message to Washington, Sir?" Schneider added.

Barnes studied the young American intelligence officer for a moment before continuing. "I think Nagy's dreaming. We're pretty far past that now. Washington needs to get focused on what's underway here and get ahead of the curve."

"What will Washington do?" Baier continued.

Barnes shrugged as he shifted his weight to face Baier. "Hard to say at this point. Given the turmoil surrounding our Allies' dysfunctional policies on Suez and Nasser and the President's focus on his re-election, I'm pretty sure he isn't looking for yet another crisis to shift attention away from the domestic scene. I think we owe it to these people to support them. This is truly a popular, democratic revolt. It's what we stand for in this world, and it harks back to our own origins as a nation. I'm going to recommend that we do what we can in the way of support with food and military supplies. Troops are another thing, of course."

Baier considered the man sprawled in the armchair to his right, sitting there in black trousers, a wrinkled white shirt, and a black and red striped tie pulled down well below his neckline. The eyes were rimmed in red, and the charge kept running his hand through his hair, now well past the ruffled stage. It was almost as though he had dressed this morning for the funeral of a close friend or family member and just returned from the service. Yet his words bore an optimism and sense of hope that stood in marked contrast to his appearance.

"We'll see what we can find, Sir," Baier said. "And good luck."

IT SEEMED LIKE Baier had been asleep only minutes when Schneider was shaking him by the shoulder, the same one that had been slapped so hospitably earlier in the day. Baier pushed his legs out straight so they extended over the arm of the sofa in Schneider's office. Then he swung them over to the floor and sat up. Then he worked his arms above his head and flapped them against the back of the sofa, partly in exhaustion and partly in frustration. Although he had had little to drink thus far, Baier felt a powerful urge to pee.

"Come on sleepy head. It's time to get back to work," Schneider announced.

"Don't you guys sleep in Hungary?"

"Not as much as you do in Austria, apparently. I thought you guys drank lots of coffee."

"We do."

"Well, they do here as well. We can grab some outside in one of the cafes that populate this city."

"Yeah, but it doesn't help much when you only get a few hours of sleep because of a drive to the border to sneak into this godforsaken country. I'm also getting hungry." Baier glanced around the office. "By the way, where is everybody? You're not working this place solo, I hope."

Schneider sat on the edge of his desk while he waited for Baier to become fully awake. "Hardly. One guy who came in a day after me is off in Gyor to see what he can pick up there on how things are faring outside Budapest. Apparently, we have someone there who is willing to report on conditions in the countryside. We can also grab a bite when we get the coffee."

"You mean a real live asset?"

"Hardly. It's just some local who hates the regime enough to pass along whatever he can pick up. The chief drives out there occasionally to collect the guy's reports and send them on to Washington."

"Not some Hungarian fascist, I hope, from the war years or the Horthy regime?"

Schneider laughed. "No, not that bad. But the guy had been in the Hungarian Army and actually fought on the eastern front with the Krauts. I guess it was his time in a Soviet P.O.W. camp that cemented his hatred for all things Communist."

"And the chief?"

"He's on his way back to Washington for consultations. Left the day before yesterday."

Baier stood and stretched. "Great timing."

"In a way, I suppose it is. Not that he'll have much he can tell them at this point, however." He slid off the desk. "Let's get moving. While you were sawing logs, I ran out to check on the dead drop. There's been another message, and our friend has some more demands."

"Bluebird? Demands? That doesn't sound right." Baier sighed. "Why is it that every missive from our man only serves to rouse new concerns and suspicions? I don't like it when he appears to be controlling the time and place of our meetings. It's like he's trying to run the operation. In fact, it stinks."

"Yeah, and there's nothing about the dead guy hanging in the old safehouse. I should say that they actually sound more like requests than demands."

"And?"

"He wants to meet later tonight."

"When and where?"

"At midnight, at the Killian Barracks."

"Isn't that a government stronghold and the scene of a very tense standoff?"

"As a matter of fact," Schneider said, "it is. Or was. I gather there been some heavy fighting there."

Meeting his asset just as the bell tolled to end his first day in Budapest. A helluva way to kick off the second one. "Motherfucker." It was all Baier could think to say.

Chapter Ten

————— ❦ —————

DRIVING TO THE Kilian Barracks, Baier and Schneider encountered plenty of evidence of the increased fighting. They had expected as much. Even as they left the office, the two could hear rifle and cannon fire as it rippled through the city. Black smoke climbed from whole city blocks and hurried away under an eastern wind. Scattered rubble was strewn across the streets, and some buildings had wide gaps blasted through the walls, opening their insides to curious onlookers wandering the streets. The few that stopped to look, that is. Most scurried through the warren of streets and alleys like mice in a maze.

"I wonder if we'll find our friends at their blockade again," Baier said.

"It wouldn't be a surprise," Schneider replied. "Although my guess is that the youth squad has changed. It's not like people have assigned duties or anything."

As the car rumbled down Tuzolto Street once more, the two Americans were shocked and saddened to see that there was little left of the barricade. "Probably a tank came this way," Schneider said.

"Jesus, but I hope those kids are okay."

A block further on and closer to the Barracks, they saw what may well have been the tank they suspected of having plowed through the barricade. It was now a blackened hulk, a small fire burning in the turret and a dead Soviet soldier in the street, arms and legs spread next to the tracks at its side. Schneider pulled the car over to the curb about five blocks later and about two hundred meters shy of the Kilian Barracks. The fighting in the area appeared to be over. At the Barracks enthusiastic crowds of teenagers and some Hungarian soldiers milled about, exchanging backslaps and hugs in the jubilation that comes with victory. There were no signs of the Soviets, aside from a few more ruined tanks and perhaps a dozen bodies. Several work details were busy removing the casualties and corpses.

"It seems we got here just in time," Schneider said.

"In time for what?"

"In time to miss the fighting. I was not looking forward to getting caught up in that."

The two Americans walked along the perimeter that the Hungarian rebels had established around the compound. One of the students from their encounter at the roadblock earlier in the day recognized the two and called them over to his post at the side of the Barracks along a broad boulevard with the ungainly Magyar name of Ullol Avenue.

"We've won, we've won," he shouted. "Perhaps now we will not need the Americans or NATO."

"Shut up, you fool." These words were spoken in broken English and came from a grizzled old man who looked to be somewhere between 30 and 60 years old. It was hard to tell with the wide-brimmed hat and bushy mustache covering much of his face in shadow and shrubbery that complimented the grime. His broad, white whiskers and deep hazel eyes suggested years of experience that Baier could only guess at. He still put the old veteran's age well past that of the students surrounding him. Bandoliers of rifle ammunition wrapped his upper body in a glaze of bravado and heroics. "You are Americans?" Schneider nodded and interpreted some of what the man said after he switched to Hungarian. "My name is Janos Szabo. Remember that. You will hear it often as we fight for our freedom."

As the older man turned away, Baier felt someone slip another piece of paper in his hand. He spun around hoping to catch the culprit only to see a small boy of maybe ten or eleven bolt down the avenue and around the corner at the end of the Barracks. He looked at the message, which contained a new address and was signed simply "K."

He showed it to Schneider. "Far?"

His companion shook his head. "Not really. It's still on this side of the Danube. It's over by the National Theater. We can be there in about ten minutes."

It took closer to thirty. Then again, Schneider had probably forgotten to take into account the time necessary to maneuver around the burnt-out vehicles and piles of stone that had narrowed passages in some paths along Jozsef Boulevard to little more than the width of their car. The slow and halting progress did help them check for any surveillance, though, and as best they could tell, their trail was clean. Then again, the AVO and Soviets almost certainly had better things to do right now.

When they caught sight of the Theater, Schneider swung their vehicle to the right and brought it to a halt on the edge of Koztarsasag Square.

"Good luck learning more of this language," Baier said, glancing up at the sign. "Man, where do they get these names?"

Schneider appeared not to have heard as he searched the buildings along their front and then to the right along the square. The Square itself was deserted. Baier thought this odd at first, since they were still close to the city's center, just blocks beyond its heart, which was known as the Inner City district. Then again, this was hardly the time for an evening stroll. Schneider finally pointed to one building that had a huge hole two floors up that yawned out to the street below. Kovacs stood in the gap in the building at the side of what was left of the wall fronting the ruined apartment in full view of the street below. He waved to the Americans.

"So much for discretion," Schneider said. "Did you ever teach this guy about the need for secrecy and security?"

"He should know that already based on his background, but I'll remind him. He does look confident, though. Let's just hope he's alone."

"Or at least not with another corpse."

The stairway rising through the first two floors was wide, like the hallway in the previous building they had visited, then narrowing for the final two floors. That appeared to be the standard architectural design in Budapest. On the fourth floor they entered the flat and found that Kovacs was indeed alone. He was now sitting comfortably in an armchair that looked out through the new view and across a city that was beginning to find some rest, and perhaps even a little sleep. Kovacs's brown slacks and brown plaid jacket were understandably covered in dust, but the man himself seemed unmarked. And unworried. He rose and offered his hand to Baier while shooting a quick glance at Schneider.

"Herr Baier. At last we meet in my city. It's is truly wonderful to see you again. A colleague of yours?"

Baier nodded. "Yes, and yes. It is a pleasure to see you again as well, Josef," he gestured towards the opening in the wall, "although the circumstances could have been more pleasant. This gentleman is a friend and colleague."

Kovacs slumped back in his chair. "Yes, well, I had hoped to welcome you to a city that was a bit cleaner and safer. But then, we are now much freer and more open. There is a great deal happening that I want you to know about." Kovacs spread his arms wide. "I hope you appreciate the irony of my choice."

"Irony?" Baier said. "How so? All I see is a bombed out flat."

"Ah, but this one has not been destroyed recently. It is what's left of the building after the battle for Budapest during the war. That's why I thought no one would suspect us of using it."

"Very clever," Baier admitted. "Does anyone else live here?"

"Oh, the apartments still intact are occupied, but there are only a few of those here."

Baier moved to the wall opposite his host and leaned back against a table that still had all four legs. He wiped the dust and bits of plaster from one edge of the table, noting how solid the piece of furniture was. That it had survived at all seemed like a minor miracle in Baier's eyes. Schneider took up a position behind Baier and closer to the door to check on any unwanted intruders.

"Yes, this is all very interesting. But first I think we must reinforce the necessity for discretion, Josef. You really need to be a bit more reserved and not announce your presence to anyone who might wander by if you're meeting with us. There may be a revolution underway, but your service and the Soviets have not given up, my friend."

Kovacs smiled and shook his head. "Yes, yes. I know you are right. I apologize. It will not happen again. I just wanted to make sure I saw you coming and that you would know it was safe."

Baier studied his asset, whose smile had not disappeared, even as he spoke these words. The man was clearly jubilant. "I see. We'll also need to find a new place to meet. The first order of business is for you to tell us what you know about what happened at the place we were supposed to meet with you earlier."

Kovacs nodded, and his eyes remained focused on the floor. The smile finally faded. "You must mean the hanging corpse."

"For one thing," Baier said. "Who was the man? You must have known him."

Kovacs looked up at Baier. "Yes, of course. You see, I

was on my way to the meeting when I realized I was not alone. Fortunately, this individual was to my front and in a tremendous hurry. He had not seen me yet, as he must have been hoping to hide in the apartment and surprise me. He was an AVO officer, who somehow had become aware of the appointment."

"How did that happen?" Baier shot up straight, his hands at his side. "Were you indiscreet at work? I hope you did not tell anyone else about our relationship."

"Else? I told no one."

"Then how did he come to know of our relationship? He met me at the border a few days ago when you failed to show. He gave a very worrisome and convincing, warning about you being in danger, Josef."

Kovacs shook his head forcefully. "I have told no one. I have been trying to make inquiries to gather information, but as you can appreciate, I'm sure, Mister Baier, that is difficult in my circumstances. I was prevented from meeting you by the work and the rapidly changing situation here in Budapest. Surely you can understand that." He glanced out the hole in the wall, then back at Baier. "I have no idea how this man came to know about us. I only know him casually. I always thought of him as one of the good ones. Not a brutal man, or even a communist."

"Jesus," Schneider exclaimed. "How did he come to work for the AVO in that case?"

"I cannot say. As I said, I hardly knew the man."

"Did you kill him?" Baier pressed.

Kovacs waved his arms in the air. "No, no. Of course not." He leaned forward. "You see, there were also some students and people from the apartment building collected nearby. They must have recognized him for what he was. They followed him upstairs. When they left about a half hour later, I rushed upstairs to see what had happened. They had been laughing and congratulating themselves on their way out. That's when I saw the man hanging there. I left as soon as I could."

"Why do you think he was there, and how did he find out about the meeting?"

Kovacs's face seemed to sink inwards, while his focus shifted from one corner of the room to another. "I...I have no idea. Perhaps he wanted to give another warning."

"Then why not speak to you directly?"

"Perhaps he thought that was too dangerous to do so during the day. Our paths do not cross all that easily."

Baier extended the note he had found in the man's pocket. "Did you write this?"

Kovacs took the note and read through it. "Yes, I did. I thought this information might help."

"But how did it end up in that man's coat pocket?"

Kovacs sat back again. "Well, I thought two things could happen, both of them good, if I slipped the note into his possession." He held his thumb up in the air. "One, if you arrived and searched the body, I knew you would find it in such an obvious place. That would serve the original purpose of our meeting."

"One of them," Baier corrected. "What was the other thing?"

"If the police or security service found it, then they might believe that he was working for the Americans. That way, if there is suspicion within the government of a spy in their midst, attention would be drawn to him."

"How would that explain the death?"

"Oh, it would be easy to convince the AVO and others that the man had committed suicide out of anguish and grief over his betrayal." He smiled. "Either that, or what actually happened." Wrinkles spread over his forehead as Kovacs frowned toward the Americans. "There has been much revenge against the AVO personnel, you know. So, you see I was making lemonade out of lemons, as you Americans say."

"Very clever," Baier conceded. "If there really is suspicion that there's a leak in your government, it might only be a matter of time before you come under that cloud. Has there been anything else to cause you concern? Anything said or done by your colleagues?"

Kovacs thought for a moment as he gazed out on the sight of Budapest at night. He shook his head. "No, not really." Kovacs's face brightened. "You see, I am now working in the central administration with Nagy and his Cabinet. I have escaped from the clutches of the AVO, as it were. That would also explain why the man would try to come here."

"Congratulations, Josef. What sort of warning do you think he had, if that is indeed why he came? I find it very troubling that an officer of the AVO somehow knew about our plans, even if his intentions were to help. How is your relationship with Gero? I hope you haven't made an enemy of him? Did he approve of the switch?"

"Oh, he had little choice. Gero is a spent force. At any rate, I think our relationship is okay. We had become rather distant of late as I lost more and more of my enthusiasm and commitment for the regime's policies. I had come to see Nagy's reformist approach as the only hope for my country, but you know all this already. We spoke of it often in Vienna."

"True, but I just hope you haven't made an enemy of the man. People like him and with the kinds of connections he has built he can still be dangerous."

Kovacs shook his fist at Baier. "Ach, his days are over, thank God. I no longer need to worry about him."

"I wouldn't be so sure, Josef. I'm sure he still has allies in the government. Not all the old Stalinists are gone, from what I understand. We may need access to the man if he and any of his cohort are planning a comeback. Access that you could provide if you're still on good terms with him."

"You mean a counter-revolution?"

Baier sank back against the table. "Whatever. Just be careful. We also need to determine how this dead man found out about the meeting. I'm sorry to keep returning to this point, Josef, but Gero or no Gero, it all sounds very troublesome and suspicious."

"Herr Baier, I'm sure that this one individual was acting on his own. He must have picked up on some hints as to what I've been doing on his own. I'm not sure how, but I will be more careful. I promise. And we were lucky, it seems, that he wanted to help us. There are clearly some good people in the old government, even in the AVO."

Baier started to speak, but Kovacs continued as though he had not noticed. "As I said, he probably wanted to help. Even if he wanted to expose me and set a trap for you, he probably wanted to make absolutely certain before he moved against me. Especially when you consider how highly placed, I am and that I am now working for the changes that people are demanding. He probably realized that an attack on me could still be construed by some as an attack on Gero and other Stalinists, or by others on Nagy and the reformers. Our party is very divided right now, and there is much maneuvering going on. The AVO itself is consumed with turmoil and fighting for its own survival. The man probably needed to make sure which way those winds you speak of are blowing."

"Do you know who he was and where he worked?"

Kovacs waved his hand in dismissal. "Yes, yes. His name was Peter Sazlo, and he worked in the AVO's counter-intelligence directorate, but his focus was more on the European NATO countries, such as the British and French, and the West Germans, of course. They still have many friends here. You Americans come under an entirely different department. He may have associated me with the Germans, or Austrians even." Kovacs grew silent, his gaze focused on the floor. "Or if he did associate me with you Americans, he may have wanted to make sure since he did not really follow your organization. He would have been required to inform the Soviet KGB of anything he knew or did. That is, if he was working against me. As you can imagine, they are in control of any work against you Americans."

Baier could not suppress the grimace that gripped his face. "Damn it, Josef, that only explains one part of this puzzle. We still don't know how he became suspicious about your activities. And who wrote the original note proposing our meeting, the one that brought me from Vienna?"

Kovacs looked up and smiled. "Oh that, one." A chuckle escaped. "I did. I had working on changing my handwriting as much as possible. I have been practicing." He saw Baier's eyes go wide and his lips thin and hard. "Do not worry, Herr Baier, I burned all those pieces of paper. In the end, I gave up and cut letters from the newspaper."

"What was the point of that? Why didn't you use any of the code words I had given you? Surely you understand how important those can be."

Kovacs shrugged. "I forgot. You have to realize how chaotic and confused everything is right now."

"Nonetheless, I am still very worried," Baier continued. "Which brings us to the need to discuss your departure. The fact that someone was on to you, even if he was acting alone, is cause enough to pull you out, given what we are up against."

Kovacs leaped from his seat. His arms waved the thought away. "No, we cannot allow that. Not yet. As for what you say we are up against, surely you are not blind, Herr Baier. All that is changing."

Baier pulled himself from the table's corner. Schneider cautioned Kovacs to keep his voice down. "How can you be so sure?" Schneider asked. "Remember, even Nagy comes from the Moscow crowd, the ones you have spoken so derisively about in the past. Didn't he spend the war years there? Isn't he a Soviet citizen? There are even rumors that he was an informant for the NKVD, the KGB's predecessor."

Kovacs stood and began to pace. "I know who the NKVD was, for God's sake. I truly believe that Nagy is changing. You don't go through something like this and not change, my friends. Many of us realize now that we cannot rely on the

USSR to act in our interests." He stopped his march in front of Baier, looking hard into his eyes. "I cannot leave now. There is so much more to do here. As I said, we are in the midst of a revolution. Haven't you noticed?"

Baier put out a calming hand. "Yes, I've noticed. Believe me. But I am also concerned for your safety."

Kovacs waved that one away, too. "Oh, please, Herr Baier. This is all so much bigger than you or me. Especially me. We have a chance to achieve something truly magnificent now. But we cannot do it without your assistance. We need Washington's help to hold off the Kremlin."

"Just what do you want us to do? What makes you think we can have that kind of impact here in Budapest?"

Kovacs spun back towards the chair, but then seemed to rethink his idea of taking his seat again. Instead, he approached Baier and leaned his hand on the table. "That is a difficult thing for me to imagine. I know so little of how your government works, and I am not sure just what it will take. Surely some kind of pressure is possible."

"What kind of pressure?"

"Pressure to force the Soviets to leave us alone and keep the Kremlin from crushing our revolt."

"How can you help in that, Josef?"

"By giving you information on what is being planned and how things are working between our government and the Soviets. This will help you devise your own policies. Will it not?"

"Sure, theoretically anyway. It will have to be really good material to push the focus away from the crisis brewing over Suez. Can you give us that?"

Kovacs nodded eagerly. "Yes, I hope so. For example, you will be interested to know that Imre Nagy is finally coming around. As I tried to explain to you just now, he has seen what the violence has done to the people's will and determination. He truly is a changed man. He plans to press the Soviets for a complete removal of all the old Stalinists and to allow him to name his own cabinet. He even wants to include non-Communists.'

"When will he do this?"

"Tomorrow. In his meeting with the Soviet advisors I mentioned in this note." He held the day's earlier missive in front of Baier.

"How do you think the Soviets will respond?"

"It still isn't clear. This is where your government can help. Khrushchev is completely confused and indecisive at the moment. I think it will come down as to which of those two emissaries is the more convincing in their reports home. If the KGB chief Serov gains the advantage, then repression will be the order, which will lead to more bloodshed and the crushing of our dream of a free Hungary."

"And the other guy?"

"If it's Mikoyan, then there is hope. He is much more moderate. I believe he is prepared to give us some room. He realizes that suppression will set back Khrushchev's plan for reforms at home and in their Empire in Europe irretrievably. So, you see, Washington can help prepare the mood and openness in the Kremlin for the right answer."

"I cannot promise anything," Baier explained. "I do not recommend policies to Washington, much less make them. I'll report on these dynamics to Washington. I'll work to keep you here and active, for now. Even that decision is not mine to make." He turned towards Schneider. "If I'm not in Budapest, my colleague Bill will work with you. We can use the same means of communication, and think hard about anything you might have done that could have tripped off the suspicions of the man who was killed earlier this evening. Please remember the distress signal if the suspicion of a mole points again in your direction. Then we'll have to get you out. And we can do it," Baier assured him. "And we will. Whether it fits with your plans or not. You can always live to fight for Hungary another day." Baier took Kovacs's hand. "We will also be giving you a new address for our meetings and a new means of communication." He glanced around the shattered apartment. "We can't meet here again. We need to establish a new point for our message exchanges."

Kovacs seized Baier's hand. "Thank you, my friend. We can do this. I truly believe it." Then he spun through the doorway and into the hall.

Baier watched Kovacs trot down the stairs and run into the street. He reminded Baier of children he had seen on the playgrounds back in America. All eagerness and enthusiasm, oblivious to the dangers of the world. Schneider stepped to his side and tugged at Baier's arm.

"Karl, there's something here I think you need to see."

The two Americans walked over to the door frame, and Schneider pointed to a small black box resting on the floor between the wall and table. Neither man had seen the package when they entered. A red and yellow wire ran from the box and ended about three feet away. Their ends had been clipped by a sharp object.

"Is that what I think it is?" Baier asked.

Schneider nodded. "You bet. Someone had planned a little surprise for us here."

"You mean a big surprise, don't you?" Schneider nodded in agreement. "How can you be sure it was meant for us?"

"Well, if it was for someone else, why is it still here? The other thing is that it's clearly been dismantled, and then left to make sure we were aware of it. It's like we have a guardian angel or something."

"Hell, I doubt that. But it certainly confirms that we aren't going to be returning to this place."

"It raises even more questions about how someone knew of this meeting, along with the previous one." Baier studied the package. "Do you think there's an anti-movement device attached?"

Schneider knelt close to the box to examine it more closely. "Hard to tell. But I'm willing to play it cautiously."

"Still, we can't leave it here."

"Why not?"

"Because if whoever owns this thing comes back to look for it, I don't want him to find it. I'd rather create some confusion over what has happened."

"Confusion? Like our own?"

Baier smiled and nodded. "Exactly." He walked into the kitchen and returned with a broom.

"Oh, that's going to help a lot," Schneider said.

"You got a better idea?" Baier tapped and then pushed the box with the broom handle. Nothing happened. He knelt down, picked the box up and walked to the open scar in the wall that emptied onto the street below. He tossed the contraption out through the hole and into the Budapest night.

"Now it's just more debris from the rebellion."

"WHAT DO YOU think?" Schneider asked as they made their way back to the station.

"I think Bluebird has let his enthusiasm get the better of his judgment."

"How so?"

"For one thing, do you really think Moscow will let a country as strategically important as Hungary go free? First the revolts in East Germany, then Poland, and now this. They've got to be shitting themselves over the spread of this virus in their empire."

"Still," Schneider replied, "there is a chance some kind of arrangement can be worked out. Something that gives the Hungarians some autonomy and freedom. We owe it to these people to try."

"Do you really think that might be possible, that changes like that can come behind the Iron Curtain?"

"Worse things have happened. I mean, look at Poland. It

looks like the Kremlin is going to let Gomulka establish some moderate changes."

"Yeah, maybe. You're starting to sound like Barnes. You do have a point, though. Granted, this is what John Foster Dulles has been promising since he took over at State, breaks in the Soviet rule that he can push back against. I guess we'll see if he puts his money where that elitist mouth is. I'm also concerned about Bluebird and his safety. I'm afraid he might do something rash to get the information he wants. You saw him. He was like a kid back there."

"If there's suspicion about a mole, then he is going to have to be very careful."

"I think we can assume that there is. No more 'if.' It's now a race between getting the information we need and the cage closing around him."

"And us," Schneider reminded him. "Do you think Bluebird can win that race? You've said before how experienced and professional he was."

Baier nodded, looking out at the darkened streets that had gone suddenly silent in the early hours of Friday, the 26th. "Yeah, but that's not the impression I get of the man right now. He's really changed since those days in Vienna. I'm afraid he may be a dead man and just doesn't know it yet."

Chapter Eleven

———

WHEN HE REACHED the Austrian border the next morning, the Hungarian guards barely looked in Baier's direction. They were probably thinking of ways themselves to join the growing flow of refugees heading west. Away from the fighting and toward freedom. To a future free of the Soviets and rulers like Rakosi and Gero. Those who did not have family to leave behind, at any rate. Who knew what these young soldiers, conscripts mostly, were planning or where their loyalties lay, especially with all the uncertainty back in Budapest? Perhaps once the sun set and darkness enveloped the area the number of Hungarian border guards would drop by a handful or maybe even a dozen or more.

It was different with the Soviet advisers. Their number had grown, as had their aggressiveness examining everyone's papers. Baier suspected it was the large numbers that were crossing over today. One of the Soviets singled Baier out and accompanied him to a guard shack about fifty yards from the crossing.

During their stroll Baier thought back to his morning

discussion in Budapest. Schneider's colleague, Jeff Simons, who had followed him on the assignment to Hungary, returned to Budapest earlier in the day, just before noon. Baier and Schneider had just finished their late breakfast of rolls and coffee after collapsing on the floor and sofa in the early hours of the morning. Forget the juice, they were lucky to find freshly baked bread as it was. Baier had taken the sofa, using the fact that he outranked Schneider and, more importantly, had gotten only about three hours of sleep over the last forty-eight. First, they had drafted and then shipped off a cable back to Headquarters. Simons had told them of how the revolt had spread well beyond Budapest, aided in no small part by the shrinking Soviet military presence as units were transferred to the capital and the borders.

"There are still some brutal AVO bastards around, though," Simons explained. "In a couple places, like Miskolc and Mosonmagyarovar, they actually fired on crowds of demonstrators, killing dozens."

"Could you spell that second one?" Baier joked.

"Actually, I can't. I just heard the name repeated a lot. Unfortunately for the AVO, several of their men were grabbed by the crowds in both places and literally torn apart."

"Literally?" Schneider asked.

"Oh, yeah. There is a lot of hate and resentment out there. Revolutionary councils or committees have sprung up all over. I even spoke with some of the members of the one in Gyor."

"How were they?" Baier wanted to know. "What do they expect will happen? Is there any sort of effective government emerging?"

"Right now, they all sound pretty confident that they have the Soviets on the run, and that Hungary will be free of the foreign occupiers in the very near future. As for effective government…well, it's hard to say. These are pretty turbulent times. Their bigger concern is getting Nagy to clean house here in the capital and get out ahead of the popular sentiment.

You know, actually lead the revolution instead of following behind it."

He might be doing just that today, Baier thought, as he marched with his Soviet guard to the small wooden shack off to the side of the crossing point. If Nagy didn't pick up his own course and pace, the refugee flow would grow into a flood. His escort, a Soviet corporal who appeared to be about sixteen years old, knocked and pushed the door open when a familiar voice barked some kind of order from inside. Baier walked into the dimly lit hut with exposed plywood walls that held a single room with a black, pot-bellied stove in the corner and a desk facing the door. The shack looked to have been hastily thrown together, without any windows and only a thin wooden door that closed with a single latch. It had to be pretty damn cold during the winters here. Baier wondered if the walls would even withstand a determined shove. Its only source of light was a single bulb hanging by a long brown wire from the ceiling. That would explain the generator Baier had seen at the back of the shed, as well as the diesel fumes. Seated at the desk was KGB Colonel Sergei Chernov, the man in charge of border security on Hungary's western boundary and Baier's partner in holding the border open for the flow of refugees that had been building since the CIA's exfiltration operation had begun a little over a year ago. The Soviet was an important cog in the machine, making sure that Baier's and the CIA's guests were let through unimpeded.

Chernov spoke a few words—no more than a short sentence—and the corporal pivoted, then left the room.

"Ah, Herr Baier, how good to see you again. How long has it been? Some months, I believe. I've missed you."

"I wish I could say that the feeling is mutual, Chernov. Although your absence does lead me to wonder sometimes just what is happening with our arrangement here. What's the purpose of this office call? Were you expecting me?"

Chernov stood and walked around to the front of the desk.

His jacket hung loosely on his shoulders. "No, no. But imagine my surprise when I saw you in the crowd at the crossing. And moving in the direction you were. You can understand why I would be interested in seeing just who all is departing from Hungary these days. I was not even aware that you had been visiting us."

"Which is how I plan to keep it. You have no need to keep track of my movements."

"Perhaps not. I am inclined to see it differently, however. First tell me how your lovely wife is doing. I assume she is pleased with our arrangement on the border crossing. It must be like old times for her."

Chernov was referring to the days shortly after the war in Berlin, when he had colluded with Sabine in running a human smuggling ring that brought hundreds, even thousands, of refugees from eastern Germany to Allied-occupied West Berlin. It was how Baier and Sabine had first gotten to know Chernov and recognized the greed that drove the man. This, plus the desire for revenge on a system that had robbed the man of his family, his siblings almost certainly dying after a life of impoverished exile in South America, having fled there after the Revolution.

"Yes, she is happy to have a purpose and work that helps to undermine your country's rule in Central Europe," Baier said. "Is that what you wanted to discuss? Catch up on old times?"

Chernov frowned and leaned against the desk. He crossed his arms, then his boots, which were covered in dust and dirt. It was almost as though he walked to the border from Budapest. "Not really. It is actually you that concerns me."

"Me? How generous, and intriguing."

The frown turned into a smile. "You see, I do care about your welfare and our profitable cooperation, Herr Baier. I thought it might be best to warn you that I am not sure how much longer I will be able to keep this crossing open and, shall we say, available for both our purposes."

"Why is that? I doubt there will be any shortage of customers. Unless, of course, peace is about to break out in Budapest."

"No, you see there is bound to be more fighting, which we believe it is in our and the world's best interest to contain. We will need to ensure that western agitators, like yourself, are not allowed to enter Hungary and aggravate an unfortunate situation."

"Does your side really think that's the cause of the revolt here?"

Chernov's smile evaporated while he nodded. "It is what I am told."

Baier shook his head in disbelief. "If that is the perception in Moscow, then there really is little hope for Communism and Soviet influence in Europe. Do your leaders really have so little understanding of the popular mood and desires in the lands you occupy?"

Chernov shrugged. "Perceptions are subjective things, Herr Baier. I'm sure your side is subject to the same challenges. In any case, I thought you should know."

"Does this mean that your people are planning to expand the crackdown? Will more units be coming into Hungary?"

Chernov returned to his side of the desk and sat down. "That I do not know. Our leadership does not share those sorts of discussions with me, as I am sure you are aware. How you choose to use this information is up to you. But remember, I did not say that border will be closed—only that I suspect that time is coming."

"Any idea how soon this might happen?"

Chernov shrugged once more. "Perhaps tomorrow, or perhaps later in the week. Then again, maybe not at all. These are uncertain times, Herr Baier."

"Then just what sort of instructions have you gotten?"

Chernov gazed at the door of the hut. "Like I said, nothing specific. But we have been told to be prepared for a rapid movement and possible change in our border situation." His face turned back to Baier, and the Russian smiled. "Then again, I am always prepared, as I am sure you realize."

Baier turned to go. "Well, thanks for that in any case. I'll think about sharing that with my superiors in Vienna and Washington." Chernov settled into his seat and busied himself shuffling a small stack of paperwork on his desk. "Yes, do that. I hope your reception in Vienna is a warm one. And please pass along my best wishes to your wife. You are a lucky man, Herr Baier." Chernov looked up from the papers to his guest. "Oh, and one more thing, Herr Baier. If you do return, please bring along a change of clothes. Those look and smell as though they've been through a battle."

HIS RECEPTION IN Vienna, however, was anything but warm. After spending the night at their place in Burgenland, with Sabine, Baier had driven back to the Austrian capital in the early hours of the 27th, a Saturday. There was still a full complement at the Embassy and among the smaller staff in the Station despite it being the weekend. Baier expected as much. Revolutions tend to do that. What he did not expect was the welcome wagon assembled in his office.

It comprised a committee of three. Two of the individuals were no surprise: Gerry O'Leary, the new station chief for Vienna, whose arrival had clearly been accelerated in view of the events across the border, and Stan Muller, the CIA's man stationed at the embassy in Budapest. He had supposedly been in Washington for consultations and had probably been rushed back for much the same reason as O'Leary. The real shocker, however, was the man in the middle of the group: Gary Peters, the head of the European Division in the Agency's Operations Directorate.

"To what do I owe this unexpected pleasure?" Baier asked no one in particular.

O'Leary was the first to move, hand extended. "Karl, welcome back. I gather you've had quite a time there in Budapest. We're eager to hear all about it."

"Of course. Stan," Baier nodded in the direction of Muller, "has some damn good officers working for him there at the moment. They're ready to do whatever they can to help keep Washington informed. The language can be a barrier, but Schneider and Simons do what they can."

"Have you ever tried to learn Magyar?" Muller asked.

Baier shook his head. "No, and I hope I never have to. That was not meant as a criticism, Stan. They've got a rudimentary understanding and ability to communicate, and some folks there have a smattering of German or English, and lots of Russian, of course."

"That's fine, Karl," Peters said. "We all know the challenges of working there or anywhere else behind the Curtain. What we—and I especially—need to know is what you found out there regarding your source Bluebird and where we see this and any other operation going from here. Your background cables were rather light on the situation with him."

Baier began to answer, but before he could get a single word out, Peters continued. "But what I in particular really want to know is why you went in there after we expressly said we did not want you to do so."

Baier maneuvered around behind the desk to his chair. The three visitors looked for a place to sit, but only Peters took a seat in the chair opposite the desk. O'Leary and Muller remained standing, moving to posts along the wall. "Gary, I made a spur of the moment decision when we received an urgent message from Bluebird. You're aware that not only had he missed a scheduled rendezvous at the border, which I had set up, but that I had received a rather ominous warning at the border instead."

"Yes, I am aware of that. We discussed it in Washington. I also understand that the message was not from him. Didn't the fact that your asset had obviously been compromised concern you?"

"Well, as it turned out, the note had been sent by Bluebird. He claims he disguised his writing in case the message was intercepted, given all the turmoil there. He does suspect that their service is hunting for a mole, so he was nervous about using our regular method of communicating in case of an interception..."

"The usual dead drop?" Muller asked.

Baier nodded. "That's right." Baier nodded again in Muller's direction. "Stan and I set that up, and Bill Schneider took over when Stan left for Washington. He's been servicing our communications with Bluebird since then. Bill can fill you in on the more recent details, if you need them. He's been servicing the drop site for the last few days, and he accompanied me to all the meetings this week. I asked him to continue working with Bluebird. Pending your return, of course."

"Well, thanks for that anyway," Muller said. "And you say Bill was with you throughout your time in Budapest?"

"That's right. I told him I squared my trip there with Headquarters. I did not want to get him in trouble with you guys. He's a damn fine officer," Baier repeated.

"That's all good and well, Karl, but this is not about Schneider," Peters continued. "Were you able to find out any more about this mystery man?"

Baier looked first at Muller and O'Leary along the wall. "Yes, well actually, we found his corpse."

"Jesus, Karl," O'Leary exclaimed.

"You what?" Peters's voice rose to a level just below a shout. "You've continued with this operation? You left Bluebird there?"

Baier let out a breath and nodded. "Bluebird refuses to leave. He's been swept up in all the revolutionary fervor and believes his mission and his future are back in Hungary." He paused before continuing and considered telling the group about the explosive device discovered at the last meeting. He decided to hold that extra detail back, knowing it would mean the end of the operation. He just hoped that he would not come to regret the omission. "There is also the matter of us having a well-placed source at the heart of that uprising, who can also report on Soviet planning and policy."

"How can he do that?" Muller pressed.

"He's been moved to Nagy's staff. He's part of the inner circle now and more valuable than ever."

"We still need to discuss your role and where we go from here," Peters said. "You may not be aware, but this Administration does not want to do anything that plays into the Soviet fear that we are instigating this revolt in their sphere of influence. Or anything that would provide them with the opportunity to claim such to the world at large. Instead, we want the world to see the revolt and the Soviet behavior for what it is."

"And that would be?"

Peters shifted uneasily in his seat. "The brutal repression of a country's longing for freedom and democracy. Period."

"Are we going to do anything to help the Hungarians? To assist this longing for freedom and democracy?"

Peters frowned, and his mouth set as though he had just swallowed something distasteful. "That's difficult to say at the moment. I can only speak for myself, based on what I've picked up in meetings with the Director. It appears that for now we've settled on a policy of 'active non-involvement.'"

"What the hell does that mean?" Baier's voice rose. He did not bother even to try to hide his puzzlement and frustration.

"I'd say that it means we will be giving most of our support to Hungary through the UN. Ambassador Lodge has already called for a Security Council discussion on the matter."

"Hell, he'll be lucky to even get it on the agenda. I mean, the Soviets do still have a veto, don't they?"

"Which if they use will demonstrate quite clearly the nature of their regime and system."

"How does that help the Hungarian people? Aren't we obligated to do at least a little more in view of all this rollback rhetoric from the Secretary of State. My God, those people at Radio Free Europe have been practically inciting the Hungarians to do more, to take up arms and take matters into their own hands. Which they've done." Baier turned again to Muller. "You are going to see some real popular courage when you get to Budapest, Stan. You'll see what I mean by all this."

Muller smiled, shifted his weight from one shoulder to the other at the wall, but he did not say anything.

"Speaking of RFE," O'Leary broke in, "they've been reporting massive desertions by Soviet soldiers in Hungary. Did you see any evidence of that, Karl?"

Baier shook his head. "Sorry, Gerry, I did not. Nor did I hear any of the Hungarians mention anything. Barnes, the charge, didn't say anything about that either. Sounds like more bullshit to inspire false hope."

"Easy, Karl," Peters said. "I don't think it's wise to throw a lot of loose accusations around. Certainly not at this point. Perhaps we should press our people to get around a little more."

"They're already out and about plenty, from what I saw."

"That may be, but right now I'd like us to agree on how we go forward with Bluebird. Stan, any ideas?"

Muller pushed himself off the wall and approached the desk. "Karl, just where did you leave things with your asset? Do you think he's compromised, or can we continue to rely on his information?"

"I raised the possibility of pulling him out after our first scheduled meeting in the city fell through." Baier explained.

"I certainly hope that particular safehouse was scrubbed. We'll obviously have to let that one go," Muller said.

Baier nodded. "That's right. Schneider is on that already. But, like I said, Bluebird is determined to stay. He's been swept up in the emotion of the revolt and thinks he can continue to provide a valuable service to us and to his country by giving us information we need to stay ahead of the game and push Moscow in the right direction."

"What is his specific role and position?" Muller asked.

"I was surprised when he told me. He's pretty high up there, as a matter of fact," Baier responded. "He claims he's working as a kind of Cabinet Secretary. So, he should have great access."

"But can we trust him?" Peters asked. "That's the important question here, Karl."

"Yes, I think so," Baier answered. "He still appears confident and unpressured. He is definitely in step with all that's going on there at the moment. He's very supportive of the changes underway. I also did not notice any kind of fear or hesitation that I would associate with him having been turned or threatened, or trying to deceive us." Baier brought his fist down on his leg for emphasis. "I know this guy."

"Maybe he's just a very good actor," Peters said.

Baier shook his head again and stared straight at his boss. "I know the man too well. Remember, I recruited him, and I've worked pretty closely with him for the last year."

"Do you think Bill can handle the case?" Muller asked.

"In a pinch. I still believe I'm the person best positioned to run this asset, but I guess an important factor will be how long the border remains open." Baier relayed the relevant points of his conversation with Chernov.

"Why haven't we provided this asset of yours with a camera or secret writing material so we can establish a safer means of communication? That would obviate the need for person-to-person meetings."

"Well, for one thing, Bluebird refuses to take a camera. He says it's too big a risk."

"Riskier than meetings in person?"

"That's right," Baier said. "He claims he does not have the time to photograph various documents, especially given how little time they spend in his possession. Not to mention how little time he has alone."

"Can't he take them home and then return them. He's not married, is he? He lives alone, right?"

Baier shook his head. "He says it's just too risky to try to take any material with him out of his office. Remember, the city is swarming with Soviets right now."

"The writing materials?"

"He also claims that he's not comfortable with that method either. He wants to meet with a human being to engage and make sure he's communicating the right information. He also says it's more timely. Things are moving at a pretty rapid pace over there right now."

"How secure is this other relationship? The one with your Soviet friend." O'Leary asked. "That's one of the things I'll need to hear more about from you later, Karl. Are we paying him a retainer or anything like a salary?"

"No, we haven't had to. As it was set up, he gets money from the bribes people pay to be smuggled out. I've passed him some cash in the past when we had an important exfiltration, or when Bluebird crossed over. I tried to make those payments infrequently and only periodically to avoid tipping him off, if possible. I would pass them along as a little bonus afterwards."

"Okay, thanks, Karl. My guess is that he could become more demanding, given the current situation. I doubt many people are paying bribes these days."

"You're probably right, Gerry. He is not my friend, believe me. I think my 'fucking Russian,' as my wife calls him, remains committed to the relationship. It's still in his personal interest. He gets a lot out of it, and he's inclined to be helpful. Look at the warning, however vague, he passed along yesterday."

"Helpful? Can we get more out of this relationship?" O'Leary asked.

Baier shook his head. "I doubt it. He refuses to become anything that would resemble a controlled source. I think he's only prepared to share tidbits now and then when he sees it being in his interest, or that of the border operation. The challenge to our operation will come when the issue is no longer in his hands."

"Which could come soon, if the fighting intensifies and the Soviets want to wall the country in entirely," O'Leary continued.

"It remains open, for the moment." Peters stood. "Karl, I understand you ran Bluebird by bringing him out of Hungary periodically because of the intense security and surveillance there. How secure is it to continue meeting with him back there now?"

Baier shrugged. "Well, it's hard to be sure, given how chaotic things are in Budapest right now. But, I believe we can use that chaos to our advantage. We just need to nail down what actually happened with the case of the hanging corpse. My recommendation is that we continue to exploit Bluebird's access and enthusiasm and then pull him out if—or when--the risks become too great."

"Fine," Peters continued. "Nonetheless, I think we should let Budapest run Bluebird for now. You can always go back in, if needed."

Baier stood and began to speak.

Peters raised his hand. "I think we need a cooling off period. There's too much of a chance at the moment that the other side could be looking for you, especially if this KGB officer is aware of your presence there last week."

"He's not going to tell anyone," Baier protested. "He became aware of it only when he spotted me at the crossing."

Peters raised his hand again. "Still, others may know as well, and having to travel in and out of the country increases the chances of you getting caught. I do not want us to have to put together another break out from Budapest." He smiled. "We know how difficult that one was and the kinds of problems we can encounter."

"I understand, Gary. But..."

"No, Karl, I think we need to have you work with Gerry in getting your new chief established in Vienna for now. You may not be aware, but Washington does not trust Nagy much more than they trust any other Communist."

"That's crazy," Baier protested. "He's announced his new government, which gets rid of some of the worst old Stalinists…"

"While bringing in some others from the back benches, as it were," Muller interrupted.

"Perhaps. But he needs to keep the Party engaged with the changes there. He's also brought in some non-Communists and other reformers. He got the Soviets to buy off on it. The man has turned a corner, damn it."

"We shall see," Peters said. "You will see it from Vienna, Karl. At least for now." He turned to the other two men. "I'd like a word alone with Karl, if I may."

Once Muller and O'Leary had left, Peters moved in close and took Baier's forearm in his hand. "Karl, do you recall when I said back in Washington that your career could be riding on how you handled this case?"

"Yes, as a matter of fact, I do, Gary. Why?"

"Well, after your little escapade in Budapest that is truer than ever."

"Gary, I'm only trying to do what I think is right for our Agency and our country."

"I realize that, Karl. I understand that you are also trying to do what you believe is right for your asset. Just make sure you do not get those feelings and priorities confused."

"I won't. And right now, they are one and the same, Gary."

Peters let Baier's arm drop to the side. "We shall see, Karl. We shall see."

Chapter Twelve

—❧—

B AIER TRIED TO follow the news coming out of Hungary on Sunday, the 28th, but he had to spend most of his time and attention on the turnover with the new chief of station. O'Leary was not quite an unknown commodity for Baier, coming as he did from Chicago's south side, where the Irish component in the city's rich cultural mixture was particularly strong. O'Leary, thankfully, was not a product of the elitist fortresses of the American East Coast, having attended the University of Notre Dame after four years at Fenwick Prep, one of Chicago's many Catholic high schools. Although Baier had grown up in a different part of the city and attended a different high school, he shared the Notre Dame and Midwestern Catholic heritage with O'Leary. This background clearly made things easier for Baier, as the two men poured over the case files run out of Vienna station and the personal histories and professional strengths and weaknesses of the people who worked there.

By early afternoon, both Baier and O'Leary decided they had covered enough of that administrative ground and broke off for the day. The news out of Budapest helped them make up their minds. Reports were streaming in about pitched battles at the Kilian Barracks and Corvin Theater between Hungarian rebels and Soviet units, and the casualties were reportedly heavy. Several Soviet tanks had been disabled, and dozens of Soviet corpses littered the streets surrounding the two hallmarks of what many were now openly calling the 'Revolution.'

Sabine had spent the night at their property near the border, which gave Baier the perfect excuse to press for a trip out of Vienna and to get closer to Hungary. "I promise to stay in Austria, Gerry. If I drive down there, I'm sure I'll be able to pick up some more about just what the hell is going on."

"How so? There aren't any journalists or government officials there, are there?"

"No, but there should be plenty of refugees. That is, if the Soviets haven't closed the border crossing."

"Do you think that's likely?"

Baier thought of Chernov and his warning from the day before. "Hard to say. But it does mean that we should get as much as we can through that crossing while it stays open."

The drive took nearly four hours. The route was easy enough as he left Vienna, but the closer Baier got to the border, the slower the pace became. He decided to take a brief detour and drive by the Austrian refugee camp at Pullendorf, which was located in Burgenland not far from the border or the estate Baier shared with his wife. When it came into view, Baier was shocked at how quickly the refugee camp had grown, as the Austrian government struggled to absorb and care for the thousands of Hungarians fleeing the fighting at home and the expected Soviet crack down on anyone who had supported the revolt. Rows of tents stretched for what appeared to be miles. They even blocked out the lines of vines that normally covered the countryside. Several wooden dormitories had been constructed, and the piles of lumber indicated that more were planned for the anticipated arrival of many more refugees. Dazed and dirty wanderers of all ages, many of them grouped as families, sat around the tents and shacks or wandered the paths between them. Feeding and care stations dotted the encampments, attempting to provide provisions and hope to those who had left everything behind. There were also several tables and stations setup to register the refugees, probably in hopes of getting an accurate count and to assemble the data necessary to feed, house and possibly integrate the newcomers.

It was a little after five o'clock when he arrived, and Sabine was not at the estate. So Baier hiked to the border a little over a mile away. He found her standing about one hundred yards from the crossing. His wife looked as though she had spent the better part of the day there. Her slacks and brown sweater had collected enough dust and dirt to pass her off as a farm hand. Or even one of the refugees. Her light brown hair was caught up in a scarf that doubled as a hat and bandana to ward off the wind. Baier circled her shoulders from behind when he reached her, and Sabine ran her hand along his arms before settling back against his chest.

"Oh, Karl, I think it may be over."

Baier stepped back and turned her to face him. "What, Sabine? What do you mean? How can it be over so soon? I heard there was a lot of fighting in the city this morning."

She nodded. "Yes, yes, but the Russians must be losing. They've agreed to a cease-fire."

"No! That can't be possible. Where did you hear this?"

"Several of the refugees who arrived a little while ago claimed they heard of talks between Nagy and the Soviets. It's all very confused, of course."

"I'll bet."

"So, I walked down to the crossing itself to see what else I could find out." She smiled and shook her head as though in disbelief. "Our Russian friend Chernov was there."

"What did our 'fucking Russian' have to say?"

Sabine's eyes went wide in amazement. Three was also a hint of disbelief as well. "He confirmed it. The cease-fire, I mean.

He said he had been called back to Budapest for new orders."

"Are the Soviets withdrawing?"

"He didn't say." She turned to study the horizon that stretched out over the east. "I find it hard to believe, Karl. It may actually be a dream coming true."

"Or simply a regrouping for another assault."

"Oh, please, Karl, let me and others enjoy the victory, even if it doesn't last."

Baier smiled. "You're right, Sabine. I never thought it would ever get this far. Did Chernov have anything else to say?"

She turned back to her husband. "He did say that the Soviets have suffered some heavy casualties. Something like five hundred dead already. They haven't even been able to recover many of the bodies. People are just throwing lime over them and leaving them in the street. Maybe those damn Russians are ready to compromise."

"Maybe so." Baier chewed his lip in thought. "Did Chernov give you any idea of when he might be back, or how we can contact him?" There had always an element of discomfort or uncertainty for Baier with the loose agreement he had arranged with Chernov over their cooperation in keeping the border crossing available not only for the flood of refugees fleeing the Stalinist regime in Hungary, but also in instituting an extremely loose oversight of that flow. This had created optimal conditions for Baier to use the open crossing to run what had proved to be a successful infiltration and exfiltration operation that provided a rare, albeit infrequent, stream of reporting from behind the Iron Curtain. It was not very insightful stuff; most of it was actually pretty superficial. Nothing of the plans and intentions of the region's leadership that the Agency aspired to collect. Consumers in Washington had occasionally expressed doubts and concerns about the value and reliability of that reporting. But considering how little else there was, it remained a badly needed source of information. That's what made Bluebird so valuable, in Baier's eyes. True, he appreciated the concerns expressed by some in Washington over the man's validity as a committed and controlled source. But you operated with the tools at hand. We deal with a lot of broken toys, a colleague had once stated. So you can't always wait for the perfect playmate.

The biggest problem for Baier was not the reporting but the questionable reliability of the man needed to keep the passage in operation: Sergei Chernov. There existed no agreed means of communication or remuneration—a point Chernov had insisted on to maintain his own flexibility and security. "I am not your spy, Herr Baier," Chernov had stated. Baier had no choice but to trust him. Thus far, at least, it had worked. And Baier remembered Chernov's words of warning just two days ago about a possible crackdown as he listened to Sabine's recounting of the Soviet assault in Budapest that very morning. Had that been his intent, to warn Baier and whomever he spoke with about the new assault? Or was there more coming, despite the talk of a ceasefire? It made him more determined than ever to regain the initiative from this enigmatic Russian he had first met those many years ago in Berlin.

"I need to go back in," he said suddenly.

Sabine's frown wrinkled her forehead, while her eyes stayed wide and very open. "Go back in where, Karl?"

He looked down at his wife's face and kissed her forehead to ease some of her obvious concern. "Budapest, Sabine. There are people there I need to see."

"Including Chernov?"

"Yes, including Chernov. If I can find him. But others as well. I think we're at a turning point here. And the information will be more valuable than ever."

"DAMN IT, KARL," O'Leary cursed. "You heard what Peters said. You're to observe from Vienna. We can't risk having you go back in there."

It was early in the morning of the 29th. Baier had gotten

back to Vienna late the night before, too late to call on the new chief. O'Leary would probably have fobbed off any decision until the following day in any case. It's what Baier would have done in his shoes.

"Jesus, Gerry, don't you think the situation has changed? Just where the hell is Peters, anyway?"

O'Leary's nervous pacing drove a small path in front of the desk in his new office. The beige walls were bare, with light spots where his predecessor had hung various prints of old Vienna. The only signs of life so far were the family photos of O'Leary's parents and siblings, and their families, on his desk. He glanced at the watch on his wrist. O'Leary had remained a bachelor, citing the difficulty of raising a family in the middle of a career that carried him every few years to a new hotspot somewhere around the world.

"He should be leaving Paris pretty soon. He had some additional meetings scheduled with the French this morning and then was supposed to head to London later today. I think he has a full plate with the Limeys for tomorrow."

"Paris? Is it about the Suez crisis those clowns have created?"

O'Leary stopped momentarily and nodded. "Yeah, but they haven't exactly been alone there. The Brits have helped. That's why he wanted to stop there as well. I think those guys are actually leading this shit storm."

"It's more like the blind leading the blind, if you ask me. And from behind. Both sides are willing accomplices pursuing their own misguided ends. Anyway, is there some way we can reach him? Maybe shoot off a cable to get his approval? I mean, we're talking here about something monumental, maybe even the end of the Soviet Empire in Europe."

O'Leary raised a hand as he studied Baier. "Let's not get carried away. You and I both know that's not about to happen, Karl."

"Who can say that? Did you expect it to get even this far?" O'Leary resumed his march. "Okay, point taken. But are you certain of your source? Will he really have the access necessary to give us the information we'll need? You're putting an awful lot of faith in Bluebird, Karl. Can we still trust him to give us some strong reporting and not just his own enthusiasm? You were not all that convincing yesterday. I'm worried that some of Bluebird's emotion has infected you as well. You need to keep a level head, Karl."

"Yes, yes, and yes, Gerry. Damn it! I understand."

"But if Gero is pushed out, what does that do to Bluebird's access? Hasn't Gero been his patron of sorts? Are you sure there isn't some residual loyalty there on Bluebird's part?"

"Yes, he was Gero's protégé. But Bluebird has been losing confidence in the old system and is fully committed to the new Revolution and its goals now. Besides, there's a deeper split in their backgrounds that goes way back"

"I thought Bluebird was a committed Communist."

"Gerry, you know as well as I that there are many different shades of that. And events like those in Hungary have a way of changing people's views and commitments. I gather Bluebird has been reliving some of the old battles between the Trotskyite and Stalinist camps that has rekindled an estrangement of sorts between the two. At least from Bluebird's side."

"Does that jeopardize Bluebird's security?"

"He says not. Bluebird claims that Gero is a spent force, a part of Hungary's past."

"And what do I say when Peters reminds us that we all agreed to let Schneider handle things for now?"

"Another good question, Gerry. But that and the others can only be answered once I get back in there and make contact." He considered the floor at O'Leary's feet before continuing. "And as for Bill Schneider. Well, I think once again we have to admit that the situation has changed drastically. Enough for us to alter our own plans. We have to stay flexible, Gerry."

"But Bill will be involved, right? I'm sure Budapest station will insist on that much."

"That's fine with me." Baier studied the floor for a moment longer before looking back up at the new Station Chief. "Do you think we can get Stan to agree?"

O'Leary nodded. "Yeah, we probably can get that much. As you say, the situation has taken a pretty drastic turn." He sighed and rolled his eyes toward the ceiling before looking back at Baier. O'Leary shook his head in a mild expression of disbelief. "I can't believe I'm saying this, but let's give it a try. I'll shoot off a cable to Stan explaining our reasons. Given what all's going on there, I'm sure he'll agree. At least temporarily. We can claim that Bluebird will expect as much, which is probably true."

"Thanks, Gerry. I really appreciate this." He approached O'Leary and took the new chief's hand. "Let's also send a cable off to London informing Peters of my push on the decision to go back in. And I will take full responsibility for this, Gerry."

O'Leary's hand felt almost limp. "I wish it was that easy, Karl. I really do."

AN HOUR LATER, Baier was waiting in front of the British Embassy on Jauresgasse , a modest residential street behind the Rennweg and across from the Belvedere Palace. He had called to set up a meeting with Henry Turnbridge, a colleague he had worked with before, most recently during the von Rudenstein case just over a year ago. The man had been replaced on that case with an officer Baier had come to like and trust more than he did Turnbridge. Fortunately, their own working relationship had survived as well. Turnbridge was an MI6 officer, and Baier hoped to get a sense of the reception that might await Peters in London and whether Hungary would play into the discussions. And how the Brits might respond. Baier did not relish the thought of working entirely alone and against the wishes of everyone in a position of authority. He hoped the Brits, as our closest allies, might be able to say or do something helpful

They met, as they had on numerous occasions during the von Rudenstein investigation, in the gardens of the Belvedere Palace because of its proximity to the British Embassy. The chilly air of late October was not nearly as relaxing—or as hopeful--as that of May, 1955. Baier gave up trying to get comfortable on the iron bench that faced the lower palace, what had probably at one time been the stables and garden house.

"Hard to say, old man, as I have not been a party to those preparations back home," Turnbridge explained as he took a seat next to Baier. "But my guess is that any discussions will focus on Suez. You are aware that the Israelis have gone into the Sinai?"

Baier nodded. "Yes, I've heard as much. I suppose you will be following shortly."

Turnbridge shifted on the bench uneasily. "It all seems to be such a muddle back there. And, of course, I can only speak for myself here..." he paused to consider Baier,"...but I would certainly expect as much. It's where the sentiment and planning have been running. You're aware of the meetings at Sevres outside Paris a week ago, aren't you?"

Baier shook his head. "Not really. That's not part of my bailiwick."

"Yes, I see." Turnbridge coughed, although Baier doubted he had anything stuck in his throat. "I probably shouldn't be telling you this, but I do want to be more forthcoming than I was allowed to be during the von Rudenstein investigation."

"Don't worry, Henry. Your secrets are safe with me."

Turnbridge moved his butt once more. "Well, that's when much of this was planned, you see. Back in Sevres, I mean. It all seems to have taken on a life of its own. I'm afraid no one is prepared to get in the way of a poor policy that has been forced on both capitals. It now has a momentum all its own."

"Were the Israelis there?"

"Yes, they were. And that has not helped either. They have

done what they could to drive this whole affair according to their needs. And, unfortunately, those interests do not square with our own in the region."

"How so?"

"For god's sake man, we've been building a relationship with the Arabs and the Persian Gulf states for decades. That will all be wiped out in a matter of weeks." He paused and glanced back toward the Upper Palace on the hill behind them. "I'm sorry to be so emotional, but I shudder to think what will happen as a result of this."

"Is anyone giving any thought at all to the events in Hungary?"

Turnbridge shook his head. "Hardly." He paused. "No, not at all from what I can see."

"So, it is unlikely to come up in the meetings with Peters?"

"Highly unlikely."

"What about at the UN? I think we're looking for your support when we introduce some sort of resolution in the Security Council."

Turnbridge sighed then smiled. "We seem to have emasculated ourselves, old man. I'm not sure what help we can provide there." He shook his head. "It's not like we have loads of credibility just now. No, I'm afraid you're on your own on this."

Baier nodded and turned to go. "I'm afraid you are as well."

Turnbridge stood. "Oh, and one other thing. I'm not sure what this means, but an old gent by the name of Rankin asked me to give you his best wishes if I see you."

Baier stopped and stared at the Englishman. "What did you say? The man's name was Rankin?"

"Yes. Does that name mean anything to you? Do you know him from somewhere?"

Baier shrugged. "We've met. Once. Did he say anything else?"

Turnbridge shook his head. "Not really. Just that he

thinks he can help. He said you should keep your eyes open."
Turnbridge laughed. "Not much in that. I mean, we all have
to do that, especially now, don't we."

"True, Henry."

"Is there anything else you'd like to say, Karl?"

Baier shook his head. "No, not really. There isn't anything
more I know."

As HE LEFT the Belvedere Palace grounds Baier strolled along
the Ringstrasse in the direction of the Parliament and *Rathaus*.
When he arrived at the *Burgtheater*, Vienna's renowned theater
sitting directly across from the park fronting the neo-Gothic
City Hall, Baier turned right and wandered around the back
of the theater to Bankgasse, where he took another right turn.
If he continued he would have shortly found Herrengasse and
the Michaelerplatz, which led directly into the imperial palace,
or *Hofburg*, and the Spanish Riding School. Like the stately
Opera House, the Burgtheater, too, had been nearly leveled
during a bombing raid in the war, but the reconstruction of the
building had been so thorough and complete that Baier could
not distinguish where the old left off and the new began. It
looked all of a piece, having recaptured the Italian Renaissance
style that had emerged from the theater's renovation in the
nineteenth century. Realizing this lent an inspiring note to
Baier's mission, as he settled into a café about a block down
the street from the theater. There he resumed an observation
post of the Hungarian Embassy he had discovered the
previous summer when Josef Kovacs had wandered into his
professional, and now personal life. The spire of St. Stephen's
cathedral rose like a beacon above the rooftops of the inner
city. Baier ordered a cappuccino, although he knew that doing
so any time after noon was considered a distinct lack of good
taste and breeding. This afternoon he didn't really care.

Baier leaned back in his seat and watched the people of
Vienna amble past his window. He remembered the warm,

sunny weather that surrounded that first meeting with Kovacs, and his own surprise at the brash offer of assistance and request for help from the disillusioned Hungarian Communist. It had been a remarkable recruitment, one that required little of Baier in terms of spotting, assessing, and developing the man. It had all come so easily. Staring into the foam that hovered over his cup, Baier asked himself if it all had not been too easy. Then he shook away the thought like an ancient heresy of self-doubt. He had gotten to know the man, and his bona fides had been established right from the outset. As was so often the case, it had ultimately come down to that gut feeling, the moment you had to make the call on the viability and veracity of your asset from your own instinctive sense of a man's worth and honesty. And Baier was more certain than ever, damn it.

He was shaken from his reverie by an odd sense of unease. Glancing up, Baier discovered a tall, well-built individual walking slowly past the café, his eyes set firmly on Baier. The man was dressed in a pair of black woolen trousers, a white turtleneck sweater, and a black leather jacket stretched by a broad set of shoulders. His square jaw was set back against a smallish chin that led upwards to a wide, square skull covered by a thick mane of black hair that had been shaved close on the side but let to grow longer along the top. But it was the eyes that struck Baier the moist, dark pupils that seemed to float on a field of ice the color of dirty water. And the look they sent to Baier was like that of an executioner, as though measuring him for a noose.

Chapter Thirteen

——⟨∽⟩——

H E MET SCHNEIDER close to where they had joined up on Baier's previous trip in. The car was parked on the same path but nestled a few hundred yards further down the road in the direction of Budapest. Schneider eyed the bag in Baier's grip. "I hope that includes a change of clothes this time. Or at least some clean underwear."

Baier smiled and tossed the small duffle bag on the seat between them. "You bet. I figured you were good for the soap and a towel, though."

"I'll see what I can do." Schneider started the engine and pulled away from the side of the road where he had parked under a small cluster of oak trees whose long, bare branches spread across the dirt path that passed for a road.

"Not exactly a scenic spot, Bill."

"Yeah, with all the troop movements you can't be too safe these days. I should warn, you, however, that Muller is really pissed right now."

Baier peered through the windshield. "Because of my sudden return and despite what we had agreed on in Vienna?"

Schneider nodded. "You got it. I thought we had best stop off at the office first thing to try to soothe his ruffled feathers."

"But he agreed to my coming."

Schneider glanced at his passenger. "Only grudgingly, Karl. Very grudgingly."

"Fine. I can live with that. Let's go talk to your boss. Am I staying at your place?"

"Yeah. Don't be shocked, but we didn't bother to check on any vacancies at the hotel you stayed at last year."

"That's okay. It was not a very pleasant place to stay in any case. Cramped and smelling of disinfectant from what I remember. Among other things. I'm sure your place is more luxurious. Probably doesn't smell any better and not much cleaner, though."

"Yeah, well, the tourist industry is not exactly booming right now." He smiled. "Then again, it never has since the Red Army arrived, so there hasn't been much demand for high quality service. Not that it would matter. There may be fewer visitors, but there's also fewer hotel staff. Fewer hotels, too."

"Any word from Bluebird?"

Schneider shook his head. "Not yet. I left a message at the dead drop, but there was nothing there yet when I left to came get you."

"I've been thinking about that. We should change our dead drop location, maybe even the contact procedure, given the surprises we encountered last week. Best not to assume our communications are still safe. I realize things got pretty hectic, but I wish we had agreed on something when we last saw Bluebird."

"Way ahead of you there, Karl. I've scouted what looks like a good location at the Eastern Railway Station. In view of the people and traffic passing through there, we'd have good cover for making the occasional visit."

"Then again, the heavy volume of people could make any counter-surveillance that much tougher. Unlike the Heroes

Square out in the City Park we've been using. Besides, I doubt we're going to be making occasional visits. With all that's happening we'll probably want to meet on a daily basis."

"Well, I'm open to your suggestions."

"No, you're probably right." Baier conceded. "It is your city, after all. At least, more than it is mine."

Schneider studied his passenger again before returning his attention to the road as they entered the capital. "Karl, what should we do about that little black package we found at our last meeting with Bluebird?"

"Have you said anything to Muller?"

Schneider shook his head. "Not yet."

"Good. I don't want to do anything that jeopardizes this operation before we know exactly what we're dealing with. I mean, we don't know who planted that thing there or why."

"Or how it got decommissioned," Schneider added.

Baier nodded. "Exactly. Or if it was even armed in the first place. So let's just play it dumb for now. And keep our damn eyes open."

WHAT STRUCK BAIER during the drive through Budapest was how arbitrary the destruction appeared to have been. The newer damage was relatively easy to identify and separate from the destruction that had yet to be removed or repaired after the Second World War. Some streets and city blocks had remained untouched by the recent fighting, as though completely unaware of the storm that had raged for a week around them. Others, however, were littered with rubble, corpses, and bombed out buildings. Sabine had been right, many of the dead had been covered in lime, probably to prevent infections and diseases like typhus from spreading until they could be properly buried. And most of those dead were Soviets. Presumably, the Hungarians casualties had been taken care of by friends and relatives.

"So, Mr. Baier, you've got some explaining to do." Stan

Muller sat upright at his desk, his white shirt pressed and starched, almost as though he was working out of an office in Manhattan. His tie was solid red, probably not the best choice of color at the moment, Baier thought. The brown office walls were covered in shifting shadows, as the sun and clouds changed positions every few minutes under the light wind outside. The room was also empty of any artwork beyond a large framed street map of Budapest on the wall to Muller's left. "As I recall, we had agreed that Bill here," he nodded in Schneider's direction, "would handle things with our asset."

'Our' asset, Baier noted to himself. That was correct, technically at least, but not only had Baier recruited the man, he had also been the only one handling this asset for as long as the man had been reporting on developments behind the Iron Curtain. "Yes, we had. And I apologize for the sudden disruption of those plans. But it seemed to me that given the new situation here, it was imperative for me to visit once more to establish a new sort of relationship with Bluebird. He will take some careful handling now that the revolt has leaped forward, as it were."

"Has Peters approved this?"

Baier grimaced and shifted his weight from one foot to the other. "Well, not exactly."

"Meaning?"

"He has been informed. I left before we heard back. Time is of the essence, you know."

"Not quite. At least not in Peters's view. Incidentally, I did hear from him. He said that you may stay—as long as I approve—to re-establish contact with Bluebird. But as soon as you leave town, you are to continue on to Washington."

"Am I being recalled? Did he say just what I'm expected back for?"

Muller shook his head. "No, he did not. And he wouldn't put any of that in a note to me, in any case. You know better than that, Karl. But I really doubt it will be for a celebration."

Baier nodded. "Yes, of course." He glanced at Schneider, then back at the local chief of station. "In the meantime, any word on how Washington is reacting to the news from here?"

"No, nothing yet. I get the impression that this is all moving too rapidly for our masters back on the Potomac. Especially given their focus on Suez right now."

"What does Barnes have to say?"

"Funny you should ask. I just got back from my return call on our charge."

That would explain the formal attire in the middle of a revolution, Baier guessed. "Is he still supportive and hopeful for the revolt?"

Muller sat back and seemed to relax for the first time since they entered his office. "I'll say. Of course, we're all supportive." He pivoted briefly for a quick glance out the window to his back. "Hard not to be. I mean, this is one helluva thing." He turned back to Baier. "But he's gone a lot further than most, certainly back in Washington. He's sent a cable to the Department advocating full support—both rhetorical and military—for the rebellion."

"Not troops, I hope. That would definitely provoke a Soviet response."

Muller shook his head and waved his hands in the air. "No, nothing that drastic. But supplies for sure. Funny thing, though, is that he doesn't sound very optimistic. In fact, I'd say he's downright worried."

"What about?"

"The Revolution. It's all so disorganized and divided. These Revolutionary Councils and Workers' Committees are devolving into little more than chatter shops with some wild ideas popping out about where to take things. People have been infected by their optimism, and many of those people want to press for complete freedom."

"Like what sort of things?"

"Like the end of communist economics and free elections

in a multi-party state. Not that you can blame them for that."

"Those issues were also in the 16 Points released at the beginning of the revolt," Schneider added.

"Okay, but some are also pushing for an exit from the Warsaw Pact and membership in NATO," Muller said. "It's actually looking kind of utopian."

"But that's to be expected in the midst of something like this," Baier objected.

"Sure. But the new government here needs to exert some control and try to calm things down if they want the Soviets to leave them alone. They have organized a single military command to try to gain control over all the disparate bands of fighters roaming the city, but who knows if any of those people will actually accede to the new structure." Muller laughed. "There's this one character, a Jozsef Dudas, who has occupied some press office here and claimed to be leader of some national revolutionary committee."

"Any followers? Who does he represent?" Baier asked.

"Mostly himself and a handful of loyal fellow adventurers, from what I can tell. But you can see the sort of problem this presents for Nagy and his crew." Muller leaned forward against the edge of his desk. "Karl, there have been dozens of AVO agents lynched."

Baier shrugged then paused, thinking of the corpse they encountered in the former safehouse. "It's hard to have any sympathy for those bloodthirsty bastards. They've done some terrible things to their fellow citizens."

"Oh sure. Don't get me wrong. I hate those pricks as much as anyone. But can you imagine how that looks in Moscow? I'd say we're a long way from having this whole thing settled, despite what people might be saying in the street. And Nagy still has a big challenge in gaining the people's confidence here."

"How so?"

"Well, there's a rumor going around that he's the one who invited the Red Army in..."

"Like they need an invitation," Schneider said.

"Yeah, sure. But the word on the street, according to Barnes, is that Nagy also declared martial law early on. You might try to run that stuff down."

Baier turned to Schneider. "It looks like we've got our work cut out for us. I'd say we get going."

Muller stood. "Just be careful, Karl. You're already in enough trouble as it is. And I don't want you to drag others," he nodded once more at Schneider who now stood beside Baier, "in with you if it gets any worse."

SCHNEIDER HAD BEEN right. The East Railway Station was a busy place. It seemed to be awash in humanity, as people flowed in from the countryside or boarded trains to flee to the west. Baier was surprised by the number of Hungarians leaving the city, now that a ceasefire had been arranged and the Revolution and the forces of democracy looked to be winning. The damage to the building from the fighting around such a strategic location did give some hint as to their concern and even desperation, though. Baier could understand if they were feeling not so much the benefits of the Revolution but more the destruction and danger it brought with it, at least for now.

"Why do you think all these people are leaving the city?" Baier asked.

"I guess those are the ones who can't believe this thing will actually succeed. They probably figure they can always come back if everything turns out well."

The two Americans wandered inside the terminal, its large cavernous hall filled with the sounds and sights of momentous activity. People, many of them grouped in what appeared to be entire families, struggled with mountains of luggage and even some furniture, presumably in an effort not to leave everything behind. Some searched bulletin boards for information on relatives, friends, or other points of contact. But many also had what Baier would describe as signs of hope and joy on their faces in wide smiles and shining eyes. Baier guessed that these people may have come into town to support the uprising and do whatever they thought possible to push the Soviets out. It was actually inspiring.

"This is a pretty good picture for the outside world to see if they wanted to capture a moment in the Revolution. It has all the right signs of hope and celebration, as well as anxiety and even some sorrow."

"Yeah, but you were also right, Karl, to point out how difficult it will be to pick out a tail in this crowd.

"Well, we'll just have to do what we can. This might also be a good place to lose one."

The two men proceeded to push and shove their way through the throng that ebbed like a herd of small, undisciplined cattle. They wandered between some of the shops and checked the train schedules on the huge board suspended over the ticket booths to see if they were being followed. Eventually, Schneider led the way down the main hallway, turning to the left at a corner about two-thirds of the way through, and headed for a bank of lockers set up along a far wall just before the left-luggage department. The human crowd thinned out slightly at this point, and Baier noticed that he was no longer jostled at every step. Schneider halted and looked back towards the main thoroughfare.

"If it stays less crowded here, we might be able to use that for a final check on any surveillance."

Baier nodded and patted his colleague on the shoulder. "Good point. I take it you think we should use one of the lockers."

"Yep. A lot less sexy than the hollowed-out arm of the bench in the park behind the statue in Heroes Square, but still pretty damn effective. Especially now. I was getting pretty uncomfortable with all the activity back there these days. There was a lot of people but not enough to blend in with."

"Sounds good. Does Bluebird know about this location?"

Schneider nodded. "Not yet. I didn't want to do anything until we were agreed on this spot." "Good," Baier said. "Then let's go make one last stop there to drop off some new instructions. Then we can find our man and get this operation rolling properly."

And find Chernov while he was at it, Baier thought to himself. The man could in no way be described as an asset, and especially not a recruited one. But he could not afford to lose a contact like that in times like these.

IN THE END, it was Chernov who found him. Baier was sitting in one of the old coffee houses that had survived the tumult of recent Hungarian history, The Turkish Emperor, set against Castle Hill just underneath the old fortress in the Buda half of the capital. It was the more historic picturesque side of the city on the western bank of the Danube. He and Schneider had stopped there after servicing the dead drop for a quick bite to eat and to enjoy some traditional local fare, a beef stew with plenty of potatoes but few vegetables mixed in. Fortunately, there was already a note from Bluebird at the old drop site, agreeing to a meeting the following morning and noting that he could try to be there by eleven o'clock but that he might be a bit late. Baier had set their own session for noon in his response, thinking that the lunch hour would provide the best excuse for his asset being away from his desk. That hour's difference would give Bluebird plenty of time to make the meeting. And it promised to be a productive one. The Americans—indeed, the world--should hear a big and important announcement from Nagy soon, Kovacs had said.

The two Americans decided to make their goulash into an early supper, their first full meal of the day. The café was dark and smoky, about what Baier expected from an eatery in the heart of Central Europe, and the menu offered mostly heavy meat and potato dishes. Baier was thinking that perhaps he should use the opportunity to fill up, since one never knew when they might eat next, and goulash seemed like the logical choice in Budapest. And there was also plenty of bread to soak up the gravy. Baier also found that he could relax in the warmth streaming from the tiled stove in the corner at the back that covered the room like a soft blanket as darkness fell over the city on an early fall evening.

As soon as they cleaned their bowls with chunks of the heavy brown bread, Schneider left to check in at the office and report on the day's activity to his boss. Baier had stated that he would wait in the café and enjoy another glass of the rich Hungarian red wine. Mostly, he wanted to avoid another lecture if Muller was in the mood or had received another missive from Gary Peters.

Not half an hour later, Baier spied Chernov strolling by with two other Soviet officers. Chernov appeared to discover Baier looking through the window at the same moment. The Russian said something to his colleagues and nodded in Baier's direction. They both smiled, nodded in turn to Baier, then clapped Chernov on the back and wandered off on their own. Chernov sauntered into the restaurant and pulled out a chair at Baier's table.

"Herr Baier, so you've come back. I'd like to say that I'm surprised. But I can't, of course."

Baier studied the Russian, wondering what his game was now. "And why is that?"

Chernov shrugged. "Because you're so predictable. At least for those of us who know you. I realized that once the ceasefire was in effect you would feel compelled to return. It should be easier and safer for you now."

"Easier and safer for what?"

"For whatever it is you are doing here. And how is your wife? It was nice to see her the other day. She is as beautiful and resourceful as ever. As I have said before, you are a lucky man."

Baier suddenly realized how little he knew about the Russian's private life. "And what about you Chernov? Is there a woman in your life? Has there ever been? Or are you married to the Party?"

"Ah, there, Herr Baier, you have me at a disadvantage. I am married to no one and nothing. Especially now that my family is gone. In some ways my personal history is a common tragedy for our century. I am adrift and looking out for my own interests now." He smiled and leaned back in his chair. "But then you probably know that already, given whom you work for. I gather that your question was primarily rhetorical."

"Not entirely. I have often wondered just what it is you believe in, Chernov."

"Once again you have me at a disadvantage, Herr Baier. I know you have your own family, and that you believe in your country, a true patriot. For me, it is less so. You might say I am stuck in that grey zone between believing and disbelieving. A man adrift, as it were." He smiled. "And I doubt that I am alone in that, Herr Baier. There have been too many absolutes in this part of the world this century, and too many failed dreams. I find it best to remain a skeptic these days."

Baier nodded, studying the man at the table across from him for almost a minute before continuing. "What did you tell your colleagues? Don't you consider it a bit risky to meet with me here so openly?"

Chernov shrugged. "I told them the truth. Or at least part of it. That we had met in Berlin after our joint victory over the German fascists and had enjoyed many common acquaintances. And that I had not seen you since then. I lied about that part." He smiled again. "Besides, with the ceasefire things are much more relaxed."

"Any more on the fate of our border crossing?"

Chernov's face brightened. "Well, now that we have a ceasefire in place, there should be no need to close the border. I have not heard anything more." His face darkened momentarily. "I hope you understood why I passed the previous message to you."

Baier nodded and leaned back, both to give himself more room but also to gain an unobstructed view of the street. He looked out over the ruins of the old royal palace, destroyed in the battle for Budapest in 1945 and yet to be rebuilt. He let his gaze drift to the Danube as it flowed south and east toward Romania and the Black Sea. "Of course. And I appreciate it. But tell me, have you done well by our arrangement?"

Chernov's smile returned. "Oh, I've done well enough. It has helped to compensate for the losses I suffered when your German namesake and predecessor left us short on our trip to South America in 1945." Chernov was referring to Sabine's first husband, also named Karl Baier. Chernov had expected a much larger share of the money that the German Baier had accumulated and hidden through a variety of black market and smuggling schemes during the war. Chernov had been involved in his own smuggling operations in Berlin right after the war, and it was how Baier and Sabine had come to know the Russian. "Your few supplements have helped, of course. But I am glad that regular payments from your side were not necessary. It will help me avoid unpleasant charges if my situation ever changes back in Moscow."

"And what have you done with your ill-gotten gains?"

Chernov wagged a finger at Baier. "Now, now. Let's not be indiscreet, Herr Baier." A frown replaced the smile, and Chernov leaned in close over the table. He motioned for Baier to do the same. Chernov's voice dropped to a whisper. "It also fortunate that I ran into you here. I have something I'd like to pass along. Some more words of wisdom, as it were."

Intrigued, Baier settled his elbows on the table for support as he leaned in close, his focus glued to Chernov to gage the seriousness of the man. "Yes, what is it?"

Chernov threw a long, slow look around the room before returning to Baier's gaze. "The AVO suspects that there is a highly placed mole in the Hungarian government, possibly within their service. There are hardliners still in place there, Herr Baier, and they have shared this thought with the KGB office here. Word has even passed to Serov. You know who he is?"

Baier nodded. "Of course. He's your boss."

"Good. Fortunately, he has been called back to Moscow, but that is probably only temporary."

"So, his attention will be diverted to the situation inside the Kremlin?"

Chernov nodded. "Perhaps. At least I'm sure you hope it will be."

"And why are you telling me this? And how did the AVO come to suspect that they have a mole?"

"You mean a traitor, don't you?"

"Hardly."

"This is no time for games, Herr Baier." Chernov's words came out more like a hiss than a whisper. "That is exactly how the AVO sees this, so you can guess how serious their search will be, regardless of any changes in the government."

"But how did they come to this suspicion?"

"I've heard that Gero left some kind of word and evidence before he was recalled to Moscow. Perhaps he will discuss this with Serov himself while they are both there. You need say no more, but if that is why you are here, then I would urge you to look into getting this mole free. You know what the AVO will do to him."

Baier held Chernov in his stare. He did not respond.

"But I would also urge you to be careful for your own and your wife's interests," Chernov continued. "They would be most unkind toward you as well."

"Thank you for your concern, Sergei." Baier surprised himself at his familiarity toward the Russian.

"Ultimately, my greatest concern is for myself, Karl. It would not be long before the AVO would know everything they want from you." Chernov paused and took in the other customers in the café. "One other thing. Please satisfy my curiosity about something."

"If I can."

"You have not discussed our arrangement or your plans here with anyone else, have you?"

Baier sat up straight. "Of course not. Why?"

"Because I have noticed some new...no, actually, old faces here of late."

"What do you mean, Sergei?"

"They are old faces but new here in Budapest. One man in particular I remember. He had been arrested for working with the British during the early years of our Revolution and was sentenced to life at hard labor in Siberia."

"Then why do you think you saw him here?"

"Oh, I am sure I saw him. He was among those released when Khrushchev began his de-Stalinization program. There were many amnesties granted. This man got one of them."

"Well, maybe he's here for the inspiration, to enjoy the freedom he sought to preserve years ago."

"Yes, and failed to do so. If I am correct and it is the same man, then he is probably here as the result of some agreement, a deal, as you Americans like to say. Remember that, Karl, if you've been blabbing to your British friends. Eventually their operations during our own revolution fell apart."

"But they did succeed in getting some very useful information back to London in the process. But more to the point, what is the man's name and what does he look like?"

"His name is Sergei, like mine. But his last name is Kalinikov. And he looks like someone who has survived years in a Siberian prison camp. You should be able to recognize that easily enough."

Chernov stood to leave, then bolted for the door when he saw his companions approaching. This had been the first time that Baier could remember seeing Chernov so close to looking worried and losing some of his composure, his natural arrogance. Perhaps it was all an act, one of the many Chernov employed to hide his true thoughts and motives. But that had not been Baier's impression. The man was clearly concerned about something. But what? It was also the first time Baier could recall the two men having ever used their Christian names.

Chapter Fourteen

⁓

THIS TIME IT was Kovacs who was late. Baier and Schneider waited almost an hour before their asset showed up at the bombed-out apartment the Hungarian had chosen for their new meeting place at the previous gathering. The rotting and broken surroundings made for a stark contrast to the exuberance Kovacs demonstrated when he entered the flat. He had on a dark blue pin-striped suit and a bright yellow tie over his white shirt. The man appeared to be almost Western. He clearly looked important, or as though he had just come from a very significant gathering.

"This is a great day, gentlemen."

"I'm glad to hear it," Baier replied. "But we need to discuss our security first. We've selected a new means of communicating, and we'll need a new meeting place. One that we will choose."

Kovacs seemed to wave off their concerns as he paced around the apartment, nervous energy pouring from his tall, thin frame. His eyes refused to focus on either of the Americans. "Of course, of course. All in good time." He stopped suddenly in front of Baier, who had once again taken his spot at the edge of the table just inside the door. In spite of himself, Baier glanced periodically at the wall to his back, even though he and Schneider had given the flat a thorough inspection for any more surprises. Schneider had positioned himself closer to the gaping window in an effort to observe the street below. "Nagy is coming around more and more to the cause and course of the Revolution."

"How so?" Baier asked.

"He has announced his new cabinet, which includes several non-Communists. We have it on good authority that the Social Democrats will cooperate with the new government. And the National Peasants Party…"

"Those guys are nothing more than fellow travelers." Schneider protested. "Like the rest of those peasant parties in eastern Europe."

Kovacs held up his forefinger, as though he was lecturing a high school class, and looked at no one in particular. His eyes were initially directed toward the floor. "They have decided to break with that tradition. They have adopted a new name, the Petofi Party. You have heard of the Petofi Circle?"

"Yes, of course," Baier replied. "The group of dissident writers and intellectuals."

"Yes, exactly. So you can see the significance in that of their commitment to our cause. And they, too, will cooperate with the government." He looked up at the Americans, his gaze shifting between them before settling on Baier. "And you would do well to remember that that party easily won our first free election after the war. They still have tremendous popular support and will be of great assistance to the Revolution."

"Glad to hear that as well," Baier grumbled.

Kovacs turned on Baier. "What is wrong with you? Don't you realize how momentous this is? And more important, Nagy will call for the complete withdrawal of all Soviet troops from our country."

Baier stood up straight. "Now that is something. When will

he announce all this?"

"Sometime around noon, or shortly thereafter. It's why I was so late. We were preparing the speech and wanted to get the wording just right. And we are no longer a 'socialist' republic."

"What about the Communist Party? It still exists, doesn't it?"

Kovacs resumed his march. "Yes, of course. And Kadar has been instructed as the new party leader to rebuild it as a more humane and independent group. Not just a satrap of Moscow."

"Good luck with that," Schneider said. "Are there even any members left? Besides those at the party headquarters."

"Oh, there are a few, of course. But it is true that most joined less from conviction and more from opportunity. But there are still true believers out there. As well as fence sitters."

"Like yourself?" Schneider asked.

Kovacs stopped his pacing and turned to face Schneider. "Yes, of course, like me. But there is so much more we can do for the people of Hungary and Europe if we shed our Stalinist packaging. I still believe in our cause. It is why I support our Revolution. And I am convinced that once the people are aware of all that we can achieve together, then we will win their support as well."

"But is this new, revamped Communist Party supportive of the changes here?" Schneider pressed. "Or are they like wolves in sheep's clothing to do Moscow's bidding?"

"No, no," Kovacs almost shouted. "We are all committed to our own Revolution now."

"So why tell us all this now if it's going to be public so soon?" Baier interrupted.

"Because I want you to report this back to Washington yourselves, with this unique perspective. Don't you think that hearing this from someone on the inside will inform your leaders better of our true intentions and goals? Don't you see how important this is? After all, someone needs to convince your people of Nagy's sincerity, of the possibilities here. Those broadcasts from Radio Free Europe are really scandalous."

Baier realized at that moment how little he had been listening to outside coverage of the events inside Hungary. He had simply been swept up by the tide of events in this country. "What have they been saying?"

Kovacs waved his arms in the air, as though he hoped to take flight. "They are ridiculous. They claim Nagy is no better than the Stalinists, that all Communists are alike."

"Well, that certainly doesn't help," Baier said.

"And it's bullshit." Schneider agreed.

"Not only that," Kovacs continued. "But they also are encouraging people to continue fighting, urging them to take more drastic actions. It is precisely what the Soviets would need for an excuse if they decided to return and suppress us."

"Can you clear something up for us, though, Josef? Why did Nagy invite the Soviet army into Budapest and why did he declare martial law early on? You understand the impact that is having on his popularity and credibility, I'm sure."

Kovacs spun towards the gaping hole in the wall and spit out onto the street. He turned back to Baier. "The martial law declaration came from others in the Cabinet without Nagy's knowledge or authorization. And there was no invitation to the Soviets. Do you really think they need one?"

"Well, it would protect them in terms of international law."

"Like they care," Schneider added.

"Speaking of our Soviet friends, what are you hearing from that quarter?" Baier asked.

Kovacs resumed his pacing, nodding his head all the while. "Good news, good news. You know that the two principle advisers here from Moscow are Suslov, the chief of the General Staff, and Mikoyan."

"The Armenian. But he's been here all along," Baier said.

"Yes, yes. But he has acted as a counterweight to hardliners like the KGB's Serov. It looks like he has the upper hand now in reporting back to Moscow and advising Khrushchev. And then there is the Friendship Treaty we and the other members of the Warsaw Pact have signed with Moscow that promises to respect our sovereignty and independence."

"Is it sincere? Do you think they'll adhere to it? Wouldn't that make an invitation all the more necessary?"

"Yes, I do believe in Moscow's sincerity. No, I mean, we all do." He stopped. "Look at what is happening in Poland. And the Yugoslavs have already secured their freedom from Moscow. This is clearly in the Soviets' interest as well."

"But how can you be so sure that Moscow sees it like that? And has Moscow made a final decision on all this? What have you heard along those lines?"

Kovacs stopped and shrugged, as though the decisions in the Kremlin were now a secondary matter. "Hard to say. It all appears to be very chaotic back there. I'm not sure Khrushchev has made a final decision." He stopped and looked at Baier again. "That's why it's so important that Mikoyan is here and has the upper hand."

Baier leaned back against the table. "Fine. But about our security."

"Our security?" Kovacs said. He stared straight at Baier.

"Yes, our security. We're taking risks here as well, you know."

"Of course. I am sorry," Kovacs responded.

"I've learned that the AVO is on to something. They suspect there is a mole in the government, and a highly placed one at that."

"How did you learn this?" Kovacs looked concerned for the first time since he had entered the flat. He buried his hands in the pockets of his suit jacket and glanced briefly out the window.

"Never mind," Baier said. "But trust me on this. We need to vary our meeting places, and we've shifted the site of the dead drops. Bill?"

Schneider stepped away from the hole in the wall and approached Kovacs, who stood rooted to the middle of the room, unfortunately in full view of the street below. Schneider explained the location of the mailboxes near the baggage drop off and claim post inside the railway station. "Number 301 will be our mailbox. For now, anyway." He passed Kovacs a copy of the key.

"But I must ask you again, Josef. Has anyone demonstrated a peculiar interest in your work, or your comings and goings?" Baier asked. "Are you under pressure at work or at home?"

Kovacs shook his head. "You know I am a bachelor, so there are no vulnerabilities on that end. And as for work, well, we are all under a great deal of pressure right now. As you can probably imagine."

"But what about the hanging corpse we encountered last week? Have you learned anymore? That still has me very worried, Josef. We can't assume that he was working alone."

Kovacs shook his head. "No, no. I explained all that I know. I have not learned anything else."

"But how did he learn so much?" Baier countered.

Kovacs shrugged. "From what little I do know of the man, he was a nosey bastard and malcontent. I do not believe he had many friends in the service. I can always explain away his acts as ones of betrayal and his killing as due to popular outrage. He is not the only AVO officer to have been lynched, you know."

"Yes, we know," Baier said. "That hardly seems fair, though. It did look like he was trying to help, Josef. He seemed genuinely concerned for your welfare. And he was still on to you, even if only preliminarily. You need to find out more about what he knew and how he knew it. But you also need to be very careful and not arouse suspicions further or draw too much attention to yourself. And how was your relationship with Gero when he left?"

Kovacs looked puzzled. Both hands were buried in his jacket pockets now. "Why do you ask?"

"Wasn't he your patron of sorts? Didn't he know you as well

as just about anyone in the government?"

"Yes, yes, but he is gone now, discredited."

"But wouldn't he still have allies in the AVO, in the government? It's something you need to consider. Please think about it, Josef." Baier paused and walked closer to Kovacs. "We will also need to increase the frequency of our meetings, given the pace of events here and elsewhere."

"Elsewhere?"

"Yes. There's a lot going on in the world, and it all ties together in places like Washington and Moscow. So be sure to check on the new dead-drop site every day in case there have been changes in our schedules or the locations of meetings. Preferably early. Will that be possible?"

Kovacs nodded. "I believe so, yes. I will try to check on my way into work, and at some other point during the day."

"Good. We'll have the new address for a secure meeting placed in the first message. Once again, Josef, please think carefully. Is there any problem with you getting out of your office every day? Will this raise suspicions about you? I mean, if there is already a hunt on for a mole this could bring up questions about your behavior."

"No, that should not be a problem. As I've told you before, it is all quite chaotic now. I can always say I'm running out to check on what is happening in the city. People do it all the time. We're in the midst of a revolution, you know."

"Well, for God's sake, Josef, remember what we told you about checking for surveillance. You've been in dangerous situations before, like in Spain. You should be able to help us here with your own security. It's important, very important."

"I know, I know."

"You should make sure you check the schedules when you go the train station, as though you're waiting for someone or planning a trip to the countryside. In fact, it wouldn't hurt if you purchased a ticket tomorrow in case anyone is watching you. We'll reimburse you."

"Or pause to scan the crowds getting off the trains, as though you're there looking for someone," Schneider added.

Kovacs nodded. "Okay, okay. I'll see what I can do. But in the end, you know, it will not matter. We, the people of Hungary, have won."

"It still matters to us, Josef. And it had better matter to you."

IT TOOK BAIER and Schneider about thirty minutes to navigate their way through the crowds and debris during the ride to the U.S. Embassy on Szabadsag Square, not far from the Parliament building that overlooked the Danube. Baier only noticed the ornate baroque architecture of the stately four-story building now for the first time. Well, he had noticed it before but never really given it much thought. He had not gotten anywhere near the compound when he had been in the city a year ago to rescue of his wife from a Hungarian prison. And during his last visit to meet with the acting ambassador, Stephen Barnes, Baier's attention had been drawn to the three Soviet tanks stationed in the square. Whether they were positioned there for some tactical reason or simply to intimidate the Americans and other foreign missions nearby, while also protecting the monument to the fallen Soviet soldiers from the Battle for Budapest, was unclear. As was the air that day, obscured by the drifting smoke that cluttered the sky and made his eyes sting.

The Embassy was clearly an impressive structure. The complex design and exterior plaster molding must have cost a fortune, even in the previous century when it was constructed. It also looked strong enough to withstand a siege, which it must have done during the battle for the city in 1945. And the neighborhood was filled with history, the most notable exemplar, however, no longer existed. That was the Tancsics military compound, destroyed at the end of the previous century to make way for the new square, ironically. The barracks had served as the prison home for numerous Hungarian revolutionaries from 1848 and 1849, including

Lajos Kossuth, the nineteenth-century Hungarian patriot and political reformer. The Embassy shared its side of the square with the Hungarian National Bank and its art deco façade. Just beyond the square and about a block south, one could see the massive neo-classical structure that was formerly the Stock Exchange. Given its original capitalist purpose, the building had been rechristened by the Soviet occupiers as the headquarters for Hungarian television.

"I have to confess," Baier said, "that I'm only appreciating this building and its neighbors for the first time." Barnes smiled and settled himself into the chair behind his desk. "Was there much damage from the war?"

Barnes shook his head. "From what I understand only the roof needed major repairs.

"How long have we been at this site?"

"Just twenty over years now. We moved in 1935."

"And the war years?" Schneider asked.

"The Swiss held on to it for us. Fortunately, they were able to accomplish some great stuff, helping Raoul Wallenberg, among others, sneak thousands of Jews to safety. Nice as the building and history is, though, the real advantage today is in the location." He turned to look out the window behind him which opened toward the Danube. "We're just minutes from the Parliament. Now that's a truly impressive building."

"We're also not far from the Communist Party headquarters. Unfortunately." Schneider added.

"Ah, but in a state such as Hungary, it helps to be near the center of real power," Barnes said.

"But for how long?" Baier asked. "Has Nagy made his announcement yet?"

Barnes nodded. "He has, indeed. And the new cabinet looks promising. He's also going to revamp the economy, open it up toward the free market. And he's effectively ended the one-party state."

"Then why is Washington holding back?" Baier pressed.

"Isn't this what we've been pushing for?"

"I think it comes to a couple things, Karl. As we've discussed before, a big one is this crap in Egypt. Given the role of our closest allies, it's understandable that the President's and Secretary's focus is on Suez, especially now that the Israelis have rolled into the Sinai."

"What's their excuse?"

"Oh, it's supposed to be a matter of self-defense. You know, clearing out guerilla camps."

"Are there any there?" Schneider asked.

Barnes glanced toward Schneider who stood to the side of the chair Baier had chosen across from Barnes's desk. They had not been invited to seats at the sofa this time, as Barnes worked his way through a pile of papers on his desk that resembled a small mountain. "I'm not sure. But they seem to be using a lot more troops and force than what's normally needed for a raid. Another reason is our pending election back home."

"You mean Eisenhower doesn't want anything to jeopardize his expected victory?" Baier asked.

"You said it, not me."

"But you're not objecting."

Barnes smiled again. "But I think the real reason is the President's concern that any material support would only provoke the Soviets, and possibly even lead to a direct military confrontation between us and the Soviet Union. And who knows where that would lead?"

"So, we're sticking with the diplomatic approach. Relying primarily on the UN? There hasn't been any change in that?"

"Well, no. Especially not now that we have a ceasefire and Soviet withdrawal."

"Have they really withdrawn, or simply regrouped?" Schneider said.

"That might be better left to your people. I can say that it appears to be the case here in Budapest, and our movement in the countryside is restricted for now. I gather your analysts have noted the movement of rail stock and shifting rail times just to the east of here, especially in Ukraine. I believe they suspect the Soviets are preparing to re-enter Hungary in force."

"Or they could be bringing resources to bear to assist with the pull-out," Schneider suggested.

"Well" Barnes sighed, "that might be something for you two gentlemen to try to pursue while you are out and about. In the meantime, our message home to Washington is that this new Hungarian Revolution is now a fact of history. My diplomats are obviously optimistic, as well as enthusiastic."

"Nonetheless, it looks like the real decision still lies in Moscow. We're hearing that there's a lot of confusion there right now. Which we'll report back to Washington in a cable, of course." Baier relayed the rest of Kovacs's message. "We'll send all of that through our channels, which sounds like it will complement much of what you're reporting."

"Good. I guess the question here is what sort of influence that is having on the Nagy government." Barnes said. "Are they being more cautious as a result, or do they plan to 'seize the day', as it were, while the opportunity is there?"

"And your own recommendations back to Washington? May we ask what those are? Beyond the reporting, I mean."

"I continue to push for more active support for the rebels, including some military supplies. I realize this could be seen as a provocation, but I honestly believe that we owe it to these people. Their courage and determination have been simply remarkable."

"But if the Revolution is now a 'fact of history,' as your people have put it, is that really necessary?"

Barnes nodded. "Good question. But if that is indeed the case, then this kind of material support will help shore up the new government."

"And the Soviets?" Baier asked.

Barnes shrugged. "I'm not sure it will make any difference. In the end, I admit that there is still a chance the hardliners in the Kremlin will win out and convince Khrushchev of the need to re-impose Soviet control. He may try a softer approach first, but if greater force is necessary, then that will come, too."

"But what do you think would tip them in that direction?"

Barnes shrugged and swiveled in his chair before settling his gaze back on Baier. "I'm not really sure at this point. There is the fear of contagion, of course, but the Kremlin has shown some real flexibility in handling the Polish situation. It probably depends on how far the Hungarians push things."

"But then what's the point of shipping in military supplies if it could lead to a battle that can only end in a Soviet victory and a lot more Hungarian deaths?"

Barnes leaned forward, as though he wanted to reach across the desk to the two CIA officers. "As I said, they deserve as much here. But as a follow up to your question, we also need to ask ourselves just where the decision point rests in Moscow and what all the factors are that lie behind it. At what point does Khrushchev conclude that a full military suppression here isn't worth the cost? Not only in military losses, but also in world opprobrium and the loss of prestige and influence." He sat back again. "I dare say the USSR would already have lost a lot more in all three categories if our friends hadn't behaved is such a similar fashion over Nassar and the Suez thing."

Baier and Schneider considered one another for a moment, before Baier turned back to the charge. "Is there anything else you'd like us to work on in our meetings?"

"Yes, exactly the things you've been picking up so far. Namely, this government's intentions. Also, how united is it? And what can we discern about Soviet plans and intentions, particularly as the Hungarians see them? What sort of impact will that have on their own decisions here in Budapest? I've discussed this with Stan, and I'm sure he'll keep you informed."

"As we will him, of course. He would have joined us, but he couldn't get away from another commitment," Schneider said.

The two Agency officers turned to go. Then, almost as an

afterthought, Barnes called them back and passed a slip of paper to Baier. "I don't know if you've seen this already, but it will certainly not make matters any easier. Either for Nagy or Khrushchev."

Baier and Schneider read the report that a junior officer had apparently given to Barnes just before their arrival.

"Jesus," Baier exclaimed. "So, a mob has killed more AVO officers." Baier looked at the charge. "But this has been going on for days. Why would this be any different?"

"It's the scale and the brutality. Past incidents have involved one or two, or sometimes even a handful of AVO thugs. Now they've slaughtered 23. And they did it by stringing them up by the feet and setting them on fire. Not only that, but then the crowd savaged the corpses. Hacked at the limbs and snuffed their cigarettes out in the bodies. That sort of thing."

"Where did this happen?" Schneider asked.

"I believe it was over at Republic Square, near the Eastern Railway Station," Barnes said. "Apparently the mob broke in and seized control of the Budapest city Communist headquarters."

Baier turned to his companion. "I think we'll need to move up our next meeting with our friend. This is unlikely to go unanswered. And it's got to be sending ripples through the government here."

"Oh, and one other thing, gentlemen," Barnes added in conclusion. "Be careful out there. The Revolution may be a fact now, but there is still plenty of opposition and lots of bad guys still on the streets."

"Thanks," Baier replied. He knew full well how right the charge was.

THAT EVENING BAIER walked carefully to the Eastern Railway Station to use their new dead drop location for the first time. Remembering Chernov's warning, he moved slowly and cautiously, doubling back every few blocks or halting at a store window along Rakoczi Boulevard to look for familiar or repeating faces in the other people strolling on the broad avenue. And there was one face, he noticed, three times, in fact. The man had a thin mustache that matched his closely cropped light brown hair, and deep, sunken eyes that looked to have suffered from a lack of sleep or heavy anxiety. Maybe both. When he no longer spotted his unwanted company Baier circled the splendid marbled hallway inside the giant arch that marked the entrance to the train station that stared down Rakoczi Boulevard as trams and a handful of automobiles wandered past. He waited another fifteen minutes to make sure his shadow really had disappeared, hoping that the fellow had given up when it became clear that Baier had made him. Baier thought of Chernov's comments about new and old faces in town, but this individual did not appear to have spent any time in Siberia. And he had not been that old, more like someone in his forties.

Only then did he go to meet Schneider, who trailed a few blocks behind Baier as insurance that they had picked up any and all followers.

"Do you think we're clear?" Baier asked.

Schneider nodded. "Was there only one on you? I had my own pair for a while."

"And?"

"And I'm pretty sure they broke off when yours did. It looked to me like they concluded we were coming here on real travel business." Schneider glanced around the cavernous hallway. "Do you think our guy can handle the surveillance?"

"I do worry about that. The guy has done a lot and has proved his worth. But his emotions are still the weak link, in my view. Especially if suspicion is turning toward us. Do you know if this kind of surveillance was normal before the rebellion broke out?'

"Stan told me once it was usually a lot heavier. This almost seems too light. Then again, he was our only guy here permanently. So it must have been easier for the AVO."

"But given the altered circumstances…"

"Like having to worry about their own skins?"

"That, but also the things we've heard and seen about suspicions of a mole. The surveillance should actually be heavier now."

"Yeah, I suppose you're right."

The two Americans sat in the main hallway for another twenty minutes, then strolled past the ticket counters and visited three platforms, as though looking for someone or a particular arrival. When they were reasonably confident that they were free of any additional tails, they swung by the mail and baggage area. Baier quickly deposited a coded note for Kovacs while Schneider kept watch on the crowd surging through the station.

"Good?" Baier asked.

Schneider nodded. "Yeah, I'm pretty sure." He sighed. "At least I'm sure we picked out the shadows we know of. They're gone at any rate, and I didn't find any new ones."

"Unfortunately, we can only ever be sure we've picked up the ones we've seen," Baier said. "I'm hoping it's what we discussed, that the AVO is too pressed by other matters to devote much in the way of resources to counter-intel operations. As you said, 'given the altered circumstances…'"

"Yeah, let's hope they have other things on their minds right now."

"You mean like staying alive?"

"Yeah. And worrying about their own futures."

Chapter Fifteen

———— ∽ ————

"WHAT'S THE PLAN for today, boys?" Stan Muller asked. They were strolling in the square behind the Parliament building, a massive structure that sat on a cliff overlooking the Danube like some medieval fortress. Which made a lot of sense, considering the events of the past nine days. It was now the last day of October, and no one, but no one could have foreseen how fast and how far the popular dynamic would carry the Hungarian revolt. Baier had become completely absorbed in the events of the last few days and the Kovacs case. Too excited and exhausted, he had not written much of anything in the cable traffic, leaving the intel reporting to Schneider. Given his lack of sleep and sporadic meals, Baier's adrenaline had carried him this far. There was no telling how much longer he could continue at this pace. He had relied almost entirely on Muller to report on his activities to Vienna and Washington, reviewing the messages only to ensure their accuracy. It only occurred to him now that he had sent and received no word from Sabine since his return to Budapest. She would be worried sick, and he was stung by pangs of regret and anger at himself.

"Before we go into that, Stan, would you ask Vienna to get word to my wife that I'm still alive and well. She's probably concerned as all hell since I haven't been able to communicate with her. I can't really guess when I'll be back. Depending on your agreement, of course."

"You haven't tried to get through to her at all? Not even a phone call?"

Baier shook his head. "Nope. As you can no doubt guess, I do not want to do anything to confirm to anyone who might be listening in--at either end--that I am here and active."

Muller nodded. "Sure thing, Karl. We'll do our best to reassure her. And given the course of events here, I can certainly agree to having you stay a bit longer. At least until we get our new operational relationship with Bluebird established so Bill here can take over. Depending on how long he stays, of course. Then I can handle it."

"Thanks, Stan." Baier patted the local station chief on the shoulder. "I appreciate that."

"You also might be interested to learn that the reason I missed your session with Barnes yesterday, was that I had my introductory meeting with the new British and French chiefs stationed here yesterday."

"And? Any more on the Suez imbroglio?"

Muller smiled and punched Baier lightly on the arm. "Good choice of words, my man. And, yes, there was some more. The decision was made yesterday in London and Paris to invade Egypt in support of the Israelis."

"Like they needed an excuse," Schneider said.

"That's my feeling as well," Muller stated.

"Feeling?" Baier pressed. "I also doubt that the decision was only made yesterday."

Muller nodded. "I agree. And yes, it is pretty much of a gut instinct. I haven't had as much experience as you have with those people, Karl. But that feeling is also based on some conversations I had with an old friend of yours, Karl. Ralph Delgreccio."

"My old boss from Vienna? Excellent. How do you know Ralph?"

"We graduated from the ops course together. When he heard you were here on temporary duty, he reached out to offer his support for your work and professionalism. Ralph's a good man, as you are no doubt aware, and it certainly helps to have him in your corner."

"Absolutely. But what did our good allies have to say?"

"Well, I gather the French are already bombing Egyptian positions, and the British troops have been pre-positioned in Cyprus, along with a small naval flotilla. We should hear more today, probably about an actual move into the country."

"And what have they got to say about events here in Hungary and the impact their Suez adventure could have on the Alliance and Soviet policy?"

Muller shrugged. "They say it's unfortunate but can't be helped."

"What's unfortunate? The Hungarian revolt or the mess in Suez?"

"I'm pretty sure they meant the mess in the Middle East and their inability to do much up here."

"So, MI6 and the French are not active in Hungary on the developments here?" Muller shook his head and stared at the ground. "What a bunch of fucking amateurs," Baier exclaimed. He thought of Rankin and assumed the man must be acting as a free agent in this. If he was doing anything at all.

"Yeah, it certainly looks that way now. But what about your next meeting with Bluebird? When is that and what do you plan to press him on?"

Schneider spoke up. "We serviced the drop site before meeting you here, chief. We've got a new safehouse not far from the apartment shell Bluebird had selected. We needed to get control on the security for this op back into our own hands.

This time it's a room at the Hotel Astoria."

"Just how secure is that? It sounds kind of public."

"Exactly. It should provide a plausible cover. Bluebird is going to be having an affair. And in case we're followed, it's also credible for us to be there, given that it's still a hub of social activity in town. Has been since it opened in 1914."

"You know it was also the spot where the Hungarians announced the formation of their National Council back in October of 1918."

"You mean as a prelude to their independence from the Hapsburg Empire?" Baier asked.

Muller nodded. "That's right. And you know how that turned out. Let's hope it's not an omen for this operation." Muller frowned. "But isn't it also kind of close in? Further out would be better to run a counter-surveillance route."

"In this city now? With a revolution going on? You've seen what the streets are like. Besides, it saves us on time, which is important now. And more important, it makes it easier for Bluebird to get there."

"You still need to do your due diligence on these matters. Let's not get careless. When's the meet?"

"Later today, during the lunch break," Baier explained. "Presumably, that's when the man would arrange for his liaison."

"Well, keep me informed. I'll pass along any worthwhile nuggets to Barnes."

THE ASTORIA WAS indeed a busy place. And very public. Dozens of guests and visitors mingled in a lobby encased in green and white marble or passed through the lounge and hallway in a rush of frenetic activity that could have meant anything from love and sex to political conspiracy or entrepreneurial ambition. Or maybe just a drink and a good meal. Baier danced through the crowd and swung to the right of the reception desk to the red-carpeted stairway leading to the higher floors. Short of breath from the trot up the stairs, he pushed his way through the door of 424 and waited for his asset. Schneider positioned himself with a cocktail in a comfortable arm chair near the lounge to double check on any possible tails on Kovacs.

Today, their asset was right on time. Baier checked the hallway through the peephole when he heard the knock, then opened the door to a worried and distraught Josef Kovacs. The contrast with the man he had seen just twenty-four hours earlier was astonishing. His clothes gave little clue—a brown woolen two-piece suit, the ubiquitous white dress shirt, and the same yellow tie from yesterday—but his face was etched with lines of anxiety, and his eyes would not settle down.

"Mikoyan has been recalled to Moscow."

"And Suslov?"

Kovacs nodded and started to pace the room. "Yes, yes, him as well. But Mikoyan is the key."

"Why was he recalled?"

"I...I can't be sure. I can only hope that it wasn't because he has been relieved, or even arrested." His face brightened, as though the thought had occurred to him for the first time. "Perhaps he will be there for consultations. Because his words are valued." The man's mood darkened just as suddenly. "But I cannot be certain. There is much turmoil among the Soviet Union's allies."

"How so?"

Kovacs stopped and stared at Baier. "Haven't you heard? Some 300,000 demonstrated in Warsaw yesterday in support of the Revolution here. And students in Romania and Czechoslovakia are protesting as well."

"Is there fear inside the Kremlin of possible contagion from events here in Budapest?"

Kovacs resumed his march around the room. "I don't know. But I would suppose so now. I heard mention of some kind of codename. 'Whirlwind.' It sounds ominous. But I do not know for certain. I'm not sure anyone in our government does. That's what worries me."

"How so?"

"The Russians would not speak of it in our presence. They even refused to meet our eyes."

"Everyone's eyes? Even Nagy?"

"Well, no, not everyone. Some appeared to be in close conversation with the Soviets at times. People like Munnich, the Interior Minister, and even Kadar. It's like in the days of Rakosi. You're no longer certain whom to trust."

"That's definitely something you'll need to find out about for our next meeting. How is Nagy taking this?"

Kovacs stopped and grab a seat on one of the two armchairs by the small table in the corner of the room. Baier noticed that he chose the seat with its back to the paneled doors that opened on to a small ledge and railing. Anyone who actually tried to use the narrow balcony would probably end up in a sorry state, Baier thought as he studied the window. It wouldn't take much to find yourself tumbling over the waist-high railing to the street below. Only then did Baier realize how thin everything appeared in the room. Not just the balcony, but the panels on the door, the mattress on the bed and the linen and pillows. Even the cushions on the chairs felt thin. It was like the interior failed to live up to the promise of the ornate and historic building. He walked over and pulled Kovacs away from the balcony door and into the chair set back against the wall. Kovacs sat leaning forward, his hands dangling between his legs.

"Oh, he remains very confident. He is even talking about leaving the Warsaw Pact."

Baier had taken his own seat in the armchair to the other side of the entrance to the bedroom. He stood at Kovacs's latest news. "He what? With whom did he discuss this?"

"With us, of course. But also with Mikoyan. I think he may have only been testing the waters with the Armenian. And there is something else."

"What is it?"

"The French and English have begun their invasion. I am sure that will increase the pressure on Khrushchev."

"To do what?"

"I can't be sure. But certainly you realize that Khrushchev must avoid looking weak. Stalin has not been dead that long."

"But what about the popular mood? The Soviets have left Budapest, and the mood on the street is pretty damn joyful. As you were yesterday. The people of Budapest sound pretty confident still, but I'm not so sure of you now. What has changed? You seem to be a lot more worried today."

Kovacs shrugged and sat back. His arms rose and dropped to his side. "Nothing in particular."

"Except for Mikoyan's recall."

Kovacs nodded. "Yes, that of course. But Nagy is not worried. He even said to Kadar that he believes we have pulled it off."

"The same guy who may be in the know on this 'Whirlwind' thing? You sound a lot less certain yourself, Josef."

"Well, I am concerned over recent developments, like the slaughter of the AVO people at Republic Square. It is not the sort of thing that will reassure Moscow."

At this moment Schneider entered the room. He and Baier exchanged a quick glance, and Schneider shrugged. He did not look concerned or worried. "Look, Josef, I think we will need to meet again tomorrow. Will that be possible?"

"I will certainly try."

"Come to the same room. How does later in the afternoon work for you? That way you'll be able to report on the day's developments." Kovacs nodded his agreement. "Good. Let's say 5 o'clock." Kovacs frowned. "Okay, 6 then. And I want you to see what you can find out about 'Whirlwind' and possible divisions within your government. What is the relationship between Nagy and Kadar, for example?"

"It's been excellent so far."

"Maybe so. But if there is pressure from Moscow or events begin to move too quickly, the Kremlin will be looking for allies here, people they can work with to create divisions. We'll need to know if they are successful.

"Yes, I will see what I can learn."

"Also, what is Moscow saying? Has anything changed? They'll probably continue to be supportive and soothing. But listen for any shift in tone, any inconsistencies. And what about rumors of rail movements and railroad stock just east of here, like in Ukraine? Are you certain they've withdrawn their troops?"

"I think so. I haven't heard anything different." "They wouldn't be preparing to bring more in?"

"No, I don't think so. At least I have not heard anything along those lines."

"Well, there is something else. And I cannot emphasize this enough. You need to be very careful."

"Should I try to bring you any documents if I think they are truly significant?"

"That would be helpful, of course, but we'll need to know the context surrounding them. Who drafted them, what kind of support do they have, are they reflecting current or future policy, or just some debate? But most important, Josef, is that you not do anything to jeopardize your safety. You are too valuable to us."

Kovacs nodded and stood. "There is something else that has me worried today." He hesitated.

"Yes? What is that?" Baier stood and walked over to Kovacs.

"I...I believe I was followed here today."

Baier shot a glance over at Schneider, who frowned and shook his head. "Why do you think that?"

"I can't be sure. But I recognized the man from the day before, when we met at the bombed-out flat."

"He was at that flat and you didn't say anything? Damn it,

Josef. What did he look like?"

Kovacs shrugged, as though he was describing someone remarkably ordinary. "Tall and thick, like he has been well fed, which is surprising, especially now. Longer black hair pushed straight back and hidden under a large hat. Clean shaven. Casually dressed in a black leather jacket."

"And you've seen him before? Any other time than yesterday?"

"Yes, actually. Now that I've thought about it. I think I remember him from my time working for Gero in the AVO."

"Oh, great." Baier spun toward Schneider, then back to Kovacs. "Did he follow you here? All the way?"

Kovacs shook his head. "No, I don't think so. He seemed to turn off a block or two away."

"In that case, you need to stick with the story of an affair. You may be single, but your girlfriend is married. You, of course, are honor-bound and must withhold her name, if anyone asks. You can make something up about her being the wife of a party member. That might deflect further questions about her identity."

Kovacs nodded and moved to leave. "Okay, I will stick to our story. They may wonder why someone with my history as a bachelor is now engaging in such a thing."

"Tell them you've been swept up in the romance of the times."

Kovacs smiled for the first time that afternoon. "Yes, that's a good one." He even laughed lightly. "The romance of the times..."

After he left, Schneider waited for about twenty seconds, then followed Kovacs to the lobby and into the street. Baier entered the bedroom and messed up the sheets on the bed to make it look like it had seen some heavy use. Then he went to the bathroom and moistened the towels, open and wet the soap to make it appear as though that, too, had been used. Only then did he leave the room. The key remained on the coffee table, as though it had been forgotten after an afternoon of passion.

IT WAS DURING his walk back to the Embassy that Baier discovered that he, too, had a new tail. But this one had a familiar face to it. That 'fucking Russian' Chernov was proving to be a source of concern and cause for caution, and not just the means to an end at the border between Austria and Hungary. His repeated and unannounced meetings with Baier were becoming a little too frequent for comfort. They were also feeling just a bit ominous. How could Baier be sure that they were not observed, that Chernov himself was not under suspicion? He did seem to have useful information to impart, though. But why now, all of a sudden? Perhaps it was time to set up a schedule of meetings if this was going to become a regular thing. It would certainly be more secure than these chance encounters, if that's what they were. Baier slowed and let Chernov catch up to him at the Russian's own pace and convenience.

"What is it this time?" Baier asked when Chernov finally joined him along the sidewalk that ran the length of the wide and busy Bajcsy Zsilinszky Avenue. They were four or five blocks short of Szabadsag Square. "I'm assuming this was intentional, and not mere coincidence."

Chernov reached out for Baier's arm to slow their pace. "You are correct, of course, Herr Baier. I do not have anything of great significance to tell you. But I did want to let you know of my plans."

Baier stopped at this and turned to Chernov. "Your plans? What do you mean? And why should I care?"

Chernov smiled, then let it pass. "No, it is nothing that dramatic. But you should definitely care. I thought you might like to know that I am being sent back west again."

"West? How far? And isn't that in the wrong direction?"

Chernov shrugged. "That depends on the objective and

purpose. I will be at the border once more. You may interpret that as you like and do with it what you like."

"I'm not sure how to interpret that, Chernov. But the things that spring immediately to mind are not good ones."

"Be that as it may, Herr Baier, I cannot say for certain how long I will be there, or how long I will be able to keep our crossing open. Probably for several days at least. In case you should need to depart suddenly."

Baier looked puzzled. "Why would I need to do that?"

Chernov shrugged again. "That I cannot say. But we shall see. You never know how things will develop."

"Now it's my turn. Have you seen much of your old-new friend from Siberia?"

Chernov stopped and studied the street traffic before turning back to Baier. "No, I have not. But that does not mean anything, Herr Baier. I suspect the man is still around."

"Why?"

The smile returned. "That should not be your concern. The real question you need to be asking is why he came in the first place."

Baier turned to continue his walk. "Well, thank you for that, Sergei. I will do just that. And you're right. You never do know how things will unfold."

As he continued on toward the Embassy, Baier wondered if he had been too harsh or curt with Chernov. The man appeared to be trying to help without giving too much away. Which was understandable. He was, after all, a Soviet officer, and one in the KGB to boot. Baier decided he would need to take the Russian's hints a bit more seriously. With the shift in Kovacs's mood and the revelation that he had held back information about a possible tail there was certainly enough to worry about.

Chapter Sixteen

———

THE FIRST DAY of November opened with a grey sky, and Baier had the sense that the air was overcast with more than just clouds. He was used to the cloudy skies of Central Europe, having lived there on and off for roughly ten years now, but this particular morning had a more ominous feel to it. There was certainly enough on just about anyone's plate to worry about, especially for the people of Budapest and Hungary, not just for Baier. At the same time, there was that pervading sense of euphoria that had arrived with the prospect of victory and the expectations of what Hungary's newfound freedom would bring. Baier was not immune to those same feelings of joy and hope, but he also recognized the seriousness of the danger behind what was now coming into a sharper focus after the meetings with Kovacs and Chernov, that there were decisions being made far away from the joy and excitement of Budapest. And these were being formed in an atmosphere of turmoil and confusion with no warning of when those decisions would fall, or what their outcome would be.

Nor could he allow the popular euphoria to cloud his

judgment. He was determined to remain focused and active. Baier and Schneider spent much of the day running their own counter-surveillance routes—Muller was right, carelessness posed as great a threat to their operation as anything-- searching for any tails that would lead them to conclude that the AVO was on to them personally. Kovacs was another matter entirely. Suspicion did seem to have settled on him, although whether it fell to him alone was another question.

"We may have to shut this thing down," Stan Muller said the next morning. "This is getting too risky. And not just for Kovacs."

"Understood. Believe me, Stan, the last thing I want is to end up in an AVO prison cell."

"I want you guys to raise this with Bluebird when you meet him later today. Do we have an exfiltration plan?"

"Of course," Schneider said. "That was one of the first things we drew up."

"But it's contingent on keeping the border open with Austria," Baier added. "If the Soviets shut that down, he will not be the only one in danger of getting stuck here."

"All the more the reason to press Bluebird on this. Are his finances secure?"

Baier nodded. "I've been depositing his pay regularly into an Austrian account. He should have plenty to start a new life in the West."

"Good." Muller paused. "At the same time, there are still a lot of positive signs out there."

"Like what?" Schneider asked.

"Well, for starters, they cleared the prisons of political dissidents and opposition figures. Even Cardinal Mindszenty has been released. I just wish our Radio Free Europe friends in Munich would stop pushing him as the true leader of the Revolution. Those guys are so out of touch."

"True, true." Baier agreed. "And that makes our reporting from Bluebird all the more important. It will give Washington a more accurate picture of what's going on here."

"And hopefully in Moscow as well," Muller added.

THE ASTORIA WAS, if possible, even busier than the day before. Part of that, Baier was sure, was because of the timing. Late afternoon/early evening would be an opportune time to enjoy what the city now had to offer as gusts of freedom seemed to sweep away Hungary's recent past of oppression and deprivation. Paradise had not arrived all at once, of course. The shelves, for example, were not yet full in the stores around town, but the new government had lifted the regulations forcing farmers to export the bulk of their foodstuffs. That had originally been designed so the national treasury could afford the country's industrialization and its payments to Moscow. But one did notice nowadays that more was available to the average Hungarian, even if the selection and quality still needed some improvement. But even that little bit played to the sense of confidence and optimism that had enveloped the city. And the full restaurant and brimming cocktail bar at the Astoria presented just two examples of that buoyant mood.

As before, Schneider waited in the lobby for Kovacs to appear, while Baier secured the room upstairs. He did not wait this time to ruffle the bed sheets and use the towels and soap. It was the first thing he did once he stepped inside. One could never foretell how much time there would be for such measures at the end of the meeting. Especially now, with Kovacs apparently under suspicion.

Today, however, Kovacs was only fifteen minutes late. And he actually appeared more relaxed.

"How did the day go for you? Any signs of suspicion or increased attention on you?" Baier asked.

Kovacs marched immediately to the armchair Baier had placed him in the day before. "No, it was much easier today. Everyone was very, very busy, you see."

"Because?"

"Have you not heard? Nagy has announced that we are leaving the Warsaw Pact."

"What? Why now? Isn't that a bit sudden? Couldn't he wait a bit, you know, like when the Soviets have had some time to digest all that's been happening here?"

Kovacs shook his head. "Not at all. I told you before that he was seriously considering it. He met with Andropov twice today…"

"The Soviet Ambassador?"

"Yes. We were seeking assurances that the Kremlin will honor its commitment to withdraw all of its troops from our country."

"And?"

Kovacs spread his hands wide and then collapsed them in his lap. He sounded suddenly resigned, fatalistic even. "Andropov agreed, of course. Which came as no surprise to Nagy. I'm less certain, but for now I am willing to share in Nagy's confidence and hope."

"Because of Andropov's assent?"

Kovacs shrugged. "It's certainly not definitive, but rather what one would expect of the Soviet Ambassador. The man lived for years in the Soviet Union, you know, where you learn to dissemble and equivocate. He may be sincere or simply stalling. Only time will tell. That is why the next few days are so important."

Baier nodded and grunted. "Yes, I understand. We all do. That's one reason Washington distrusts him. But do you think this background and cunning of Andropov may be less of a factor here, that Moscow is no longer holding him back? Could it be that he is resigned to the success of your uprising? Do you believe that he will actually recommend that Hungary be allowed to enjoy the fruits of its Revolution?"

"I for one am not sure either way. Regardless of Andropov's feelings or intent, he alone will not change anything. You see, the Prime Minister believed he had ensured that commitment earlier and was confident of his deal. But the real decisions are being made elsewhere. I am not sure how significant Andropov's agreement or approval really is."

"What do you mean? He is the Soviet Ambassador, after all. His views must reflect those of his superiors in Moscow."

"Well, we have had reports of Soviet units crossing our border, moving in from Ukraine, and Andropov continued to play dumb with us. He said he did not know anything about that since he was not a military man. Earlier he had said that the Red Army was only moving to ensure a peaceful and stabile withdrawal."

Baier remembered Chernov's words from the day before about his redeployment to the west of the country. "Are there reports of any other Soviet troop movements?"

"Yes, of course. They've been sitting in the western parts of our country and have yet to move from there." Kovacs paused and smiled. "Then again, you could say that there has been no movement there in any direction."

"Still a cause for concern. You seem quite relaxed about all this."

Kovacs nodded. "Yes, of course. But, you see, when Andropov remained so non-committal early today, Nagy threatened to pull out of the Warsaw Pact. And then when he continued to play his game this afternoon, Nagy made a public announcement to that effect." Kovacs's face beamed. His mood abruptly shifted. His eyes seemed to dance as they sought out Baier's face. "We are now a neutral country."

"But how will the Soviets respond? Has he thought that through?"

"Don't you see? We have tricked them. By withdrawing from the Warsaw Pact, we have outmaneuvered Moscow. They cannot invade a neutral country. We have appealed to the four Allied powers from World War II and the UN for a guarantee of our independence and neutrality. Like Austria."

"Well, good luck with that. Was there any resistance in the

Cabinet? What about Kadar or any of the holdovers from the previous government? And any more on this 'Whirlwind' thing?"

Kovacs stood. "The vote was unanimous, Mister Baier. Everyone is committed. Kadar, too. Some were a little less enthusiastic than others, but in the end, everyone went along. And as for 'Whirlwind'..." Kovacs waved his hands in the air "...no one was speaking of that today."

"What have you heard from Mikoyan? How is his visit to Moscow going?"

Kovacs thought for a moment before responding. "I have not heard of anything about his trip. Moscow has gone quite silent for us. We can only hope that Mikoyan is holding to his previous line in support of our changes and new status."

"But that did not include Hungarian neutrality and withdrawal from the Warsaw pact," Baier said.

Kovacs nodded. "True. Nonetheless, I am sure he will understand that the hardliners in Moscow drove us to this point."

"But again, Josef, how do you explain these Soviet troop movements at your eastern border? If they're accurate, that is."

Kovacs shrugged. "Perhaps they are a pressure tactic. I would not put it past the Kremlin to try something like that. But tomorrow will tell. For now, though, I must hurry back. We are very, very busy, as I am sure you realize. Shall we meet again here? Same time?"

Baier nodded. "Yes, we should meet again, and at the same time. That way you can fill me in on the day's events, which I'll report to Washington. Your information is invaluable, Josef. Tell me, though, were you followed again?"

Kovacs shook his head vigorously. "No, not today. Not that I saw, in any case. And I was cautious, as you had instructed. I took my time. It was why I was a little late, you know. I checked on possible followers several times but never found any."

"Have you had to use your story about your love affair?"

"No, not yet. No one has asked about my movements. I'm not sure anyone has even noticed."

Baier would check with Schneider about any possible surveillance when he left. "Nonetheless, we need to discuss getting you out of here. I can't stay much longer myself. It's getting too hot."

Kovacs looked puzzled. "At this time of year? Don't be ridiculous."

Baier smiled at the misunderstanding. "No, I'm sorry I used an American colloquialism. I meant that it's getting too risky politically. There are too many worrying signs out there. The AVO may be on to you, and we need to protect you. Besides, I'd like to go home and see my wife."

Kovacs drew himself up to his full height of 6 feet and three inches. "Mister Baier, I could never leave Hungary. This is my country, my home."

"Josef, you may not have a choice."

IT COULD NOT have been more than a few minutes after Kovacs left when the pounding at the door began. Baier had decided to stay behind and help himself to a drink from the bottle of brandy he had brought along, the better to convince anyone who came after that there had been a liaison between Kovacs and his mystery woman. He finished his first glass, poured himself a second, and strolled to the door, glancing through the peephole before opening it. An unfamiliar, rotund and heavy face locked in anger, rage almost, stared back at him.

Baier walked back to the table and set the glass down. He looked around the room and remembered that there was no other way out. He returned to the door and noticed that Mr. Big Face was still out there. Baier had no doubt that this individual was from either hotel security or, even worse, the AVO. Hopefully, not, but his chest tightened at the thought. Either way, even if it was only the detective, this clearly spelled the end of the use of the Astoria. Deep inside, though, Baier knew it was not just some hotel dick. It had to be those pricks from AVO. Things had just gotten even more serious and dangerous for Kovacs, Schneider, and himself. God knew what else was going on if AVO felt secure enough to make this move.

Damned if was going to just give up, though. He would still try for an escape. He hoped that Kovacs had not been detained as well. And Schneider?

Baier positioned himself against the wall so that he would be behind the door when he opened it. He fastened his grip on the door handle, jerked it inwards, and reached around for the man's coat collar. Thankfully, he was able to grab a fistful of material and pull the man into the room. Baier's visitor was heavy set, and his weight propelled him downwards faster than he could resist. Baier fell heavily on the man's back and slammed his skull into the floor. The visitor grunted in pain, then groaned. Baier felt quickly for a weapon, pulled a Makharov loose and leapt for the hallway.

Figuring that the man had not come alone and that elevators would be watched, Baier bolted for the stairs. At least he would be running downhill. He emptied the weapon of its clip and the round in the camber, then tossed the pistol down the laundry chute located in the wall by the landing between the third and fourth floors. Scrambling down the stairs two and three steps at a time, Baier aimed for the back entrance used by the staff and for deliveries. That, he was sure, would give him the best option for escaping. If the man really was from the AVO, the main lobby would surely be crawling with AVO thugs, and perhaps even a few KGB officers as well.

He probably should have tried the elevator and the lobby. Maybe the local security service would have been hobbled by the presence of so many civilians, especially if they had been celebrating the success of the Revolution. A few might have even attacked the AVO bastards. Lord knows it had happened frequently enough. But in the end, Baier knew that discretion and subterfuge offered him his best chance of escape.

It was not enough, however. They were waiting for him as soon as he pushed his way through the double doors at the back of the hotel that led from the kitchen. The air reeked of garbage, which struck Baier as fitting, given his company. A muscular set of arms grabbed him from behind, squeezing the air from his lungs. Baier tried to stomp on the man's foot to loosen his grip, but the heavy boots cushioned the shock of the blow. Then he threw his head back, hoping to make contact with the man's nose. That actually worked, but the brute still held on despite the cracking bones and howl of pain. Within seconds, other arms and hands arrived to help the wounded thug, and Baier felt a fist that must have been forged from steel sink into his stomach. A knee rose for his crotch, but Baier was able to deflect that with his thigh. It still hurt like hell.

Baier looked around and saw his colleague Bill Schneider already being pushed into a black Zis limousine. Baier was hustled to an identical vehicle and tossed into the back seat. Someone roughly the size of a small mountain was already in the back waiting for him. Rough hands that could have built a Soviet dam or steel mill on their own seized the back of his neck and forced Baier onto the floor.

KGB or Hungarian, Baier wondered. The cars suggested the former. These limousines were normally used for the VIPs behind the Iron Curtain. But then a voice from the front seat spat in heavily accented German that Baier vaguely remembered from his visit a year ago. When he looked up, Baier found the square face of the man he had recently encountered in Vienna. He was even wearing the same white turtleneck and black leather jacket. At least, it looked like the same sweater and jacket.

"As you fucking Americans say, it's payback time, asshole. I was in the van during your big bad prison break last year."

Oh shit, Baier thought. So they remembered him. "I don't

know what you're talking about."

"You also broke my compatriot's nose back there. You will pay for that, you fascist prick. Just wait to see what we will break of yours."

The hulk in the back seat grunted in approval at his buddy's words.

So, it was the AVO after all. Still, there had been no sign of Kovacs. That was good news at least.

The creep in the front seat laughed and nodded toward his colleague next to Baier. "This time we outsmarted you, Mr. American Asshole. Gero was smarter than you and that traitor had thought. He worked with Serov all along to set this up once he suspected your buddy of betraying us."

"I don't know what you're talking about. And you're the one who's an asshole." Baier smiled in turn. It wasn't much of a response, admittedly, but it was the best he could do under the circumstances. "Really."

Baier wondered about the guy in the hotel room. He remembered courses as a junior officer at the Agency when the instructors had cautioned against using force or violence, against trying to play the hero. You're on their home turf, they had warned. The other side will always be able to bring more to the game than you. It was these words of wisdom he had applied when confronted at the border by the Soviet team last year. Maybe Sabine's absence this time around had removed that sense of caution on his part. As far as the AVO was concerned, his efforts tonight had probably succeeded only in making them even angrier. Shit, now they'd have two scores to settle.

"We might even be able to pay you back at your home."

The words dropped on Baier from the front seat like an anvil. "What the fuck do you mean?" Baier could feel his rage boiling like an ocean volcano. "You had better not cross that line, you prick, or I will personally break your goddamn neck."

A heavy shoe pressed Baier's head against the dirt-lined floor of the Zis. "It is you who have crossed the line, you American son-of-a-bitch."

All Baier could do was let his anger and spit spill across the mat under his face.

THE CAR RODE for about twenty minutes. Then it turned and drove down what seemed like a country lane, slowly over a bumpy dirt path. When they stopped, the same gnarled and muscular hands pulled Baier up from the floor and threw him out the open door. He wondered if those were the hands that would interrogate him. He stood on unsteady feet. His legs tingled as the blood worked to regain its circulation. They appeared to have arrived in a cemetery. That did not bode well. Baier craned his neck and saw Schneider emerge from the Zis that had departed the Astoria at the same time as his own. Both Americans were pushed toward another vehicle, this one more of a prison van. Square and white, it looked vaguely familiar to the one that had transported Sabine from her prison in this very town. Did the Hungarians have a sense of poetic justice?

Just then another car pulled up, this one a dirty white Mercedes. That car drove up alongside the Zis Baier had just rode in. Two men stepped from the German car and were immediately surrounded by a small crowd of men in suits, all of them of a smaller build than his own traveling companions. Baier was surprised, stunned almost, to recognize Janos Kadar and Ferenc Munnich, the party leader and Interior Minister in the Nagy government, respectively. My God, were they being arrested as well? Had the entire government been overthrown?

But then Baier noticed Yuri Andropov, the Soviet Ambassador. He walked over to the two Hungarians and embraced them. With a round of handshakes and more hugs, Munnich and Kadar slid into Baier's Zis, which then sped off out of the cemetery.

Baier and Schneider were shoved into the back of the van.

Without another word, their new transport drove away in the opposite direction.

Chapter Seventeen

~~~

WHEN BAIER AWOKE, he had no idea what time it was, or even what day. He lay on the cot under its single woolen blanket for several minutes, waiting for his eyes to adjust to the darkness. The blanket stretched only as far as his ankles. There was no pillow. There was also no sunlight, which did not mean that it was night. Only that there were no windows. He could tell almost immediately that the cell was damp. That came from mold and mildew, the smell of which was almost nauseating. But the last thing he wanted to do was vomit. There was no way to clean it up. And if he thought the smell was bad now...

If he had been seized on the night of November 1, it was at least the 2nd. Then again, he had no way of knowing how long he had been out. He thought of the possibility of drugs, but then could not recall having drunk or eaten anything. Nor had an injection been administered, as far as he knew. Baier rubbed his arms to see if there was any soreness but felt nothing. All he remembered was stumbling towards the cot after marching around his cell for the longest time to wear off the anxiety, anger, and occasional desperation he felt. Eventually, he gave up and collapsed on the hard, cold bed they had provided. At this point, his adrenalin must have expired. He remembered nothing more beyond a sudden and overwhelming sense of darkness.

Slowly, the memory of his arrest—if you could call it that—returned. The prison yard had been dark, almost cavernous. He assumed he had been delivered to a prison; no announcement had been made. In fact, not a word had been spoken by his captors after their van left the cemetery. The hulking creep and square-faced asshole who had ridden with him from the Astoria must have joined those in the front of the van, because afterwards they had together jerked Baier from the back and half pulled, half escorted Baier as he stumbled down two flights of stairs to some sort of cellar, where he was sure he now rested. It was almost as if they had practiced their delivery. He assumed there had been no shortage of opportunities to do so. The darkness of the prison yard must have been intended either to block Baier and Schneider from recognizing where they were or to prevent others from seeing the new arrivals. Maybe both. He wondered where Schneider was now. Probably in the same dank cellar, maybe even next door. Baier would try to work out some sort of communication code in his head before trying to pound on the wall to determine if anyone was residing on either side.

Fortunately, the man-mountain and the nemesis from Vienna who had thrown his threat from the front seat of the Zis had yet to return. At the moment, Baier suffered only from a sore shoulder that had come from being thrown into the cell and banging into the cot. He was pretty sure there would be a bruise, but at least it was not dislocated. Maybe they were waiting for his nerves to go before the interrogation began. He thought of Sabine and her incarceration. Was this the same prison, the same cell even? Hell, he had no way of knowing, sitting here alone and ignorant of anything beyond the prison door with its metal grate just above eye level. He guessed the opening filled a space of about two or three square feet. What he did know for certain was that he would use the memory of his wife's time in whatever hellhole she had occupied as inspiration to keep his sanity and resolve.

After what seemed like hours—Baier realized then how distorted his sense of time had become so early into his incarceration—a face appeared at the grate. It shouted something in Magyar, which Baier could not understand. So he continued to lie there. Then a wooden tray was held in the opening when the grate had been pulled back, and more incomprehensible Magyar was shouted through the door. Fearing the guard would simply let the tray fall, Baier stood and walked over to the door. He took the tray and stared at his new companion. "I want to talk to somebody from the American Embassy."

"Ha!" At least he could understand that. No interpretation was needed.

"You have no right to hold me here. I am an American citizen, and I have broken no laws."

The grate shut. Footsteps echoed down the hallway, growing dimer with each step.

Baier sat back on the cot and contemplated the food: a bowl of thin, watery soup with a finger-sized piece of what looked like fat swimming at the edge. A chunk of brown bread offered a little more sustenance. He looked over at the bucket in the far corner that he assumed was meant to serve as his toilet and decided to forego the meal for the moment. Perhaps he would save it and wait for his hunger to grow bad enough to the point where he would feel compelled to eat. He set the tray on the floor, slid it under his bed, and lay back down.

After an interval of what was probably another thirty minutes or so, he stood and felt through his pockets. All his documentation and money was gone, as was his wristwatch. Then he recalled the search in the courtyard shortly after their arrival. That figured, of course. The watch especially would have been nice, if only to keep some track of time. His wardens clearly did not want that. He decided to pace the limits of his cell again, both to do a little exploring with a clearer mind and to keep his body active. He tried to think back to the exercises his instructors had demonstrated during the training courses that put you through situations like these to see what he could pull up that might help in a real-life situation. But the uncertainty was too great, and he found it difficult to focus. He returned to the cot, grabbed the spoon from his tray, then returned to the walls running along the sides of his cell. He tapped numerous times on each wall to see if he could discern a response. He also hammered with his fist occasionally, hoping to find some way to get the sound to penetrate what seemed like miles of concrete. Yelling through the grate brought no response. He listened for what seemed like minutes at a time between each signal but received only silence in reply.

Eventually, Baier returned to his cot, ate the bread, then fell asleep once more.

The sound of a door opening woke him up. It was not just the grate this time, but the whole damn thing. Baier was initially too groggy and unable to focus. But after a few minutes his mind cleared, and he found a young woman standing by his side. Schneider had once told him that Hungarian women could be very attractive and even sexy. This one certainly matched that description, at least in Baier's exhausted eyes. Still, he figured the move here was pretty transparent. Her dress was short, riding above her knees, and the blouse was only buttoned a little more than half way up from her waist. It also looked to be about two sizes too small. She wore medium-length blond hair that was pulled back from her forehead and pushed behind her ears. She wore no make-up, but didn't appear to need any. To Baier, this made her even more attractive. Maybe it was the surroundings.

"Are you comfortable?" She asked.

Really? "No. And I want to talk to someone from the American Embassy."

"I cannot help that." Her English was halting and heavily accented. But at least it was not Magyar. She bent over Baier to give him a direct view of her cleavage. Baier couldn't help staring at first, but then remembered himself and averted his eyes. "Would you like to be clean?" She asked. "I can wash."

"That's very kind of you, but I do not plan on staying long. I'll bathe at home."

She did not appear to have understood much beyond the word 'bathe.' She stood and walked to the door, where a bucket of soapy water waited. She bent down to fetch that, lingered so that Baier could admire her rear end, then returned to his cot. Baier shook his head and held up his hand, palm out. He shook his head. "No, thank you."

She shrugged, set the bucket down and pulled his tray from beneath the bed. "I bring more food." She left Baier with a smile when she departed.

Baier sighed. At least this was better than getting the crap kicked out of him by the hulk from the evening before and a collection of his buddies. Too bad they hadn't been lynched when the crowds had the chance.

The sexy temptress never did return. Baier spent what felt like a day or so, alternately sleeping, rubbing his grumbling stomach, pacing the cell, counting the steps in an effort to get a sense of the measurements and size, and tapping on the walls to establish some kind of communication with the world beyond his own narrow confines. Again, he had no idea of how much time had elapsed. Luckily, he had only had to use the bucket to urinate thus far.

After one of his roundabouts, Baier saw the door open. His eyes had adjusted enough, so that he could now see pretty well in the dark. A Soviet officer entered his cell, dragging a chair behind him. The epaulets suggested he was with the KGB. So, they're going right to the A-team, he thought. Baier also wondered just what this would be like. The KGB as good cop, and the AVO as bad? That's how he would guess for them to play it.

"You don't remember me, do you, Herr Baier?"

Baier stared through the darkness but struggled with any form of recognition. "No, I'm afraid not. I apologize if we have met before."

The Soviet set the chair in front of Baier's cot. "Well, I have to admit that the meetings were brief. There were only three. In each case, we were near the Austrian-Hungarian border, and it was about a year ago." He paused to see if this helped. Baier's puzzled frown indicated it did not.

"Two of those times you were in a vehicle. Once in a jeep and once in a Ford. The third time you were running, accompanied by your wife and two American CIA agents, one of them badly wounded by a gunshot."

Realization finally dawned. Baier clearly remembered the man now. In the first two instances Baier had been casing the border near the von Rudenstein estate when he had been investigating the death of the Austrian aristocrat and plotting his wife Sabine's rescue from this very city. The third occasion had been the flight afterwards. In the first two cases, the Soviet officer had issued a friendly warning to Baier about straying too close to the border. Or at least Baier had assumed it was friendly. On the third, he had simply saluted once Baier and his party had returned to Austria, demonstrating his complicity in the escapade and subsequent border crossing. Was he also an ally of Chernov?

"When will I get to speak with someone from my embassy?"

The Soviet shook his head. "You won't. Other arrangements have been made. Besides, you are not here under any diplomatic capacity."

"What the hell is that supposed to mean? I am still an American citizen. Don't tell me the Nagy regime is complicit in this kidnapping."

"Oh come now, Herr Baier. You know full well what you have been doing here and the legality—or lack thereof—of your actions. Just be happy that we are handling your case, and not the AVO. They were very eager to get their hands on you."

"Oh, tough shit if I roughed up one or two of their boys." Baier tried to muster a sense of strength and invincibility to match his initial anger. "It's all in a day's work."

"That's not how they see it. Especially with the death of one of their own. You do recall the hanging corpse in that apartment?"

Baier sat upright. "I had nothing to do with that. And neither did my colleague. Where is he, by the way?"

"Oh, he is fine. He has already been returned to your Embassy. He does have diplomatic standing, so he is covered, as it were. You, however, do not. At least not in this country. And our AVO brethren do not see your part in the death of their colleague quite so innocently. In fact, they claim you are at fault and have notified the local police."

"He was already dead by the time I got there. Am I going to be tried for that? Hell, if he really was AVO the Hungarians would celebrate me as a hero if you tried."

The Soviet smiled while he studied Baier's face. "Not anymore, I'm afraid."

"What does that mean?" Baier laid his head back on the cot. "You are just full of riddles today, aren't you?"

"Decisions have been made. Nagy will be removed and our leaders in Moscow have agreed on Kadar as the next premier. Some in the Kremlin wanted Munnich, the Interior Minister and a real hardliner..."

"I know who he is."

"Of course, you do. But Khrushchev thought that Kadar would be more humane and make it easier to re-establish the old regime. The Yugoslavs also convinced him that Kadar, who was imprisoned and tortured by the fascists, would have more credibility here than someone who spent the war years in the comfort of Mother Russia."

"The Yugoslavs? What do they have to do with any of this?"

The Soviet officer shrugged. "Comrade Khrushchev wisely thought that getting them to agree with his move would add greater credibility among our allies in Europe. The final decisions were made just a few days ago on a nice secluded isle off the coast of Yugoslavia with Tito and his leadership. Time will tell, but they were probably right."

That would explain why he had gotten no warning from Kovacs. "But what about the Hungarian military and freedom fighters?"

The Soviet shrugged again. "That is being taken care of as we speak. The military leaders have been lured to our base at Tokol, ostensibly to continue negotiations over our withdrawal. They will be met instead by Comrade Serov and a contingent from the KGB, who will arrest them. That effectively decapitates the Hungarian military."

That son of a bitch Serov apparently had been one busy bastard, Baier thought. "And the Red Army?"

"Already on the move. The problem from our perspective—and yours in particular—is that the Austrians have already closed the border. That will complicate things."

"So, I'm being sent home?"

He nodded. "Of course. The Hungarian police will be looking for you, and I doubt your Embassy will be able to protect you. Besides, you must realize that neither Comrade Chernov nor I want the AVO to interrogate you. Believe me, you would not last long. I don't care what sort of training you have had in these matters. In fact, Chernov was incensed that you were even seized. He wasn't sure whether to blame AVO greed and overconfidence or your own incompetence." He smiled. "It was probably some of both, don't you agree?"

"How did they find out?"

"Find out what? That you were running an agent here?"

Baier said nothing.

"The AVO had their suspicions for some time, but it took them a while to focus on Mr. Kovacs. They pulled one step ahead of you after you set up your dead drop at the Eastern Railway Station. Before that you seem to have covered your tracks very well, as best we can tell. They have not shared much with us on this operation, which has us a bit concerned. You were probably lulled into a false sense of security because the surveillance was very light, or non-existent."

"Then how…?"

"No, you see they were able to recruit that man who ran the baggage claim department at the station. Surely, you tried to recruit him and offered to pay him well enough to ensure his loyalty?"

Again, Baier did not respond.

The Soviet laughed. "They probably offered him more." He shrugged. "It happens. Not everyone is dedicated to the cause of freedom, you know. In any event, they had you well covered after that." He paused and glanced around the cell before continuing. "Tell me, though, what you know of the hanging corpse. Apparently, he had been there several days before he was found. The neighbors complained about the smell."

"I guess he was in the wrong place at the wrong time."

"Meaning?"

"Either he was identified as AVO and despite his good intentions, he was lynched by a local mob. Or it was a set up by those pricks."

"The AVO?"

Baier nodded. "That's right. If it was them, they must have thought he was a mole or associated him with the Revolution in some way. So they killed him, making it look like popular revenge."

"And if it was someone else?"

Baier shrugged. "Then the locals found him and handed out some of their own rough justice." He studied the KGB officer.

"Do you really need to be asking me about the AVO and their role in this?"

"Sadly, yes. At least at the moment. You see, we have our own means and interests here, but you have tripped a number of wires, as it were." The officer smiled, then pursed his lips and frowned. "I have one more question about the corpse. Why then and there?"

"I really don't know." But Baier did know. Or at least he thought he had a good idea at this point as to the why of there and then. It was part of the complicated game of trust and openness between case officer and asset, the strength and depth of which you could never be sure.

Baier studied the floor, chewing his lower lip. Live and learn. A lesson for the training courses, once he got back home. If he got back home. He was dying to ask his visitor about Gero and what the old Stalinist may have known or guessed about Kovacs, or when he began to suspect his old protege. But that would have betrayed too much, even taken as a confession of sorts. He would wait.

"I know you are dying to ask about your source but are too professional to do so," The Soviet continued. "You are afraid you will give him away. Well, Mister Kovacs has not been touched. Not yet anyway. The AVO is probably waiting for the victorious Red Army to restore order in Budapest before they move against him. They also probably want to see if there are others cooperating with him. Besides you, of course. If they move prematurely they may only scare him and any others off. As he is Hungarian, I'm afraid there is little we can do for him."

"Why did they suspect him?" Baier would stick to his shaky cover story of an affair as long as possible.

"Oh come now, Herr Baier. He was caught red-handed, as you say. He was at the Astoria."

"People go to hotels for all sorts of reasons. Maybe he was having an affair or just dinner with friends. Who is the source of the accusations?"

The KGB officer smiled and wagged his finger. "Surely, you do not expect me to reveal that. I know little, in any case. As I said before, the Hungarians have not been very forthcoming. But I do know that Gero had begun to suspect his loyalties once Nagy returned to power and Mr. Kovacs moved from the AVO to a new post in the Nagy government. I gather your friend was too open in his enthusiasm. At least that is how I put the pieces together from what little I know. I imagine Gero also felt betrayed by his protégé."

"Well, then, can you tell me what day it is?"

"Certainly. It is late in the afternoon of November 3."

Hungary's Revolution against the Soviet occupation had lasted just twelve days, Baier thought. Longer that anyone would have thought possible thirteen days ago, but a lot less than anyone would have guessed just yesterday. Would anything the Hungarians had achieved survive, or would this country and all of Europe plunge deeper into a well of conflict and confrontation? Baier brushed those thoughts away to concentrate on his more immediate problems. Like surviving prison and staying out of the hands of the AVO.

The Soviet stood and held out his right hand. "Come." He reached into his jacket pocket and retrieved Baier's wallet, passport and watch with his left. "I believe these belong to you."

Baier took the items. "Thanks. And my jacket?"

"It's in the car."

"Where to?"

"Someplace not here. I'm sure you'll like it, if only for that."

In spite of himself, Baier let a smile escape as they made their way down the corridor toward the stairs. "Oh, by the way, thanks for the entertainment."

"Entertainment? What are you talking about?"

"The Hungarian girl. Pretty transparent, but still a welcome interlude."

The KGB officer smiled in turn. "Oh that. I didn't think

that would go anywhere, but I didn't expect you to complain. It certainly beat having a couple thugs try their methods. And believe me, they were eager to do so. Besides, you're slipping, Herr Baier."

"How so?"

"She was Moldovan, not Hungarian."

"Oh, yes, of course." Baier stopped after the second flight of stairs. Like he could recognize the difference. "Hey, you never told me your name."

"Andrei Lukovich. I am Ukrainian. And in case you're wondering, my family broke apart after my father's death during the great famine that Stalin induced for his collectivization in the 1930s. He had been a kulak. My sisters died in the war. The Germans had shipped them west to work in their factories, but they died in early 1945 from an Allied bombing raid on Cologne. So you can see that I have no great love for the Soviet system either. I also despise the West, unlike Sergei Chernov. Still, it was luck, I guess, that brought me and Chernov together. For our mutual advantage, you see."

"Yes, I do see. Are you interested in doing anything more against the Soviet system?"

Lukovich shook his head and smiled. "No. As I said, I despise the West almost as much. There's simply too much baggage in my personal history, as with so many others in this part of the world."

They walked for a minute or so. "Where are we going?" Baier suddenly asked.

Lukovich smiled. "We have safehouses in the city, too. But we will have to blindfold you for the journey."

How wonderful, Baier thought. Blindfolds in this part of the world rarely lead to anything good.

Chapter Eighteen

———❧———

WHEN BAIER AWOKE the next morning, the sun was just coming up on a hazy grey horizon broken by patches of black smoke. He thought at first that it must be raining, claps of thunder echoing through the city. Then he realized it was cannon fire. He rolled off the sofa where he had spent the night, collapsing shortly after his arrival. Baier glanced around what appeared to be a living room, well-furnished and with an array of framed watercolors—pastoral scenes mostly with lots of birches and an odd oil portrait of Catherine the Great over a fireplace—lining the walls. He had seen next to nothing of the flat when his guards removed the blindfold the night before. This morning, everyone appeared to have left. He lay on the sofa and listened for a minute or so to see if he could catch any sounds of movement or conversation from elsewhere in the apartment. Nothing. Now that was odd.

Baier stood and moved to check out the rest of the rooms before deciding on his next steps. His first act, however, was to walk to the window to look outside. Jets roared above the city's skyline, and explosions rocked the ground. This must be the

Soviet invasion that Chernov, Lukovich, and others had hinted at. Baier wondered if the Hungarians were putting up much resistance, and who was winning. From the sound of things, there was clearly a battle going on, but he guessed that the Red Army was probably a lot better prepared this time around. So much for the confusion in Moscow that everyone had spoken of earlier and the half-assed attempt at military suppression the Soviets had initially employed.

He quickly moved away from the window, mostly to avoid presenting a target to some overeager Central Asian or Mongolian conscript, but also to look around his new prison. If that's what it actually was, given the absence of any guards. When he entered the kitchen Baier was surprised—almost pleasantly—to find a man in plain clothes—presumably a Soviet security officer—sitting at a table drinking a cup of tea and listening to what sounded like a news report in Russian. The KGB guard had his back to Baier and sat hunched over a radio tuned to an incredibly low volume. Perhaps he had not wanted to disturb his 'guest.' Suddenly the man bolted around and took in Baier's presence with a smile.

"It has begun," he said in passable English. "It will be over soon." The smile widened. "November 4, 1956. Remember this day in history."

Baier nodded but did not return the smile. "I see. Congratulations." The Soviet was in his shirt sleeves and looked to be in his early twenties. He held his cup of tea aloft with a questioning look on his face. "Yes, please." Then Baier remembered one of his two words of Russian. "Da." He hoped to have a chance to deliver the other—"Nyet"—soon.

He left the kitchen and found the bathroom at the end of a long hallway that separated two furnished bedrooms on either side of the passage. The other apartments Baier had seen in the city had only a single bedroom. Baier searched the space around the sink and bath tub, then he inspected the toilet tank attached to the wall approximately seven or eight feet above the floor. He tugged lightly on the chain, then made a quick adjustment.

Baier returned to the living room where he had spent the night. The extra living space reinforced his impression that the KGB was able to maintain much nicer safehouses in Budapest if all of them were as well-stocked and comfortable as this one. It was almost luxurious for this part of the world. Again, it struck Baier as odd that there was no one else in the flat.

His wallet and passport were on the floor next to the sofa, and his jacket hung over a chair on the other side of an end table at the foot of the couch. Baier picked those up, slid into the jacket, slipped on his shoes, and walked back to the kitchen. He tapped the Soviet officer on the shoulder and spoke slowly and loudly, as though this would make his words more understandable.

"Could you come with me? I think there is something wrong with the toilet."

The KGB officer looked puzzled at first, but when Baier repeated the word 'toilet' several times followed by 'kaput' the man recognized Baier's problem. He smiled and nodded, mumbling something about 'Hungarian plumbing.'

Oh, I'm sure it's not up to Soviet standards, Baier thought, as he picked up a rolling pin from the kitchen counter. "For the pipes," he said.

The KGB officer led the way back to the bathroom, Baier close behind. He squeezed through the doorway to keep himself near the Soviet, who immediately stood on top of the toilet seat to inspect the tank that extended from the wall above. He pulled on the chain, which failed to release any water, thanks to Baier having dismantled it just minutes earlier. The Soviet looked at Baier, who shrugged. He stepped down, Baier pointed to the pipe running from the toilet to wall, and the man bent over to study that more closely. That's when Baier brought the rolling pin down hard on the back of the Soviet officer's skull. The KGB man collapsed across the toilet.

Baier searched his antagonist to be sure he was unarmed, then he ran back to the kitchen, where he found a roll of string in the top drawer next to the sink. It probably wouldn't last very long, but at least it would give him a head start.

Baier hustled back to the bathroom, where the Soviet had not moved. Baier wrestled his bulky body—the guy must have weighed over two hundred pounds—into the bathtub, and then tied his feet and hands as firmly as he could. Baier sincerely hoped he hadn't killed the guy or fractured his skull. The man had been friendly and obliging enough to make Baier feel guilty at having harmed him. And he did not want to add to the list of those who already felt they had a score to settle with him.

BAIER HAD NO idea where the Soviet safehouse was located, but he quickly discovered that he was just about a mile north of the area around the Parliament building. Thankfully, that put him on the right side of the river to get himself back to the U.S. Embassy. That looked to be even more important since the Red Army appeared to have seized control of all the bridges over the Danube. Baier followed the course of the river toward the Parliament, whose massive structure was impossible not to see in spite of the smoke that hovered over Budapest like a bad storm. Baier thought of going inside the building to see just what was happening and the state of the Hungarian government but reconsidered when he saw it surrounded by Soviet troops. Shortly afterwards, an official looking Hungarian, whom Baier recognized as Zoltan Tildy, Nagy's deputy, marched outside with a white flag. After a brief conversation, Tildy shook hands with a Soviet officer, and the two men—followed by a phalanx of Red Army troops—marched back inside the building. Apparently, Baier had just witnessed the surrender of the Hungarian seat of government. Just as well, Baier thought. The Hungarians were probably heavily outnumbered and outgunned. Gone were the T-34s, replaced by the more modern and better equipped T-54s. And there were lots of them. Clearly, the Soviets had taken a much more serious and thorough approach this time around. These had also been the first Hungarian troops Baier had seen, and he wondered if any of the Hungarian units had put up a fight. Or was the resistance relying again on the patchwork groups of young volunteers to run from building to building and toss Molotov cocktails from the rooftops? If so, the constant whine of jets making bombing and strafing runs overhead and the reverberations of cannon fire suggested they would not have nearly the success the Hungarians had enjoyed during the last round of fighting.

Baier slipped through the streets that ran a block behind Parliament and made his way to the American Embassy at Szabadsag Square. There was a crowd of reporters, civilians, and Soviet officers gathered at the front of the building. Most of the crowd appeared to be Hungarians, however, either local civilians or government officials. Baier used the attention out front to slip around to the back gate, where the Marine guards recognized him and let him pass once he showed his diplomatic passport. All hell had broken loose inside, which is about what Baier had expected to find. Most of those inside were being hustled to the basement for safety, while a handful of American diplomats and staff rushed along hallways and in and out of offices, probably trying to glean the latest information on developments outside to report back to Washington. They were also probably trying to ascertain the status and safety of any Americans in the city, as well as any of the local staff or American diplomats trapped in the fighting. Fortunately, family members had been sent home weeks ago. Baier took a back stairway to the fourth floor and headed for Stan Muller's office. The chief sat at a desk along the wall to the right of the door. Bill Schneider was pacing back and forth in front of the window but turned when he heard Baier enter. He immediately ran over and grabbed Baier's arm.

"Karl! Thank God you're safe. Are you hurt at all? Did those bastards rough you up?"

Baier patted his colleague on the arm, then turned to Muller. "No, I'm fine. It was actually all pretty low-key and kind of odd."

"How so?" Muller asked.

Baier recounted his ordeal in the car, the long wait in the prison cell, the visit by Luykovich, and the transport to the alleged Soviet safehouse.

"Alleged?" Muller pressed.

"Yeah, I say that because it was so well-appointed. And they did not seem to be very concerned about my being there and finding out where it was located." He recounted his escape. "I just hope the guy's okay. I wasn't sure how hard to hit him. I only wanted to knock him out and not give him any permanent damage."

"Oh, Karl, I guess you're just a lover and not a fighter," Muller laughed. "Still, you did alright."

"Perhaps. But I'm also someone who does not want to make any more enemies than necessary, and someone who has to rely on cooperation from some in that organization to keep a very valuable operation going." He paused and jerked his head in the direction of the Embassy's main entrance. "What's with the crowd out front? Are we expecting an announcement from Washington or something?"

Muller stood and walked around his desk, shaking his head. "Nothing beyond the usual words of regret and outrage. No, the crowd is out there because of the Cardinal."

"The who?"

"Cardinal Mindszenty. He showed up here around six o'clock this morning requesting asylum with a handful of priests."

"And? Is he going to get it?"

Muller nodded. "I assume so. I gather there were some discussions along that line in Washington already. Word came in before the Cardinal even got here that we should expect his arrival." Muller laughed. "Hell, it's the least we could do after leaving these people in the lurch."

"And after all the unhelpful prodding from RFE," Schneider added. "Those guys were actually promoting Mindszenty as the real leader of the Revolution."

Muller motioned with his head toward Schneider. "Bill and I spent the night here and went down to help smuggle his retinue into the building past a cohort of AVO and Soviets assholes outside." He smiled. "At least we won that battle."

"What about Nagy and the rest of the government? And how is the fighting going?"

Muller sat back against the edge of his desk. "Nagy found asylum at the Yugoslav Embassy this morning around the same time the Cardinal showed up here. I gather the Red Army started to roll in just after midnight."

"The Yugoslavs. Why the hell them? From what I picked up from Lukovich, those clowns worked it out with Khrushchev that Kadar would be the guy to replace Nagy even while the negotiations between the military chiefs were supposedly going on over the Soviets' withdrawal."

"Well, where would you go? At least it's not the East Germans or Bulgarians or anyone else in the Warsaw Pact."

"Why not here? He and the Cardinal could plot their revenge."

Muller shook his head. "Sorry, but I don't see that in Nagy. And it would only confirm in many peoples' minds that this uprising by the Hungarians was all a set-up by the West."

"And the fighting? My one guard back at the apartment claimed that it would all be over soon."

"He's probably right. I hear the Soviets are not exactly being careful in their responses to any attacks. The jets and tanks are blasting away at will. I'm not sure what's going to happen to the rest of the government, but I doubt anyone involved in this rebellion against the Soviets is going to have a very bright future."

Baier paused to study the chief of station. "Nor does anyone who's been working for us."

"You mean Bluebird?"

Baier nodded. "That's right. I need to get him out."

Muller moved back behind his desk. "It's probably too late for that, Karl."

"I still need to try, Stan. I should have moved earlier, as soon as we found that body. Kovacs had been compromised or close to it, but I wanted to keep a source active who was so close to the action. I made a big mistake, Stan, and I need to fix it."

Muller waved his arms wide. "Are you kidding? In this mess? How the hell are you going to do that? You'll get yourself arrested again, Karl. Or possibly killed. And I am not going to be responsible for that. Our exfiltration plans are all for shit now anyways, and you know it."

"I can still do it, Stan. Damn it, I—no, we—owe this guy. He's dead meat otherwise."

"Karl, our priority is getting you out first. And that's what we're going to concentrate on for now. You and Bill put your heads together and come up with something pronto on that. No later than this afternoon. This city is going to be awash in Red Army troops for the foreseeable future, and I do not look forward to having you as a houseguest. The Cardinal and his gang are going to make this place overcrowded as it is. And you're already in enough hot water back home. Besides, there's Sabine to consider. You can imagine, I'm sure, what must be going through her head right now."

Baier looked at his feet, then the floor. Then he muttered half-aloud, "I know, Stan, I know."

Bluebird wasn't the only person on his conscience. It all added to the pressure he felt to get this thing resolved as quickly as possible.

OUT IN THE hallway, Baier turned to Schneider. "Bill..."

"Don't even say it. I know what you're going to do anyway.

Regardless of what Stan says. And you're going to get me in all kinds of trouble."

"No, Bill, just help me locate Bluebird's address. I'll take care of everything else. I know what Sabine would expect me to do. But I have to move fast."

"I already know the address. I had looked it up before you returned during this latest go-round in case the dead drops didn't work and we needed to find him. I'll write it down for you and show you where it is on the map." He paused. "I have to warn you, though, it's a bit out of the way. And in this fighting, I'm not sure how you'll get there."

"Thanks, Bill. I'll find a way."

Chapter Nineteen

BUT SCHNEIDER COULD not keep himself away. About a block from the Embassy, Baier heard a voice puncture the noise of battle at his back that called out his name. When he turned he saw his colleague trotting in Baier's direction.

"In for a dime, in for a dollar," Schneider said.

"Don't sell yourself so cheap," Baier answered. "What's up?"

"There's no way in hell I'm letting you wander off and get lost in this mess. I'd never be able to look myself in the mirror again." Schneider motioned towards the rest of Budapest in front of them. "It's going to be a long hike, so let's get going. You don't mind if we don't drive, I hope."

"Not at all. I don't relish the thought of being used as target practice by some young Soviet kid. Lead the way."

Schneider was right. It was a long hike, especially with the frequent stops to avoid Soviet patrols and bombing runs. They walked for over an hour to a street around the corner from the Yugoslav Embassy that ran about a mile almost directly behind the Parliament. Along with the Eastern Railway Station and Parliament building, the Yugoslav Embassy formed a neat triangle that was the scene of a good deal of the fighting going on in the city. It was also close to the AVO headquarters. Just the site of that building sent a shiver down Baier's spine and through his stomach.

The two Americans continued to creep through the streets of what was now a battleground. But it was one without distinct lines of demarcation. You never knew what you might find or encounter, especially with the overwhelming noise and curtain of smoke that hung over the city. Soviet tanks and troops were everywhere. The two Americans dodged from building to building, as though they had joined the young workers and students who had provided the bulk of the Hungarians' fighting force for the past two weeks. It struck Baier that he must resemble those young warriors, seeing as how he had not changed his clothes in three days now. And he couldn't remember the last time he had washed. The extra clothes he had brought along were sitting clean and safe back in Schneider's apartment. He had hardly eaten as well and probably looked emaciated and exhausted to anyone who might notice them. The funny thing was that he rarely noticed how tired and hungry he was. He was just thinking about it now for the first time since his return to Budapest. Adrenalin and danger formed a rare and at times intoxicating narcotic.

Schneider at least appeared to have had the chance to shower and change out of the clothes Baier had last seen him in. Gone was the dust and grime that had encased Baier since they were dragged away from the Astoria so many hours ago. Schneider did not look any more rested, though. Together they almost certainly made a tempting target to the conscripts from the far-flung steppes of the Soviet Empire now running around Budapest and shooting indiscriminately at just about anything that moved and wasn't wearing a uniform similar to theirs. Even without their car, the Americans were not safe from the kind of exposure that could draw a line of lead. Baier wondered what the young soldiers had been told about their mission and whom they had allegedly been sent to fight. Probably Nazi hordes or Western imperialists like the CIA. It made Baier all the more cautious, realizing their chances of talking their way out of danger were pretty damned slim.

When they reached Kovacs's apartment block, the two Americans were shocked to find that little had been left standing. Fortunately, there were no Red Army troops around. And there was an eerie silence that hung over the area, the rumbling of battle having moved to other parts of the city. But this building had been nearly leveled already, presumably by the jets screaming overhead.

"Shit! All that walking for nothing," Schneider yelled. "What a fucking waste."

"Do you suppose our man is somewhere in that?" Baier asked. He pointed toward the rubble that littered the ground in front of them.

"Who knows? But that's as good a guess as any." Gunfire echoed in the air around them. "I understand the fighting is still pretty vicious over at the Killian Barracks and Szena Square. The Russians probably want to capture those areas that had emerged as the heart of the Hungarians' resistance and rebellion against the old regime." Schneider glanced around. "I imagine it's probably why we're not seeing any of their forces here anymore. This place has already been secured, as far as they're concerned."

"And those are the same areas the locals are likely to defend as much as they can to build some kind of legacy."

"Yeah, so let's avoid those spots and get the hell back to the Embassy."

They swung around several blocks behind the AVO headquarters on Stalin Avenue, running along parallel roads toward the Parliament building. When they crossed Lenin Boulevard and reached the major thoroughfare on Bajcsy Zsilinszky Avenue Baier stopped and pulled at Schneider's arm.

"Bill, wait a minute. Hadn't Nagy moved his government's seat into the Parliament? You know, as a symbol of his commitment to the people and the Revolution?"

"Yeah, so what."

"But Bluebird was highly placed inside Nagy's administration."

Schneider shook his head, his eyes wide and his face wrinkled in a deep frown. "Don't tell me. If you're going where I think you are with this shit happening all around us…"

"Then it stands to reason that he was in the Parliament when this whole thing broke apart this morning," Baier continued. "We need to check it out."

Schneider waved his arms in the air in obvious exasperation. "But that place has got to be crawling with the Red Army, man. You'll get us killed for sure."

"No, look, Bill, this is not Berlin in 1945. This isn't the site of some big final battle like with the Reichstag."

"But it's still an important symbol, and the Soviets will be there in force. There's no way we can get in there without being seen."

"But the fighting there is over. In fact, it never really began. I saw the Hungarians surrender this morning when I was returning to our place."

"It's still a bad idea. And Muller will shit if he finds out we've been in there. I'm already screwed as it is."

"Then what's to lose?"

"Aside from our lives, you mean?"

But Schneider took his place beside Baier as the two men ran the last three blocks to Parliament Square. A large crowd, a mixture of Hungarian civilians and Soviet Army troops, had gathered in front of the main entrance. Baier had no way of knowing if the civilians were outraged citizens here to protest the Soviet invasion or willing satraps of the Kremlin, but he figured it was best to avoid the group in any case. Instead, he and Schneider skipped around to the left, aiming for a side entrance. This one also had steps leading to a basement.

The door was unlocked, and the two Americans slipped inside. They walked past discarded boxes and broken furniture like they belonged there, their eyes focused on the path in front. They hopped up the first stairway they found, which brought them around two corners and to the main staircase behind the front entrance. It was a gorgeous blend of red carpet and gold leaf. It was also crammed with people, about a third of them Soviet soldiers, racing up and down the stairs. Fortunately, they were all too busy to notice the uninvited American guests.

Baier and Schneider beat a quick retreat back the way they had come. The original stairway took them up four more flights and to an ornate lobby with more gold paint or leaf and led to the Deputies Council Chamber. That room was eerily deserted, a symbol, Baier thought, of the Soviet's system's contempt for democratic governance. But that system also had the whip hand today with its superior manpower and firepower, so they did not linger.

"Where to now, O fearless leader," Schneider pressed. "This place has got something like 600 rooms. At least."

"How the fuck would I know? This is my first time here. It's your town." Baier paused and took Schneider's arm. "Look, Bill, I'm sorry." He shook his head to clear out the exhaustion and frustration. "We can't get after each other. Let's think a bit. Where are the offices? Isn't that the most likely place Bluebird would be holed up?"

"If he's even here. Which is an incredible long shot." Schneider glanced up and down the foyer. "Damn it, Karl. Okay, okay, there are offices on the floors we passed. We can check a few on our way back out."

The first floor down held very few open offices. Baier trotted along the corridor, looking in the few—no more than four— that were not locked and dark. He could not find anyone at work or even sitting in their office. Not that he could blame them. It was the same on the floor below.

On the third one down, however, their luck changed. This hallway opened on to more offices that appeared to be open—almost a dozen at least—and in one Baier found Kovacs huddled behind a desk and staring at the floor. His shoulders were shaking, and his head periodically bobbed up and down. The Hungarian asset looked up as Baier broke into the room. He was a shattered remnant of his earlier confident and at times jubilant self. The man had been severely beaten, his face a blend of red and blue patches around his cheeks and temples. His lips were swollen. At least he was not bleeding, as far as Baier could tell. Baier ran back to the door and signaled for Schneider to join them.

"Good Lord, Josef. What happened to you?" Baier asked. "Who did this?"

Kovacs's face was streaked with dust and tears, and his eyes were red from weeping. "The AVO. Who do you think would do something like this?"

"Where are they now? Are they coming back?"

"I'm…I'm not sure. But they told me to wait. That was two hours ago."

"Why did they let you go or let you stay here alone?"

"I…I'm not sure. They said something about helping them ferret out other traitors. I have been a fool, Herr Baier. I never really thought it would come to this."

Baier moved closer to his asset and pulled a chair from the window over to the desk. He sat down and put his arm around Kovacs's shoulder. He thought back to his conversation in the prison cell with the Ukrainian. "Josef, you knew why the man who met me at the border had come to me. The same man we found hanging in the apartment. You knew how he had found out about you, didn't you?"

Kovacs looked at Baier with red eyes and tear-streaked cheeks. He nodded. "Yes. He had been on a team that was looking for the mole. When he realized the evidence was pointing at me, he approached and tried to help."

"Why didn't you tell us? We could have helped, we could have gotten you out. Instead we walked into a trap."

Kovacs stared out the window for a few seconds before turning back to Baier. "I thought it did not matter anymore. I was sure we had had won our freedom and that the AVO would be crushed." He paused and fought back new tears. "I was committed to our cause. I was so sure. I never meant to hurt you."

Baier stood. "Well, come on. It's not too late. We're getting you out of here."

Kovacs held up his arms. "No, wait. Where are you taking me? I have nowhere else to go. This is my home."

"This will be your grave if we don't get out of here," Schneider said.

Baier and Schneider eased their asset up from his chair by his underarms and walked slowly to the door.

"Okay, we need a story in case we're stopped," Baier said.

"You mean when we're stopped," Schneider responded.

"Whatever." They draped Kovacs's overcoat over his shoulders. "Look, we'll claim that you were beaten by Hungarian soldiers when you tried to prevent them from firing on the Soviet heroes in the square below. Tell them we're taking you for some medical attention. How's your Russian, in case that's who we meet?"

Kovacs nodded. "It's good, of course. We all had to learn it at some point."

"Well, it could finally come in handy today. Let's go."

And it did come in handy. A troop of Red Army conscripts and their officer intercepted the three men just as they reached the basement door by which Baier and Schneider had entered. Kovacs mumbled something in Russian, which Baier hoped was the story they had agreed upon. He felt very relieved when the Soviets all patted Kovacs on the back and nodded their approval to Baier and Schneider. Then they hurried from the building.

As the three men limped past the Communist Party headquarters just blocks from the American Embassy, another one of those damned Zis sedans pulled up alongside them. It was black, of course. It screeched to a stop, and three men in Soviet uniforms jumped from the vehicle. Baier cursed. One of them was his new friend Lukovich.

"Herr Baier, you are like some kind of bad virus. You just keep coming back no matter what we do."

"Your buddy Sergei said I was like a bad penny once."

Lukovich shook his head. "No, you're worse than that. A penny is too cheap. You are much more trouble. I think you and your friends will need to come with us." He looked hard at Baier. "By the way, the man you assaulted is in the hospital with a concussion. Why did you attack him? I told you we were going to put you over the border into Austria."

"I'm sorry to hear that," Baier said. "I truly meant him no harm. But you can understand my eagerness to get away. I guess I'm just too impatient."

"Perhaps.   But   he   was   seriously   injured all   the   same.   It   was   very   foolish   of   you."

"In that case, I will come with you. But let my friends here go. We rescued a colleague who had been injured by some careless fire from your troops today, and we need to get him to a doctor at our embassy.

Luykovich walked over to study the other two. "You," he pointed at Schneider, "may go. I remember you from last night. The other one stays with us."

Schneider drew himself up to his full height. "I'm not going anywhere without my compatriots."

Lukovich stepped in closer, his face inches from Schneider's. "Don't be a fool. You are in no position here to make demands." He pointed at Kovacs. "And I know this man. He is not a compatriot of yours." He turned back toward Baier. "And you can tell your superiors that we will deal with Mr. Baier accordingly."

"According to what?" Schneider argued.

"According to what he deserves."

Lukovich spat those last words over his shoulder. The other two Soviet KGB officers marched over to Baier and Kovacs, seized their arms and led them to the limousine. A yelp of pain from Kovacs and a curse from Baier were the last things Schneider heard from the two men.

AT LEAST THIS was not the same prison cell he had occupied the day before. In fact, it wasn't a prison cell at all. More like an interrogation room. As best he could tell, it was the same complex. He had been blindfolded when they arrived the other night, and back then the air had seemed darker than an endless night. But despite the presence of light and more open space, this one still stank of mold or mildew or something clammy. The dark grey walls were probably designed to hide the moisture and dirt, while also casting the place in the depressing image of another lost night and, more than that, lost hope. Baier figured it was intended to remove you from feeling any connection with your own world on the outside. It was about what he had expected. A large table occupied the center of the room, along with two chairs facing each other on either side of the table. A single light bulb hung from a thin, black electrical wire above the table. There was also a lamp on the table pointing at the chair where Baier sat. Fortunately, it was turned off at the moment.

Once again, there were no windows. Just a door that had been bolted shut once the two KGB officers from the car had brought Baier to the room and sat him in the chair. Actually, it was more like he had been thrown into his seat. The two guards had gone, and Baier had been waiting there for about an hour. He still had his watch and documentation this time.

A Soviet officer entered and shut the door. He took a seat opposite Baier. The man was a complete stranger to Baier, and he wore the uniform and insignia of a major in the infantry.

Maybe all the KGB officers were busy torturing Hungarian rebels. Baier doubted it, though. They had the AVO for that. Which made the use of a regular Army officer all the more puzzling. The Soviet placed a pad and pen on the table between them. His broad shoulders and large peasant-like hands suggested he was the not the sort to take his time in getting what he wanted out of the session. His face was hard and impassive, as though it had been sculpted by a Soviet architect with a heavy use of concrete. Maybe he was going to be the bad cop.

"We shall use this to write out your confession." The Soviet drew the tablet and pen toward himself.

"My what?" Baier forced out a smile. At least this guy's English was pretty good.

"Do not be so smug, Mr. Baier. You know exactly what you have done."

"Perhaps you should remind me. It's been a long day."

The officer pounded his fist on the table hard enough to make the pad and pen jump. "It has been a long day for all of us, Mr. Baier. But it has also been a good and glorious one for the Soviet Union." He pointed an index finger at the American. "Less so for you. And it has been more than just a day."

Baier shrugged. "Okay, so two days."

The Soviet sat back. "I can see this is going to be difficult. At least at the beginning." He stood and walked around to Baier's chair. With a movement almost too quick for Baier to register, he slapped Baier hard across the face. Twice. Once with the front, and then even harder with the back of his hand. Hard, boney knuckles stung Baier's cheek and mouth, and he noticed the warm and salty taste of his own blood dripping through his lips. The movement had shaken loose a strand of the officer's thick black hair, which had been smoothed back over a long skull.

"I do not have the time or the patience for your silly, little games, Mister Baier." He pushed the disobedient hair back in place. "Now let us proceed."

"Fuck you, asshole." Baier hoped his voice sounded stronger than he felt. "I am an American diplomat sent here to assist my compatriots at the American Embassy during a time of intense pressure and danger. You cannot hold me here and subject me to this sort of treatment."

The Soviet relaxed in his chair once more and smiled. He smoothed his hair, as though he wanted to make sure it obeyed the next time around. "We can do anything we like right now. Especially to someone like you, who, despite what you say, has no diplomatic standing in this country whatsoever. You are not on any approved list of diplomatic missions in Budapest." He sat forward again. "We do know you have been running imperialist espionage schemes here, ones designed to embolden the Hungarian people against their natural allies and guardians from the Soviet Union."

"Don't make me puke, asshole."

"Oh, that can be arranged as well." He reached for the pad and pen and began to write. It was in Cyrillic script, so Baier could not even try to read it upside down. "Let us begin by stating your name and profession."

"Which you'll probably get wrong. Like everything else so far."

The Soviet continued as though Baier had not spoken. "Oh, I'm just listing your past assignments. You know, those in Berlin, and London, and Washington. I'll finish here with your current work in Vienna, work that culminated in your nefarious activities against the People's Republic of Hungary."

"Which people would that be? Those inhabiting the Kremlin?"

"Among others. Now, I'd like you to provide the details of your work here over the last week or so. In particular, who have you met with and what have you instructed them to do. What day did you arrive here in Budapest?"

"Like I said before, asshole. Fuck you."

The Soviet stood once more and returned to Baier's side. This time he reached down, pulled Baier upright by the collar, and delivered a blow to his solar plexus that left the American gasping for breath. The man was obviously very strong. Those shoulders and hands were matched with strong, muscular arms that handled Baier like a small package. Baier found himself marveling at this almost as much as he did at the Soviet's mastery of the English language, articles and all. The name tag said 'Savinkov.' Baier assumed this meant he was Russian. Hopefully, not another 'fucking Russian.' The thought made Baier wonder just where Chernov was and what he knew about this whole affair. The Russian dropped Baier back into his seat and returned to his own side of the table.

"We can go on like this all day and even longer if you persist in insulting me and denying your crimes, Mister Baier."

"I haven't committed any crimes." Baier struggled to push the words out through the pain in his mid-section.

"Oh, and what about your assaults on the Hungarian and Soviet security officials? Those were especially egregious since they were only trying to ensure your safety."

"I was acting solely in self-defense."

"Come now, Mister Baier. They have filed sworn statements to the contrary. Whom do you think our superiors will believe?" He paused to consider the American. "But more importantly, I want to know the details of your meetings with a particular Hungarian official," he consulted a notepad that he had pulled from his jacket pocket, "by the name of Josef Kovacs." He looked up at Baier. "That man is currently being interrogated by my colleagues in the KGB. Soon it will be the AVO's turn." He smiled again at the thought.

"I don't know who you're talking about." Baier studied the Soviet in turn. "And why is this of interest to a Soviet infantry officer, in any case?"

The Soviet scribbled some more on the pad. "I'll take that as an admission of guilt."

"Oh, piss off, you piece of shit." Baier realized his anger was directed at himself, as much as at the Soviet, for revealing an interest he should not have shared. He wondered how soon before his exhaustion and disorientation would lead him to make additional and possibly more serious errors.

At that moment he heard the door to the room open and shut. He turned to see his nemesis from the last two days enter the room. This Ukrainian guy Lukovich had an awful habit of appearing at the worst possible times. But at least he was not the guy Baier would expect the KGB to send in for some rough treatment. No, he was actually more dangerous than that, Baier suddenly realized. This guy had some insight and intelligence. Baier struggled through the pain he felt from the blows to his face and stomach to pull his wits together. He needed to rein in his anger and be on his best guard. He bit his lips and clenched his fists, as though the physical exertion would help.

That was why Baier was stunned when Lukovich spoke.

"Have you mistreated our guest, Comrade Savinkov?"

"Not at all, Comrade Lukovich. The American must have slipped when he was brought to this room."

"Has he revealed anything yet?"

Savinkov sighed and studied the pad. "Not really. He continues his stubborn and ultimately futile resistance."

This was all stated in English, presumably for Baier's benefit.

"I see. Then perhaps you should get him a cup of coffee or a glass of water. It is probably a good time for a break." Lukovich turned to Baier. "Are you hungry?" Baier shook his head. "Do you smoke? Would you like a cigarette?"

Again, Baier shook his head.

"Yes, of course, Comrade Colonel." The Russian got up to leave. Lukovich nodded and smiled at Baier. He waited until the other Soviet officer had shut the door behind him before continuing.

"Ah, Herr Baier, what am I to do with you? You know I

cannot afford to allow this interrogation to continue. What would you do in my place?"

"I would never be in your place. You know that."

"Then what do you suggest?"

"How about letting me go? We can explain all this as another unfortunate misunderstanding. These things happen in the heat of battle, you know."

Lukovich shook his head. "No, I'm afraid it will not be that easy." He paused, then raised his finger, as though the thought had suddenly occurred to him. "No, I know what we are going to do. We are going to drive you to the border and release you back into Austria. In fact, we will push you, literally, over the border. And I will oversee this personally to be sure you do not pull another silly escape." He rubbed his hands together as if he was washing them. "No, I will not let you out of my sight. That is the simplest solution. After all, it's not like you entered this country legally, is it?"

"And my colleagues at the Embassy?"

"We will inform them in our own way, of course. Don't worry. They will not be left in the dark."

"But I thought the border had been closed. Wasn't there some nonsense about guarding against a western invasion?"

Lukovich waved his hand. "You needn't worry about that. Fortunately for your side, there are no NATO troops massed at the Austrian border. In fact, we've reopened that border to allow all the malcontents to leave. It will make for a more stable and happier Hungary. Don't you agree?"

"Like hell it will. It will make for a more pliant but more miserable population. And you'll lose the most talented and energetic people."

Lukovich stood and extended his hand to assist Baier. "That, Herr Baier, is not my problem. However, you are. One that I plan to solve now."

Baier stood and brushed away the Ukrainian's hand. "I'm not leaving without my Hungarian colleague."

"I doubt that will be possible. We are about to turn him over to his countrymen."

"Then get him back. You know I will come back for him."

"If you do, I will not be able to help you again. Instead, I or someone else will have to kill you."

Baier shook his head. "No, you won't. By then it would be too late."

"Too late for what?"

"Too late to save yourself. Or Chernov for that matter. You said once you did not want the AVO to get their hands on me because of what they are bound to learn."

Lukovich nodded. "And?"

"Well, they'll learn plenty from my friend as well. He's been using that same exfiltration scheme I set up with Chernov for the last year. So, it wouldn't be long before your friends started putting the pieces together and informing Moscow in the process."

Lukovich sighed. "You know, Herr Baier, you are what your countrymen call a real son of a bitch. I'll see what I can do."

"What about the other guy who was here? Savinkov?"

Lukovich shrugged. "We do not need to worry about him. Surely, you've noticed that he has not returned." Baier glanced around the room, as though the Russian might be hidden somewhere. "I told you before that we had our own means of finding things out about this operation. This officer was instrumental in doing that. I assume you have not heard the name Boris Savinkov before."

"No, I haven't."

Lukovich frowned, then smiled. "You Americans need to study your history more." Baier started to speak, but Lukovich waved him away. ""You see, his father was this Boris fellow, who led a rebellion against the Lenin government shortly after our own glorious Revolution. He was part of a plot hatched by the famous Sidney Reilly. You have heard of him, I'm sure."

"Yes," Baier said, "I have heard of that one."

"The father was shot, of course, and his son had to survive and grow up on the heartless steppes of Central Asia. Have you been there?"

Baier shook his head.

"Well, it is almost as cold as Siberia. And just as desolate. It seems our Comrade Major has been working to win his way back into favor ever since. That probably explains why he was so impatient and rough with you. He also wants to enter the KGB, but he has yet to work away the stain of his father betrayal."

"Why isn't he coming back?"

"He has been detained by something else. I saw to that before I joined your little party."

As far as Baier could tell, it was the same damned Zis he had been riding around Budapest in for the past two days. It certainly looked and smelled the same. The floor at his feet appeared to be littered with the same dirt and cigarette wrappers, and the air carried the sickening scent of some kind of disinfectant. He was really getting to hate this car. Even the leather upholstery felt cold and hard, as though it might crack open any minute. God knew what might crawl out. Probably his own fears and doubts to match the pervasive despair of the Soviet repression evident in the streets of Budapest.

Kovacs was already slumped in the back seat. His face had a fresh set of bruises, and his lip was bleeding. Baier wondered what the rest of his body looked like. He slid in beside his asset and looked into the Hungarian's face.

"Are you alright, Josef? How badly have they hurt you?"

The Hungarian looked up at Baier slowly, as though any sort of movement was painful. "Where are they taking us?"

"They're taking us away from here. To freedom and safety."

"Are you certain?"

Baier nodded and placed his arm around Kovacs's shoulder. The car pulled away from what must have been a Soviet base on the outskirts of Budapest. There was a steady movement of trucks carrying Red Army troops speeding past rows of plywood barracks. The air was full of shouts and curses in Russian. Or at least, Baier assumed it was Russian. Not all the soldiers looked to be from Russia proper. He almost expected to hear some Asian languages or dialects, not that he would have understood or recognized them.

"Yes, I am. I've taken care of you, like I promised. We're going to Austria. You can start a new life there."

Tears dripped down Kovacs's cheeks. "No, no. Hungary is my home. I cannot leave. We have so much to work for, to build a truly socialist state."

"Josef, that dream is over. Look around you. The Stalinists have won. And there will be many more of your countrymen in Austria. You can settle in amongst them. And I will stay in touch to make sure you're safe."

"We shall see." He wiped at the tears and looked at his hand when it dropped to his side. "I'm not sure I can stay away, but we shall see." He stared out the window for a minute or two, then began whispering, as though he wanted to hide what he had to say. "Erno, Erno, I misjudged you."

Baier leaned in close. "What is it Josef? What are you trying to say?"

Kovacs looked up at the American with red-rimmed eyes and a look of despair. "I underestimated Gero. Again."

"Again?"

Kovacs nodded. "Yes, once again. The first time was in Spain, when I misjudged the man's capability for cruelty. This was the second time."

"How have you misjudged the man now?"

"He guessed at what I was doing. I'm not sure how, but he seemed to know. He was the one who set that man you found on my trail. I am sure of it."

"What man was that, Josef? The one from the border?"

"No. No, not him. He meant to help. The older one, the Russian. The one who looked like he had been worn down by time, by his history. That's why I was not that concerned at first. He's the man I saw following me these last few days in Budapest."

Baier sat back. "Josef, you never said. What Russian? You should have shared this with me. Don't you see why I insisted on keeping me informed?"

Kovacs shrugged and coughed. "I realize that now, of course. When it's too late."

"But how would Gero know of any of this? Why do you think he was behind all this?"

"The man was evil. He could smell the presence of good in his environment."

"He recognized your change in mood and purpose over the last year," Luykovic interrupted. "The man was naturally suspicious, so he followed his instincts. It was how he survived the years of Stalin, Beria, and Rakosi and others like them. He shared those thoughts. Near the end."

"Shared them with whom?" Baier asked.

"With some at his level in our government, as well as a few in his own organization. I think he spoke mostly with Serov. But there were others who suspected something was up. Chernov, for one." Lukovic studied Baier's face and smiled at the shock. "Do you feel betrayed or let down? You look distraught."

Baier stared out the window at the passing countryside. When he turned his face back towards his Ukrainian host, Baier bit his lip to avoid saying anything.

Lukovich's smiled faded, but his eyes stayed wide and bright. "Oh, come now. It was only bits and pieces he was able to pick up. It was what he was trying to warn you about."

The car rode slowly westwards through the Hungarian countryside. Lukovich sat in the front on the passenger side, almost certainly to make sure that he and his organization would be rid of Baier. Finally. And expulsion really was the easiest option. Murder would be far too messy and would almost certainly invite retributions. But he clearly wanted the American out of Hungary and out of his hair. The drive, however, seemed to be taking longer than any of Baier's previous forays into Hungary from the west. There were multiple detours and roundabouts the driver kept taking, often it appeared on Lukovich's instructions. And they had plenty of company from Soviet military forces moving, for the most part in the same westerly direction.

"Just where are you taking us? Is this your scenic tour?"

"Don't be ungrateful, Herr Baier. Our troops have encountered stiff resistance in Gyor, as one might have expected. This has required troop movements along the roads toward Hgyeshalom, where I had intended to push you across. There is fighting there as well. So we are swinging a bit west of that."

"What's the new goal?"

"Well, there has also been some intense fighting further to the south, so we'll need to avoid going too far in that direction. I'm surprised these fools insist in resisting the inevitable. They will all be crushed, of course."

"Maybe for now. But perhaps they also want to leave a legacy for the future."

"Oh please." Lukovich stole a glance at his driver. "You know that History is on our side."

"Oh, for sure." Baier snorted. "Maybe you're the ones who need to study the past a little more thoroughly. And with a more open mind."

Lukovich turned to study the way ahead. "In any case, I guess we'll aim for the region around Sopron." He pivoted to look at the American and his companion. "That should be familiar to you. I guess you might call it poetic justice to use that the same old crossing point, eh?'

"Yes, very much so. But will it be open? And for how long?"

"Of course. For now at least." The Ukrainian turned to stare into the eyes of Baier. "We shall see about the future, but I certainly hope it remain open for those desperate enough to flee our workers' paradise. Today you might also meet your

Russian friend there."

"I think that would be more poetic than just."

Once they arrived and climbed from the car Baier was astonished by the virtual sea of humanity rolling in a westward tide. If Chernov was there, Baier doubted he would ever see him. Thousands were pushing their way across the border into Austria, their dream of a free and independent Hungary crushed. There were Soviet border guards present, but not one bothered to ask for identification from any of the refugees. They probably did not want to do anything that might hold up the rush. Baier wondered if any of the Soviets had seized the opportunity to join the throng moving westward.

Just as he reached the border and saw his first Austrian soldiers, Baier thought he caught a glimpse of Chernov. But the moment passed, nothing more than a fleeting image that faded almost immediately into the land he had just left. Kovacs got some sympathetic looks from the others struggling alongside them and from the Austrian border guards. But the two men proceeded without any difficulty past the Austrian authorities. Baier paused to ask Kovacs if he could walk further.

"Yes, I believe so. But how far?"

"Not more than a mile or two. I have a house up the road a bit. We can recuperate there for a few days before traveling on to Vienna and registering you with the authorities there."

And he would get to see Sabine. Perhaps she would be at the house, but Baier had no way of knowing. Not right after escaping from the chaos that had been Budapest. Baier was sure she had been as worried about him, as he had been about her when their roles had been reversed over a year ago. He tried to move Kovacs along as quickly as possible. That Muller had not been able to contact her was indeed worrying. But given the turmoil of the last few days there was no way of knowing for sure what may have happened.

It all reminded him of how much he missed her. He remembered this now that his return had become a reality, now that his every movement was no longer accompanied by the sounds of battle, or the urge to accomplish his mission, or even the desperation of surviving. In all the excitement and danger his thoughts had been focused on the events in Budapest, on his work with Kovacs, the dangers he and Schneider had confronted, his seizures and escapes. But now, he wanted nothing more than to fall into her embrace, to feel the warmth of her body and presence.

He put his arm underneath Kovacs's to help him as they started to walk down the road. Up ahead Baier saw his wife waving to him at the side of the road. She was smiling. He felt all his muscles relax at once in a wave of relief. But then the words from the darkness of the Zis returned, and Baier realized they would rarely have such moments of peace and surety in their future. The risks, the danger would always lurk somewhere in the background, at the edge of their lives. He had made enough enemies now to know that the element of uncertainty and anxiety would be with them as long as they continued in this work, in this part of the world. It was the life they had both chosen.

It was a decision that he still believed had been the right one. Despite the hardship and danger and disappointment, all that he had witnessed over the last two weeks convinced Baier of the need and the importance in the responsibilities and leadership his country had chosen. He also remained convinced of the role his organization had to play and the contributions, however small, that he could make. There were imperfections and shortcomings, to be sure. But despite all that, he would do what he could sustain the commitment he made nearly ten years ago. Perhaps most important, Baier knew that Sabine would be there to work at his side.

Chapter Twenty

"WELCOME BACK. AT least for now." O'Leary, the new station chief in Vienna rose from his chair, walked to the front of his desk, and offered his hand to Baier. The two men stood an arm's length apart and studied each other for a few moments. Then O'Leary broke their pose and returned to his seat.

"We missed you here, Karl. There's a lot you should have been doing on this side of the Curtain. And, as you've no doubt heard, Headquarters is mightily pissed about your escapade in the East."

Baier tried to relax. He slipped into a chair across from his new, if temporary, boss's desk and crossed his legs. He was still exhausted from his journey out of Budapest and return to Vienna. It had been two days since he left the Hungarian capital. One day to recuperate with Sabine at their estate and calm Kovacs's fears about starting a new life in the West, and another to make the trip to the Austrian capital and get his asset registered with the local authorities. Today was Baier's first visit to the office since his return to Austria.

"I know, Gerry, I know. But I couldn't do anything else. I had to contact Bluebird and then get him out. Given the unusual, hell, even historical circumstances there I made a command decision all on my own. We needed to learn what he could tell us. Besides, I wouldn't have been able to live with myself otherwise."

"Karl, I get it. I won't ever admit this to anyone else, but I probably would have done the same thing. Or at least been sorely tempted. But Headquarters doesn't feel that way, not after giving explicit orders to the contrary. I have instructions to put you on a plane home. Your tour here is over."

"And the border operation I set up? Is that going to continue?"

"Yes, as far as I'm concerned. We will still need to use that to move people back and forth over the border. Will your Soviet contacts be willing to cooperate further if you're not around?

"I think so. They were never driven by any personal loyalty to me."

Well, our Soviet and Hungarian friends may have other ideas at the moment. Things look like they may already be tightening up there. But that may have something to do with the fighting. I expect things to get very tight along that border and others in the region for the immediate future. Hopefully, the situation will relax after a bit, and we can resume our cooperation with your assets. I'll reach out for you when the moment is right."

"You can continue to use our place nearby as a debriefing and relocation center, if necessary." Baier wondered what Chernov and Luykovich were up to now, if they were even still in Hungary. His chances of reestablishing contact, however, were pretty slim at the moment. "There is one other issue that I need to address, Gerry."

O'Leary threw himself back against his chair. "Oh, hell, Karl, what is I now?"

"I need to nail down just who betrayed Bluebird. I've been

able to figure out the AVO's part, but the Soviets appear to have had their own, separate source and known knew more than they ever should have about this operation."

"I thought that asshole Gero was responsible."

"True, but only partly. Gero's suspicions set off the search and helped bring the focus on Bluebird. But the Soviets knew far too much at the end. And it looks as though they were running a separate operation on this case from the AVO, with neither side telling all that much to the other. Unfortunately, both of them were a step ahead of us at the end. It made it even more difficult to pull anything off. I'm surprised we were able to do as much as we did with Bluebird."

"Are you sure you didn't just fuck it up? You didn't let your tradecraft lapse in all the excitement of the revolution, did you? It would be understandable."

Baier leaned forward. "Yes, Gerry, I'm sure. We were meticulous about our counter-surveillance and making sure the dead drops were secure. We did hit a bump at our final location, but that was because those fuckers knew where to go and whom to bribe. They each knew too much, and they knew it too fast at the end. Both in their own way. It never should have happened so quickly. They were way too sure all of a sudden. And I'm going to find out why."

"I'm surprised those guys didn't cooperate more with each other."

"I got the impression that the Soviets and the AVO did not like or trust each other all that much. It might be worth keeping that in mind for the future."

O'Leary rose again, an obvious sign that the conversation was over. "Fair enough. I should remind you, though, that you don't have a whole helluva lot of time for anything else, Karl. I'll give you two days to pack up and make your arrangements here. Will Sabine be leaving with you?"

"Of course. We've been separated too much lately."

"I'M SORRY I can't give you anymore, Karl," Henry Turnbridge said. They were strolling past the Hapsburg's Imperial Palace in the direction of the Volksgarten, which stood practically next door. The cold November wind swept in from the east, forcing both men to pull their coat collars tighter around their necks to ward off the chill. "We generally don't keep up communications with retired officers. Especially old farts living in seclusion and fantasizing about their adventures from years ago."

"That sounds a little harsh. This Rankin fellow did a lot of good work for your service and country, from the sound of it."

Turnbridge sighed. "Perhaps your right. I suppose I'm just bitter at how this whole affair in Egypt turned out. I might add that your lot was not very helpful. You certainly played hardball with us, and not just at the U.N. I thought the Pound was going to collapse for a moment there."

"You were warned. If your ears had been open, you would have known well in advance that we were not going to tolerate such a horrible misadventure. Sadly, you may have shifted the dynamics of the Middle East in an entirely new and more difficult direction for all of us."

"Yes, well. I'll leave those sorts of judgements to the people who pay my salary. And I suppose your right about your government's actions on this. I'm just bitter and frustrated."

Baier shifted their direction back toward the Palace. He was scheduled to meet Sabine at the Spanish Riding School. "But about Mr. Rankin. You had no other communications from him beyond the first one to pass along with his greetings?"

Turnbridge halted and studied the ground littered with brown leaves. He moved several about with the toes of his right foot. "There was one other message. I did not pass it along, of course, as I was told you were out of town." He looked up at Baier. "No word where you had gone, though. Very mysterious, that."

"Need to know, old chap. What did Rankin have to say?"

"Only that he had found someone who might help. An old hand, apparently."

"Did he give a name?"

"No. He did not. Need to know and all that, old man. And I apparently did not have the need on that end either." Turnbridge paused. "Did you ever meet up with anyone who might have fit that description, vague as it is?"

"Not that I'm aware of. But he may have met up with me. In a way."

"Yes, very mysterious, that."

BAIER REMARKED ON how much the Lake District had changed in just a month's time. The subtle colors of autumn had been replaced by the harsh tones of an approaching winter. Baier thought about how beautiful this area would be after a snowfall, wondering how much it actually received on average. The hills along Lake Windemere's opposite shore were now brown and grey as the trees had lost their foliage, and the water in the Lake seemed cold and forbidding. It was certainly dark enough. The tourists were also gone, or nearly so. The café by the lakeside dock was empty, except for two couples and a solitary tea drinker at the window. Baier took a seat at a table on the street side of the building, away from what would have been the natural place to sit, enjoying the view of the water and the boats cruising from one end of the lake to the other. Baier was tempted to purchase a ticket for the ride to Grasmere to visit Wordsworth's two homes. He had promised himself he would do so ever since that English Lit course his freshman year at Notre Dame. But his mind was not on poetry at the moment.

Baier heard the jingle of the bell as the door opened, and Rankin limped in. It took him a minute or two to navigate the tables and chairs and reach Baier.

"Sorry, I'm late. But my arthritis has gotten worse since you were last here. It does this every winter."

"I'm sorry to have inconvenienced you then," Baier replied. "We could have met at your place."

Rankin waved the thought away, as he dropped his coat over the back of the chair next to his. He was wrapped in a thick, gray, and woolen turtleneck sweater that hung past his waist and covered about half his rear end. Loose brown corduroy slacks reached down to a pair of scuffed leather boots. "Nah. It's good for me to get out of the bloody house now and then. Besides, you said you'd pay for the tea." He glanced at Baier's cup. "You're not drinking that godawful swill you Americans like, are you? I can't abide the stuff."

Baier held his cup aloft in a mock toast. "Yes, I'm a coffee man through and through. But tell me, just what did you mean by the messages you passed to Turnbridge?"

Rankin signaled to the waitress for a pot of Earl Grey, then turned back to Baier. "So, you got them? Good man, that Turnbridge."

"You know Henry?"

Rankin shook his head. "No, he was just a name someone gave me when I inquired about Vienna. Glad to hear he made the connection."

"Well, not exactly. I received the first message, but only heard the second after I had returned to Vienna. I never really understood either one. Until today, that is. I thought about it long and hard on the train from London."

Rankin's tea arrived, and he waited for the waitress to return to her station by the bar before continuing. "And what did you conclude?"

"That your outreach screwed the operation. Not intentionally, of course, and not entirely. There were other factors and players involved. But it cost us dearly, all the same. How did you know I was in Budapest?"

"Hell man, where else would you be? You were operating out of Vienna. You had told me that much. With all hell breaking loose just a few hundred miles to the east it wasn't hard to figure the rest out."

"And how did you come up the individual you found, and what did you expect he could accomplish?"

"I had gotten back in touch with an old accomplice from my time in Moscow during the Revolution in 1917 and 1918. He had been sent to Siberia but was pardoned by the Khrushchev gang as part of the destalinization. There were a lot of people allowed to return home." He nodded in appreciation. "It was a good thing for those poor saps."

"How did you know to reach out to this person? You didn't exchange phone numbers and addresses when you left, did you?"

Rankin stirred his tea and cream. "No need to get smart, young man. No, he reached out to me when he returned to Moscow. Said he felt he had an unpaid obligation since our operation had gone balls up back then. Said he wanted to try to make things right."

"But I thought you said it was Reilly's fault."

"And so, it was. But you know that in this line of work you can never be sure, that there are always unanswered questions. So, I guess he felt he might have done something to wreck the operation we had established. I tried to reassure him, but he was pretty damn insistent."

"And? That insistence didn't set off any alarms for you?" Baier had not touched his coffee since Rankin's arrival. When he took a sip, it had gone cold. Baier set his cup back on the table and off to the side.

"Not at all. Damn it, I know the man. I still trust him. So, I gave him your name and told him to see what he could do to help."

"Anything else?"

Rankin sipped his tea, then shook his head. "Nope. But you should be thanking me, not complaining. He said he managed to get to Budapest…"

"Odd that, don't you think, considering all that was going

on?"

"Well, yes, but remember, this man was an old pro. Anyways, he said it was a good thing he found you. Said, you were in need of some help. In 'bad need,' was what he actually said."

The Russian Kovacs had mentioned. Now it made sense. "How so?"

"Well, for one thing, you and some other fellow were about to walk into a trap some AVO people had set. It was in an apartment. An AVO thug had gone in there first and planted a bomb, apparently. My pal snuck in after him, knocked him a good one on the noggin and dismantled the whole device."

"And what else did he do to the AVO officer?"

"He didn't say. But he was worried that you and your pal had been found out by the locals, so he contacted someone in the Soviet command he knew he could trust from the old days to see what he knew."

Baier shoved his coffee even further away and leaned in close. Rankin's eyes were clear and settled, his face calm. "And who was this Soviet officer?"

"That's where more good luck came in. It was the son of a Soviet officer who had worked with us against Lenin and his crowd. His father had been General Boris Savinkov. An honorable gentleman, if I ever met one."

"And you think this 'honor' had carried over automatically to his son? That nothing had changed?"

"Sure. The son and my man had been in touch throughout his childhood. Well, as much as you can when one is sitting in a camp in Siberia. My guy was a sort of father figure to the poor fellow. The kid had to grow up an orphan, you know."

"Where is your friend now?"

Rankin shrugged. "I don't rightly know. I haven't heard from him since the Soviets rolled back into Budapest. But he said he had been able to straighten out a few things with this Savinkov fellow."

So, the sins of the fathers are not always visited on the sons,

Baier thought. Sometimes, they change and get spread a little wider. He considered this man and the errors in his thinking that had been dulled by years of retirement and nostalgia. He had become convinced that his memories were all the reality he needed, that he retained all the knowledge and judgment necessary to operate in a world forty years older than the one he had known. Should Baier explode in rage, shake the old man from his failed certainties?

He watched Rankin sip his tea and grimace at the heat the liquid still held. Would the operation have turned out any differently if he had never approached the old Brit, never bothered to take the train to the Lake District? Perhaps not. The overwhelming Soviet force, Bluebird's history and personality, the man's own desires and love for his country, as well as Baier's drive for more and more information to feed to Washington at a critical juncture in European and world history had dictated the outcome as much as anything. Certainly more than the musings and memories of some former British spy ensconced in his retirement in the English countryside. But Rankin's 'assistance' certainly hadn't helped.

Baier paid the bill, then left the old man to his delusions.

Chapter Twenty-One

———— ✦ ————

IN THE END, Kovacs could not stay in Vienna, or anywhere in the West for that matter. He had always told Baier that his heart rested in his native land, and that he would always be drawn back there. Baier realized now that that homesickness was what had allowed Baier to convince Kovacs that he should return to Budapest that cold autumn evening in Vienna back in 1955. "You can help fight the Stalinists in your party, in your country," Baier had said. Kovacs had believed him, but there had been more to it. In any case, they had been able to work together toward a mutual goal, for a while at least. So Baier wasn't really surprised when word came from O'Leary that Kovacs had done a flip and swam against the current of humanity that was fleeing Hungary through the border opening that the Soviets left clear to ensure the departure of the 'malcontents and fascists,' as the Kremlin called them. The man actually returned home.

"Doesn't he realize he just signed his own death warrant?" Delgreccio asked. The two men were seated at the bar of the Old Ebbit Grill, just a block from the White House and the Treasury Department. They were meeting Sabine for a Christmas Eve dinner at the Washington Hotel just around the corner on 15th Street.

"The man's always been a true believer, Ralph. Not only in Communism, or perhaps we should say Socialism. But also, in the power of that movement to reform itself."

"I'd say he's a bit naive there, wouldn't you? I mean, how else can you interpret the Soviets' brutal repression of the Hungarian Revolt, but that the system is incapable of self-correction?"

"You know, he may have been lured back when he heard that Kadar had offered an amnesty of sorts to those who supported the Revolution."

"An amnesty of sorts?"

"Well, yeah," Baier said. "He promised that no harm would come to anyone who supported it. And then on the 21st, Kadar gave his assurances to the Yugoslavs in a letter..."

"Where Nagy was hiding in their Embassy in Budapest, right?"

"Yeah. And Kadar publicly promised that Nagy would be able to live in Hungary in peace. The timing's about right. Bluebird returned to Hungary on the 23rd."

"The day before Nagy left the Yugoslav Embassy."

"That's right. And then Nagy was shipped off to Romania and his execution four days later."

"But Jesus, Karl, how many Hungarians died during their Revolution at the hands of the Soviets? I mean, those fuckers were hanging rebels from the spans of the bridges over the Danube as a warning against future revolts. Wasn't Bluebird aware of any of this? You can forget any more talk of destalinization or liberalizing the Soviet system. And there certainly won't be any loosening of Moscow's control over its satellites. Probably not in our lifetimes anyway."

"I'm afraid you look to be right on target about that, Ralph. I wish Bluebird had come to the same conclusion. As far as deaths go, at last count it was well over 100,000. And I wonder how many of those were under the age of thirty. The Soviets and their puppets can forget the future generations in eastern Europe, if you ask me."

"I haven't asked because I know what your answer would be anyway. And I agree. At least half of those killed had to be students and young workers. That would be my guess. Precisely the kind of people they would need to build their worker's paradise. Presumably."

"And a like number were arrested," Baier added. "God knows what will happen to them."

"Do you think your pal Bluebird was among them?"

Baier stared at the holiday traffic crawling by on 15th Street as merry Washingtonians made their way to the department stores like Woodward and Lothrop for their last-minute shopping, or were escaping from office parties and on their way to neighborhood or family gatherings. He sipped his old-fashioned and turned to his good friend and colleague. "I really don't know, Ralph. It's hard to tell. But I think it's probably safe to assume the worst. I really wish he had stayed put."

ON BAIER'S FIRST day back in the office after the New Year, where he had joined Delgreccio's Middle Eastern Task Force, a cable from the station in Vienna was sitting on his desk, covered in a brown folder with a Top Secret stamp along the upper edge. It had been sent overnight. The message explained that someone unknown had tossed an envelope into the window of Bill Schneider's car in Budapest as he drove to work the day before, on January 2. The envelope had been addressed to Karl Baier. Inside had been a letter written in German, but with the poor grammar one would expect from someone struggling with a foreign language. Clearly a non-native speaker. The letter explained that Baier's "old Hungarian friend" was living in internal exile as a postal clerk in the city of Csepel. 'We are watching out for his welfare,' the author claimed, 'protecting him from the vengeance of the Karhatalom. We will ensure his continued isolation and safety.' The letter had been signed simply, "L."

Baier smiled at the irony of it all. Csepel had been among the last holdouts against the Soviet invaders, not surrendering until November 11. And the revamped AVO, now labelled the Karhatalom, had embarked on a savage set of reprisals that had swept away thousands. But Lukovich had at least been honest when he said that he and Chernov wanted to keep Kovacs out of the clutches of the Hungarian security service, whatever its name.

The letter also had contained a postscript. "C has been recalled to Moscow." That was all it said. No explanation as to why, whether he had been promoted or arrested. Baier smiled again, thinking about how upset Sabine would be when she heard that Chernov was back in the Soviet capital. She would clearly hope he had been sent farther east, all the way to Siberia. Or shot altogether. She still hated that 'fucking Russian' despite all the help he had provided at the Hungarian border and in Budapest.

"Hey, enough daydreaming," Delgreccio shouted from the hallway. "We've got a staff meeting to attend. And I don't want you do anything to bring more unwanted attention to yourself right now. We've got to keep your head down, way down."

Baier had been staring out the window as he pondered the message in the note, his gaze fixed on Roosevelt Island sitting in the middle of the Potomac directly across from the window in the hallway. By now the trees were bare, and the small forest was little more than a barren nest of grey branches surrounded by slow moving brown water, like the ruins of an abandoned medieval castle. He pulled his attention back to the world running alongside E Street in downtown Washington.

"Sorry, Ralph. I wasn't exactly daydreaming. Just wishing some things had turned out differently, I guess."

"Well, don't go getting all maudlin about your future. Not just yet. I'm sure that someone with your background and skills will be in demand again. We just have to bide our time. It's not like freedom is about to break out across all of Europe anytime soon."

"Thanks for the encouragement, Ralph. But I was also thinking about the operation in Budapest."

As the two men marched down the hallway to the conference room at the other end of the long, winding corridor, Delgreccio handed Baier a report from London. "Then you'll be interested in this. The Brits finally decided to share this with us. Apparently, Bulganin had sent a note to the Egyptians on November 4 that Moscow was getting aircraft ready to attack Britain and France unless they withdrew from the Sinai."

"And the Brits knew this way back then?"

Delgreccio nodded. "Apparently. And are only telling us now." He blew out his breath. "I guess it's a good thing we've resumed intel sharing with our cousins."

"Do you think this is why the Brits pulled out and took the French with them?"

Delgreccio shrugged. "Who the hell knows? I'm sure there were a whole lot of reasons London finally called a halt to an operation that wasn't going anywhere anyway."

"I thought it was our refusal to support the pound sterling after they squandered most of their monetary reserves."

"Oh, I'm sure that played a big part, as did our refusal to support them at the U.N. But let me ask you this, my man. Do you think the Soviets would have gone through with it?"

Baier shook his head firmly. "No, I don't. They could barely handle a ragtag group of Hungarian students and workers. Why take on two of the most powerful members of NATO? Especially when it would risk bringing us in." Baier thought for a moment. "No, they must have guessed that the game was up for the Brits and Frogs, so they just wanted to look tough for their new Arab friends."

"Well, in that sense the Hungarians did help us."

"How so, Ralph?"

"They hobbled the Soviets, almost as much as our friends hobbled us at a really critical juncture."

"And now the British Empire really is dead, especially in the Middle East. We can expect the rest of their colonies around the world to begin drifting away. T.E. Lawrence must be turning over in his grave."

"Hell," Delgreccio said, "he helped create this mess. Let him turn and then turn some more."

"And now it's fallen to us," Baier said. "I just hope we don't screw it up as badly as our British and French allies did."

Photo by Didi Rapp

BILL RAPP RECENTLY retired from the Central Intelligence Agency after thirty-five years as an analyst, diplomat, and senior manager. After receiving his BA from the University of Notre Dame, an MA from the University of Toronto, and a PhD from Vanderbilt University, Bill taught European History at Iowa State University for a year before heading off to Washington, D.C. *The Hapsburg Variation* is the second book in the Cold War Spy series featuring Karl Baier. Bill also has a three-book series of detective fiction set outside Chicago with P.I. Bill Habermann, and a thriller set during the fall of the Berlin Wall. He lives in northern Virginia with his wife, two daughters, two miniature schnauzers, and a cat.

For more information, go to www.BillRappsBooks.com.